WHIPS AND CHAINS

SAINT VIEW MURDER SQUAD
BOOK 2

ELLE THORPE

WWW.ELLETHORPE.COM

For Tasha Myers.
Thank you for your endless support through the years

1

VIOLET

"Three..."

My heart thumped against my chest, terror climbing its way up my throat. I stumbled, my back hitting the cold steel wall of the abandoned warehouse.

The man came at me, his footsteps faster and faster. Bloodied knife still clutched in white-knuckled fingers.

"Toby!" It was a desperate plea to my best friend. A feeble attempt to snap him out of the instinct that had convinced him only one of us could make it out of this alive.

It did no good.

Tears streamed down his dirt-smudged face, but he didn't see me. He didn't see Violet, the girl he'd made it through high school with. He didn't see the woman who'd sat on the couch beside him for the best part of his twenties, eating candy and watching *Grey's Anatomy* until we both knew every scene word for word.

All he saw was survival.

All he heard was the unknown, unseen threat that

whispered in his ears from speakers hidden high above our heads, promising his death if he didn't kill.

"Two..." the distorted, robotic voice taunted us.

I twisted, trying to get away, but there was nowhere to go. No safety to be seen in dark corners. No one coming to save me. No one to hear me scream.

Toby grabbed my arm, the deadly knife between us, covered in blood from the man who'd already lost his life tonight and now lay headless in a pool of blood across the room.

The speaker let out its final warning.

"One."

Toby's dead eyes were the last thing I saw. The best friend who'd loved me so fiercely was gone, replaced by a man I no longer recognized.

I closed my eyes, giving in to a fate I never could have imagined, even in the worst of my nightmares.

In the cold warehouse, the psychopath watching us finally fell silent, waiting for my final moments to play out.

I waited for the plunge of cold, sharp steel that would end my life.

Waited for the pain.

Toby gurgled.

An out-of-place sound in the silence of the room.

My eyes flew open just in time to see him slump to his knees in front of me.

The knife stuck firmly in his neck.

"No!"

He collapsed completely, his head hitting the concrete floor with a sickening thud.

But it was nothing compared to the horror of that

knife, wedged firmly in his neck, blood running from the wound, instantly covering his throat and collar.

I fell to the floor beside him, instinct taking over through the panicked screams inside my brain. I pressed my fingers around the wound, horrified when they came away sticky and wet.

Toby's eyes stared up into mine.

The Toby I knew, not the cold, checked-out man from just moments earlier. The Toby who had loved me for a decade. The Toby who was more my family than anyone else.

The Toby who had just sacrificed himself so I could live.

"What did you do?" Tears blurred my vision, but I could do nothing to wipe them. I needed my hands for the desperate bid to save my best friend's life.

Blood trickled from the corner of his mouth, and he tried to speak, but no sound came out. Just gurgles while he choked on his own blood.

I sobbed harder. His life was slipping away in the blood draining from a gash too deep for me to stem.

Anger suddenly coursed through me, powered by adrenaline. I shook my head at him. "You are not dying here tonight, Toby Horton. You hear me? I won't allow it! You're going to hold on until help comes and then you'll get all fixed up and we'll be back on that couch watching doctors fall in love until we're old and gray."

My shouts echoed around the empty warehouse.

But no matter how hard I pressed at his neck, no matter how much I willed him to hold on, I could see the inevitable.

This wound was going to kill him long before anyone

would find us. There was no help for me to get. Our phones were useless, and the warehouse doors were locked until one of us died.

A blazing anger for the psychopath watching us roared inside me. But I pushed it away, knowing that pain and fear and resentment would have to wait.

Because my best friend was dying right in front of me. And all I could do now was comfort him.

Tears rolled down my cheeks. "Did I ever tell you the first moment I realized you were the best friend I was ever going to know?" I tried to smile at him reassuringly.

He stared up at me, eyes wide with fear, hands fluttering and jerking as he struggled uselessly. "It was the day you brought me one of your jackets. We were maybe sixteen, and I'd outgrown the one I'd had, and my foster parents had refused to buy me another. They kept insisting they weren't going to buy me more clothes if I just kept getting fatter and I would have to lose weight instead. So I'd been going to school in layered long-sleeve shirts through most of the winter. I don't think anyone else noticed. Or maybe they had and assumed the fat girl was always hot and didn't need anything warm."

I removed one hand from the gash on his neck because I knew it wasn't really doing any good. Instead, I brushed his hair off his sweaty forehead, ignoring the stripe of blood it left across his brow. "But not you. You noticed and without being asked, you helped. You brought me a jacket that was warm and so clean it smelled like heaven. You told me it was old, from the back of your closet and you never wore it anymore, so it was no big deal. But I found a receipt in the bottom of the bag you gave it to me in, and realized you'd bought it for me. It wasn't expensive, but that shitty job you'd had at the bakery had paid so badly, it was probably months' worth of your wages."

One of my tears landed on his cheek. "You'd been saving up for a car. Remember the one you always talked about? That old black thing Mr. Chen down the road said you could buy from him because you spent so much time staring at it every day when we walked to school? You wanted it so bad. But you always put me first, even back then."

And he'd done it again tonight, in the most selfless act I could have ever imagined.

He was a better person than I could have ever hoped to be. He might have been the friend who gave me shit about my favorite color being pink or my cheap taste in wine, but he was also the friend who would lay his life down on the line for me.

Literally.

Tears streamed down my face, half a lifetime of memories all featuring him flashing through my brain in a blinding display of friendship I'd been so lucky to have. I pulled his head up onto my lap, cradling him as his breaths stuttered, slowing, his end drawing near.

His lips moved, his voice barely audible.

I shook my head. "Don't try to talk."

But Toby, stubborn as always, ignored me and tried again.

I bent my head, bringing my ear closer to his lips so I could hear the barely whispered words.

"I'm sorry."

"For what?" I whispered back.

His lips moved again. I strained to listen, but I couldn't catch his words.

The light in his eyes drained away, and his body fell limp.

It took a long moment for me to comprehend that he was gone.

A howl of pain lit up inside me, but when I opened my mouth, it wasn't a sob or tears or even screams that came out.

It was red-hot, blinding anger.

I pushed to my feet, spinning around in a circle, glaring at the shadowy ceiling where I knew there were cameras watching every movement I made. "You happy now?" I shouted to the madman who'd set this whole thing in motion. "Are you fucking satisfied, you sick piece of shit?"

A mechanical whirring came from the door. The distinct sound of the lock disengaging.

But I didn't run for it. I didn't even reach for the handle.

Instead, I slumped down on the floor with my best friend and held him until I went numb.

LEVI

"*The omelet is out of the frying pan!*"

That one ridiculous sentence repeated over and over in my head while I pushed my bike through the quiet, middle-of-the-night streets of Saint View.

I was going to kill X and his ridiculous code names if anything had happened to Violet.

I tried to quell the rising panic in my gut that told me something was wrong and reminded myself I was overreacting. So she'd created a distraction and slipped away with her bestie. She was probably just out at a club dancing, but the fact she wasn't answering her phone was stressing me out.

Though that could also be explained by the fact she was barely speaking to me right now. She probably would have ignored my calls even if her phone was on. It was why I'd been sending her letters instead. Though for all I knew, she'd been burning those or dropping them directly into the paper shredder.

But none of that mattered. She'd managed to give X the slip and now she was out somewhere, unprotected, and with no idea of the danger she was potentially in.

I gunned the engine, pulling into her street in record time.

X's ice cream van was still surrounded by a crowd of children and their parents. It seemed like half the neighborhood had shown up and it had turned into something of a street party, with music playing from a portable speaker and groups of people milling around the lawn while kids ran around crazy on a sugar high.

X stuck his head out the window. "Levi! Help me!"

I took in the chocolate sauce smudged on his face. "Not a chance." I needed to get up to Violet's apartment and see if there was any indication of where she might have gone. There weren't many clubs in Saint View, but for all I knew, she and Toby had hopped an Uber into Providence or gotten on the late bus into the city.

She could be fucking anywhere by now.

"Why are you going inside? They went that way!" X pointed down the road as he handed another kid a sloppy-looking ice cream sundae.

"Unless you can sniff her out, then I'm going to go inside and see if I can work out where they might have gone."

X waved his hand around his face. "I'm actually a little stuffed up in the head at the moment. Think I caught a bit of a cold when I was out here soaking wet the other night. It was so cold. You know, since I wasn't really wearing clothes."

I ignored him and was almost at the apartment doors when X shouted, "Oh, for the love of ducks and geese!"

I glanced over my shoulder just in time to see his apron fly out the server window, quickly followed by the rest of his lanky body. His feet hit the ground, and he glanced at the maybe twelve-year-old kid who'd caught his apron and said seriously, "The ice cream gods have chosen you. The plastic spoons are in the first drawer and we're fresh out of soft serve."

A groan of complaint came up from the rest of the people waiting on their sugar fix.

The kid just stared at him.

X made a shooing motion with his hands. "Go on then! Start serving, young padawan!"

The kid's eyes were about as wide as dinner plates as X shoved him up into the van and then took off running after me.

He caught up, and I raised an eyebrow. "You know they're going to clean you out, right?"

"I know. But I can't stand there serving fucking ice cream another second while she's out there somewhere alone." He shook his head. "I'm an idiot. I should have gone after her straightaway. But I didn't want to freak her out after…"

I stopped walking. "What the fuck happened between the two of you the other night? You came out of Violet's apartment soaking wet, half-dressed, and so upset about something that you sent Whip in to fix it."

X's face clouded over, and he clutched the back of his neck, squeezing his eyes shut as if he were reliving the scene. "I choked her."

I froze. "What?"

He opened his eyes, and they were filled with remorse. "I know. I know, okay! You don't need to fucking look at me with all that damn judgment in your stupidly pretty eyes." He peered at me, moving in closer. "I can see why Whip keeps staring into them, you know. They're insanely green."

I shoved him off me. "Focus, would you?"

He sighed. "I'm fucked in the head, okay? Is that what you want to hear? I can't be alone with women because every time I am, all I can think about is killing them."

Red-hot anger coursed through me. "You knew this and you let yourself be alone with Violet? You could have hurt her!"

"Don't you think I know that? I already hate myself, Levi! You don't have to worry about that. I'm never going to be alone with her again."

His expression was filled with so much remorse it was practically palpable. But I didn't have time to baby his feelings. I stormed up the stairs, X following close behind, until I got to Violet's apartment. I grabbed the door handle, but it was locked. I did a quick scout around for a spare key hidden in the light fixture or the dying potted plant at the end of the hallway, but there was nothing.

X watched me, and when I shook my head, he lifted one foot and kicked in the door.

The lock sprang free so easily we both winced. She may as well have left it wide open. A toddler could have broken that lock.

But worrying about Violet's apartment security, or lack thereof, was the least of my current concerns. I stormed inside, calling out just in case she and Toby had returned, but the apartment was empty.

"Levi."

I stuck my head back out into the open-plan living/kitchen area, to X holding out a note. One that looked exactly like the letters I'd been sending her. He already had his burner phone out and up to his ear, calling someone.

I took the note from his fingers, Whip's voice faintly answering X's call in the background.

Words are easy, ink runs free,
But face-to-face, we fall, we flee.
Maybe letters are our space,
A quiet world, our own escape.
But one last time, let's break the rule,
Meet me where the night is cool.
No crowds, no noise, just you and me,
A place where no one else will see.
We'll start again, the way we should,
And if we don't, then it was good.
Come alone, come when it's late,
I'll be waiting. Don't be late.

There was an address at the bottom. I snapped my gaze up to meet X's. "I didn't write this. This seems like it's from me, but it isn't."

I stared down at the note. Had she thought this was from me? Admittedly, it was the same type of paper and the same sort of font I'd been using to write her letters on Hawk's computer.

Had she slipped away from X so she could meet me and try again?

A stupid part of my heart flickered with the tiniest glimmer of hope.

But it was snuffed out just as fast.

Because if this letter wasn't from me, then it was most definitely from the person targeting us.

And that left me colder than X standing half naked and soaking wet outside Violet's apartment.

He relayed the info back to Whip, including the address.

I didn't wait for him. Knowing he'd follow, I thundered out of the apartment, down the stairs and outside to where I'd left my bike. The impromptu street party all turned and stared at us, but neither of us stopped. X's ice cream van had been overrun by kids, all helping themselves to whatever they could find, but he didn't make a move to stop them.

I threw my leg over my bike and gunned the engine.

X slid on behind me, wrapping his arms around my middle.

"Seriously?" I shouted.

"I'm coming!"

"Please don't say that when you're on the back of my bike and snuggled up against me."

"Don't worry. I'm not going to get a hard-on."

"You better fucking not!"

"I'm not Whip."

Even with the roar of the engine and the looming danger Violet was in, I could hear the laughter in his voice.

I envied his ability to provide comic relief in the most serious of situations. Sometimes, I even secretly found him funny. But not tonight. Tonight, all I did was slam my hand on the throttle, giving my bike what it needed to get us to Violet.

hip's shitty little house in the worst part of Saint View was closer to the industrial area than Violet's apartment was, so he beat us there and was already getting out of his car when X and I arrived.

He didn't stop and wait for us, just like I wouldn't have waited for him either. He stormed ahead, leaving X and I to jog after him to catch up. Our footsteps were loud in the silent night, but none of us bothered to quiet them.

We were the scariest things out here.

We were the monsters in the darkness.

But, apparently, another had joined us.

I hoped like hell whoever had tricked Violet into coming here saw us now and realized what a big fucking mistake that had been. It was one thing to mess with us. Another entirely to target her.

Huge industrial-sized warehouses loomed all around, each one identical to the last, nothing but badly lit concrete paths in between. Whip pulled out his phone and flicked on the flashlight function so we could see the numbers on each building.

We worked our way through the maze that seemed to have no end, a ticking clock in the back of my head reminding me that every second we lost trying to find the right building was another second Violet was alone with a psychopath.

Whip's flashlight bounced over something on the path ahead, before moving away again.

"Wait. What was that?" I ignored that I noticed what his skin felt like as I grabbed his arm and guided it back to where I'd spotted something.

The light lit up the dark round shape, and all three of us froze.

"Is that..." Whip choked out.

We moved in unison, as if drawn in by some sort of sick, morbid curiosity we shared.

"A severed head?" I stared down at the bloodied hair. "Yeah."

X squinted at it. "Do we like...pick it up? Is there a lost and found for body parts?"

I squatted and grimaced at the clean slice across the neck. It was face down, and that sick part of me demanded I turn it over.

I stumbled back, instantly recognizing the dead, unseeing eyes. "Oh, Jesus fuck, I know him. It's Adam Dickson. We were in prison together. He's one of the guys on the list that Trig and the others were watching. Doc said he went missing a couple days ago. They thought he'd skipped town."

I didn't know why he was here or how, but this had to have something to do with Violet. Whip was already a step ahead of me, snapped out of gruesome curiosity with the sick realization something very, very bad had gone down here tonight.

"Violet," I managed to gasp out, sprinting after Whip and X, who were already running for the warehouse door. I caught up quickly, fueled by a rising panic, and it was me who got to the door handle first.

It was me who yanked it hard, the door creaking open beneath my solid pull.

It was me who stopped dead at the sight of Violet sitting in a pool of blood, Toby's lifeless body cradled in her arms.

She didn't look our way. She didn't say a word. Just sat there, stroking his hair with bloodied fingers, her eyes unseeing.

For once in his life, even X didn't have a joke or a witty remark.

"Fuck. Violet!" Whip lunged forward.

Violet's scream was a warning of anger more than one of fear. It stopped Whip in his tracks instantly. His expression filled with desperation, and his body went rigid as he tried to hold himself back.

I took in every detail of her blank expression and repeated movements. "She's in shock."

"There's another body over by the window." Whip's gaze bounced around the room, searching for any possible danger that might still linger, even though he flicked constant little glances at Violet. "Probably headless and probably Dickson's, I'm guessing." He swore under his breath. "What the fuck happened?"

I had no idea, and I almost didn't care. All I could see was Violet.

X's expression, centered solely on Violet, was so full of heartbreak I could barely look at him. I could tell every inch of his body was demanding he make sure she was okay.

Because mine was doing the same.

But X had a hold on himself that was so rigid it seemed painful. He swallowed hard and stared at me. "Please..."

I instantly understood. He couldn't go to her. After what he'd done, he was terrified of scaring her again. But it was killing him.

"Help Whip check the room. Make sure there's nobody else here," I told him.

But my gut already said there wasn't. I could feel it in the air. The only person who'd been left breathing here tonight was Violet.

I moved toward her at half the pace Whip had. She didn't glance up, but she didn't scream either. The only sign she even noticed me at all was the quicker pace she stroked Toby's hair with.

There was no point checking his pulse. I crouched to touch his skin, and it was still warm, but he was very much dead. Clearly not for long, but there was no living through an injury like the one he'd sustained.

"Vi," I said so softly it was barely audible.

She didn't say a word, but her fingers stilled. So I tried again, my voice cracking. Her pain was written all over her beautiful face, and it was killing me. Every second she wasn't in my arms was a burning agony I couldn't even explain because I'd never cared about another person the way I cared about her.

"Vi."

I was so fucking in love with her I could barely breathe, and all I wanted to do was tell her that while I wrapped her in my arms and protected her from whatever horrors had lurked within these walls.

But I forced myself to go slowly, putting what she needed above what I did.

"It's me, Vi. It's Levi. You're safe now, okay? X and Whip are here too."

I could feel their gazes from across the room. Their fear for Violet as thick in the air as the smell of Toby's blood.

I ignored the pool of blood beneath me, because all I could do was focus on her.

She stared at the wall, barely blinking.

I couldn't help myself. The desire to touch her was too strong. I cupped the side of her face.

She jerked, another scream ripping from her mouth. "Don't touch me!"

I clasped her cheeks with both hands and forced her to look at me. "Vi, it's me."

She flung her arms up, colliding with mine, breaking the hold I had on her. She scrambled back onto her feet, trying to get away from me, Toby's head clunking onto the concrete in the process. "Don't touch me!"

Her eyes were huge. Her chest heaved with too-fast breaths. But her fingers clenched into fists, telling me she still thought she had to fight her way out of this.

"No one is going to touch you," I assured her, using a gentle, deep voice I would have used to settle a spooked horse. "You're safe. You're okay."

But shock had set in deep. Her gaze strayed to Toby, and her body tensed at every sound, every movement.

"We can't clean this," Whip muttered from behind me.

X quickly agreed with him. "Dickson we probably could, but Toby has family and friends who will miss him. We can't just sweep whatever happened here tonight under the rug. We've gotta let the cops find this one."

But all I could see was that knife sticking out of Toby's neck.

And Violet the only person left here breathing. I knew how that was going to look to the police. Whether she'd done it or not, she'd be the prime suspect. And I'd bet anything her prints were all over that murder weapon, just from the way she'd been holding Toby as he'd died. "Agreed. But we need to convince her to come with us first. She can't be here when the cops find it, and that weapon comes with us. Get the guys down here to clean her prints off anything she might have touched."

I didn't wait for their confirmation. I knew Whip well enough by now to know he'd handle it.

All I could concentrate on was Violet.

"Vi. Can you look at me?"

I waited, trying to stay patient, even though everything inside me screamed to stride across the room, pick her up, and carry her out of here. And I would if I had to. But that would only cause her more trauma, so it was a last resort.

"Vi."

Eventually she dragged her gaze to meet mine.

"That's good. That's real good, baby. We're going to take you home, okay? Nobody is going to touch you, but we need to get you out of here. All you have to do is walk. Can you do that?"

She didn't respond, but her eyes flickered to the door. That was enough for me to know she wanted out. Somewhere deep beneath the shock and anger and fear, she wanted to be home, surrounded by things that were familiar. I could see the yearning in her eyes.

"Whip's car is just outside," I promised her.

Her entire body trembled, but she stepped forward.

I cringed, watching her walk right through the puddle of blood like she didn't even see it, but there was nothing we could do about the footprints we were leaving behind. We had to trust that Trig and the others would get here in time to clean up any evidence, because all we could do now was get the fuck out.

I held the door for her and led her to where Whip had left his car. He and X moved cautiously behind her, keeping their distance but wearing identical worried expressions to the one I was sure was plastered all over my face.

Whip unlocked his car when we got close enough, and I held the door open for her. X walked around us carefully, keeping an eye on our surroundings, the knife that had been in Toby's neck now firmly grasped in his hand.

Fucking hell. What a ginormous mess all of this was. My goddamn bike was still sitting here, and I couldn't risk leaving it, but I wasn't leaving Violet either.

X held out his hand. "Give me the keys to the bike. You stay with her."

I could tell it was the last thing he wanted to do. He wanted to be with her as much as I did, but somebody had to get the bike out of here.

Normally I would have never let anyone else touch my ride, but it was the easiest yes I'd ever said. I dug my hand in my pocket and swapped the key for the knife that X wouldn't be able to hold, then got in the car with Whip and Violet.

We drove away without a word, X on my bike sticking right behind us.

"We need to get her shoes off." Whip threw me a glance in the rearview mirror, his mouth pulled into a grim line that made him seem older than he was.

I agreed. She couldn't track bloody footprints all through her apartment building. It was going to be hard enough to get her upstairs without anyone seeing us.

"Take your shoes off, Vi," I said gently.

Her eyes remained blank and free of tears. She still stared at the back of Whip's seat, but as though on autopilot, she removed the bloody shoes and put them aside.

"Good girl," I mumbled. "That's real good. We're nearly there. Just gotta hold on a little longer, okay?"

I was twitchy, being this exposed. The cops patrolled Saint View at night, searching for people up to no good and often finding many who fit the bill.

Tonight we were some of them. If a cop stopped us, there would be no explaining any of this. Not the blood. Not the knife. Not the fact Vi couldn't even speak.

I breathed a sigh of relief when her building came into view, and another when I realized the party that had been going on earlier had dissipated. The street was dark, and though I'd been concerned by the broken streetlight in the past, knowing it was a safety hazard for Violet and the other people who shared her building, now I looked at it as a blessing. It left long, dark shadows for us to slip into.

We moved slowly, no other option but to go at Violet's wooden pace.

I held my breath, hoping for a reaction out of her when she saw her building, but it didn't come.

I knew her current state was her body protecting itself from a traumatic event, but the fact she'd barely responded to us at all since we'd found her was starting to scare me.

I guided her up the stairs without touching her. We

gave her as much space as we could, the three of us sharing silent but worried glances.

Whip nudged me. "Should we call Doc?"

I shook my head. "I don't know."

She barely knew Grayson. She'd already screamed when Whip and I had tried to get close to her. I couldn't imagine that was going to be any better with a man she didn't know as well. As far as I could see, she wasn't physically hurt.

Violet walked like a zombie up the stairs, feet heavy with trudging steps. On her floor, Whip opened the door for her, the lock still busted from where X and I had kicked it in.

"I'll get that fixed for you in the morning," I assured her, trying to make normal conversation, even though this was anything but a normal situation.

Violet ignored me.

But the moment she got inside, she took her jacket off, dropping it on the floor at her feet.

With the next step, her shirt followed, exposing the plain white bra beneath.

"I'll turn the shower on for you." X hurried ahead and disappeared down the hallway that led to her bedroom.

If Violet heard him, she didn't say anything.

She just made her way toward the hallway, pulling off socks, and then her pants, leaving them in a trail behind her.

Whip picked up the clothes as she went. "I'll have to burn these, sweetheart."

Again, she didn't respond.

She took another step toward the hallway and froze, her gaze latched on to Toby's room.

Whip's arms were full of her bloodied clothes, the shower running in the background. My gaze focused solely on her.

So I saw the buckle in her knees.

Heard the howl of pain rise up her chest.

I caught her as she fell, refusing to let her hit the floor. "I've got you, Vi."

The part of me that was so damn in love with her whispered I always would.

3

———

VIOLET

I wrapped my arms around Levi's neck and pressed my face into his skin, inhaling his scent. He was warm around my achingly cold body. I was sure it wasn't just the cool night sending goosebumps across my flesh. I'd never felt a chill like the one that had set in deep, spreading through every bone and muscle and joint until it was all I could feel, all I could think about.

Everything hurt. My head. My lungs. My stomach.

The only way the pain could escape was through my mouth in screams and wails of terror and despair.

It didn't matter if I closed my eyes. I could still see Dickson's body falling headless from the window. I could still hear the psychopath's countdown. Could still smell Toby's blood, pouring from his neck.

I sobbed in Levi's arms, feeling rushing through me once more. I didn't want it. Numb was so much better, but there was no stopping it. His warmth pervaded every inch of my body, and then he was walking me into the shower, holding me beneath the spray.

I blinked, catching sight of X hovering, his concern painted all over his stupidly handsome face, and that's when I knew how rough I must look. Because X had never shown any real concern before. Whip leaned on the doorframe, an identical expression of worry drawing his brow into lines. I wanted to reach out and smooth it away, reassure him he didn't need to worry about me because I had always been able to take care of myself.

Except I hadn't. Because I'd always had Toby.

And now I didn't.

I couldn't stop the full-body shakes or the gut-wrenching pain that felt like it was going to rip me in two. Every drop of water felt like a knife spearing through my frozen skin, and yet I didn't want it to stop.

"We should give her some privacy," Whip murmured to X.

He nodded, and the two of them went to leave.

But I didn't want privacy. I didn't want to be alone. And if they left, then Levi might too.

And then I'd have no one.

I couldn't bear the thought.

"Don't go. Please don't go."

Both men froze. They exchanged looks with Levi over my head, but both of them came back into the tiny bathroom, barely big enough for all four of us.

Levi's voice grumbled through his chest. "X, help me get her underwear off. I don't want to put her down, but I can't wash her like this."

I didn't want him to put me down either. For once, I wasn't concerned with how heavy he must think I was.

He didn't act like my weight bothered him at all. But with my head on his chest, his heart beating steadily beneath my ear, it was as close to comfort as I'd felt.

X caught my eye. "Is that okay?"

He'd run out of this room just days before. We'd gone from making out, his fingers around my neck, his lips on my skin, cock so damn close to taking my virginity...to him gone and me left wondering what I'd done wrong.

But it almost felt trivial now, especially when every ounce of his attention was solely on me, and his expression was racked with guilt and remorse. We needed to talk, but I didn't have it in me tonight. Tonight, all I could do was keep breathing long enough to make it through the pain threatening to drag me under.

I couldn't give a shit who saw me naked. Two of these men already had anyway, and the one holding me had held my heart for a year.

I'd never felt safe to share my body with anyone, always covering up at the beach and pools, saying I didn't feel like swimming because I didn't want people staring at the fat chick. I'd heard too many beached whale comparisons throughout my younger years to ever want to swim or get changed in public ever again.

And yet with these three men, I was safe.

No matter what had happened between us, at my core, that was the one thing I now knew with complete certainty.

I gave X the tiniest of nods. "Yes."

He pushed the shower curtain aside, water splashing out on the tiled bathroom floor and splattering on his clothes. If he noticed, he didn't show it. He just ran his hands beneath the hot water, warming his skin up, then found the clasp on the back of my bra and undid it.

Levi leaned back against the shower wall, facing X, giving him as much room as he could. I was squished between them, a limp noodle, my body—or maybe my mind—too broken to be of any real help.

But X didn't need it. He drew my bra straps down my arms, Levi shifting me so X could get it fully off. My underwear came next, another complicated maneuver due to the way Levi was holding me, but he refused to put me down, and X just worked with it.

I should have felt vulnerable, but I didn't. I couldn't. Not when I was surrounded by the three of them, and the only thing in their expressions was a desire to help and take care of me.

Whip watched silently from the doorway, and X grabbed my bodywash from the caddy hanging from the showerhead. He squirted a generous dollop onto his palm and rubbed them together, lathering the soap up into frothy bubbles.

His gaze caught mine once more, and he checked I was still okay with all of this. My heart squeezed.

His palms on my skin were heaven. He slid them up and down my arms, chasing away the goosebumped flesh and leaving something warmer in his wake. He soaped up my legs and then ran his hands across my collarbones.

"I gotta put you down, baby," Levi whispered to me. "We gotta get you clean. You're covered in blood."

It was only then I realized the frothy bodywash was no longer white and the suds washing down the drain were tinged with a deep pink.

Dickson's blood.

Toby's blood.

I needed it off me.

I scrambled to get down, and Levi helped me stand. But it was all I could do. I leaned on the wall, barely able to hold myself up, the sight of all that blood running down the drain too much for my brain to comprehend.

The violent body shakes were back, along with the movie reel that replayed the night over and over in my head.

I closed my eyes, willing the images away, but they were burned there at the backs of my eyelids.

The only distraction X's and Levi's hands running all over my body.

Levi's fingers brushed over my nipples. There was nothing sexual in the touch, and yet my body responded like it was. X's hands ran down my spine and over my ass, Levi's fingers swept over the bare mound of my pussy.

X soaped up my hair, and I tilted my head back, falling into his strong fingers massaging away the tension headache that pounded behind my eyes and in my temples.

It was over all too quickly, the water running cold, and X reaching behind him to shut it off.

"Step out, baby," Levi urged quietly. "Whip's gonna get you dry."

It was ridiculous that I needed him to tell me everything I had to do when I'd been taking showers my entire life without his assistance just fine. And yet now, I didn't seem to be able to think at all. I just waited for one of them to tell me what to do next and was grateful they were there to do it.

Because without them, I suspected I wouldn't be

functioning at all. I'd still be back in that warehouse, sitting in a pool of blood.

Whip wrapped me in a towel and used another to rub the long lengths of my hair until they no longer dripped down my back. His fingers cupped one side of my face, tilting it up so he could look down at me. "How you doing, sweetheart? We're going to get you into bed, okay?"

All I could do was nod and let him guide me out of the steamed-up bathroom.

He'd switched the lamps and the fairy lights on in my bedroom, turning the space into the cozy den I loved. He sat me on the edge of the bed and blow-dried my hair, running a comb through the long lengths as he went, detangling it gently and carefully.

Whip brushing and drying my hair with such tenderness nearly did me in. The warm heat coasted down the back of my neck and across my shoulders, and I closed my eyes, relishing a touch I couldn't remember ever experiencing before. I never had this done when I went to get my hair cut. It was an extra expense I could never afford. I was sure someone must have brushed my hair when I was tiny, but I'd gone into care at four and I couldn't remember a foster parent ever doing this for me. I'd been on my own.

And now, suddenly, I wasn't.

When my hair was soft and smooth, Whip turned the dryer off, setting it down on the bedside table.

I glanced up at him. "Where did you learn how to do that?"

Something flickered in his expression, but he didn't answer. Just drew back the covers. "Get into bed, sweetheart."

I stood, and he unwrapped me from the damp towel. His gaze didn't lower to take in my naked body, he just urged me to get beneath the blankets.

I sank down onto the mattress, letting the softness of the sheets and pillows engulf me.

He tucked me in. "You should try to sleep. Don't worry about anything. We're taking care of it."

He went to leave, but without any conscious thought, I grabbed his arm. "Stay with me."

He didn't hesitate. Just pulled off his shirt and toed off his shoes. His jeans were next, and then his underwear. He barked out orders to the others as he slid beneath the covers with me. "Ace is on his way over here to take away the clothes and deal with my car. Everything has to go with him. He's bringing fresh clothes for all of us too."

From the corner of my eye, I caught sight of Levi and X hovering outside the bathroom, both of them out of their wet clothes and wrapped in spare towels. Their bloodied clothes, along with mine, in their arms.

Levi scooped up Whip's clothes and added them to the pile in his arms. "Got it. We'll wait for him in the living room."

Panic swept through me at the thought of them even going as far as the living room. It squeezed tight around my throat, and my heart sped up to a pace that had me gasping for breath. "Don't go. Please don't leave me."

The two men paused, but Levi's answer was quick, "I won't leave." He dropped the clothes in a pile, and in nothing but a towel, because there was nothing else for him to wear, he sank down on the little armchair in the corner of my room.

X said nothing, but he slid down the wall opposite my

bed, sitting on the floor, his gaze trained on me so intently it sent the panic inside me skittering away.

I lay back and rolled onto my side, facing Whip.

He reached up and tucked a stray strand of my freshly dried hair behind my ear. "How you doing, sweetheart?"

"Not good," I admitted honestly. I fought the way my voice wanted to break. "Really not good."

He pulled me into his arms and kissed the top of my head while holding me tight. "I know. You're going to be okay. I've got you."

And in his arms, I believed that. I snuggled against his warm chest, remembering the way we'd done this after he'd taken my virginity. Remembering the way he'd blanked my brain out so beautifully with orgasms delivered by his talented fingers and tongue, until I'd barely known the day of the week or my own name.

I wanted more of that. More of the sweet, delicious numbness I knew he could give me.

And a whole lot less of the nightmare that would live in my brain for the rest of my life

I lifted my head, lips brushing over the stubble of his beard. "Touch me."

He craned his neck so his mouth was above mine, his forehead furrowed in frown lines. "I don't think—"

I didn't want him to say no. So I kissed him instead.

For a long second, he didn't respond, but then I reached up, grabbing his face, showing him exactly how much I wanted him.

He groaned, holding me tighter, his lips moving with mine, opening so our tongues could stroke together. His hands roamed up and down my back, each swipe setting my skin alight and distracting from all the hurt that threatened to drag me down.

I needed more. I pressed against him, hooking one leg over his hip, opening myself up to him.

"Violet," he murmured over my mouth. "I'll give you whatever you need, but X and Levi are still here."

"I know."

And I didn't care.

I wanted them to watch Whip take me. They'd both rejected me, and I suddenly wanted to show them what they'd missed out on.

Whip didn't question me. It was clear to everyone in the room what I meant.

Whip got hard between us. I reached for him, stroking his cock, while he fumbled for the drawer of my bedside table. I didn't even blush as his fingers trailed over my vibrator and he found a box of condoms. One I'd hopefully bought before a date with a man who had later stood me up and then ghosted me.

Whip took one out, leaving it on the mattress behind him for when he was ready for it.

His hand lowered beneath the blankets and covered mine, both of us pumping his shaft together for long moments until his hips rolled and he was fucking into our grip.

But he pulled away all too soon for my liking, his fingers moving between my thighs instead. He found the nub of my clit, rolling it with his thumb and forefinger, sending sweet rivers of pleasure around my body. He stayed there, playing with it, an ache building inside me, demanding more. Slick arousal pooled at my center, and he scooped it up, coating his fingers in it and rimming my entrance, stretching me just a little, warming me up.

"I'm wet for you," I whispered, stating the obvious.

For a second, the words hung in the air, and embarrassment threatened to flood me. I didn't know why I'd said that out loud when he could clearly feel exactly how soaked I was, just from being naked and some clit stimulation.

But I quickly realized I hadn't said it for him.

I'd said it for the other men in the room watching us.

I wanted them to know how much I wanted this. Wanted him.

"Yeah, sweetheart, you are." Whip's voice was pure desire.

It rushed over me like warm honey, chasing away any awkwardness. His finger thrust inside me, finding my G-spot, and I gasped, leaning into the feel and loving the way that when he touched me, it was all I could think about.

One finger quickly became two and then three until I was riding his hand, my hips shifting so my clit got some friction too.

Whip's dick was hard against my thigh, and his lips were sweet at my neck when he whispered, "Need to fuck you, sweetheart. You're so damn wet, your pussy is begging for it."

"Yes," I groaned, the ache inside me so desperate it hurt. I needed more than just his fingers. I wanted to fall over the edge with him inside me, while he held me tight.

But as soon as he stopped touching me to pick up the condom, everything rushed back in.

Screams. Countdowns. Blood.

Death.

I slammed my eyes shut, willing the images away, but they didn't stop. They rained down on me in a tidal wave of horror.

I couldn't breathe.

"Violet, look at me," Levi commanded from his spot on the chair behind Whip's back.

I did as I was told, peeling open my eyes to find him staring at me. He was still shirtless, sitting in nothing but a towel tucked around his waist. His tattoos covered his skin, hard muscle beneath them. There was a white gauze bandage taped to one of his pecs. I frowned at it, wondering when he'd gotten hurt.

But before I could question it, he spoke again. "Eyes on me, baby. Don't think."

Whip slid inside me while I was still watching Levi.

I gasped at the intrusion. Whip was as big as I remembered, but I stretched around him easily, taking every inch he had to offer. He bottomed out inside me, his pubic bone colliding with my clit deliciously, while Levi watched.

I couldn't turn away from his impossibly green eyes. They held me captive, heat flickering behind them, setting them ablaze as he watched another man take me.

The orgasm built inside me, thrust by thrust. Whip had me on the perfect angle, one that had me desperate, until my hips were moving just as quickly as his, my leg still hooked over his hip, anchoring him to me, keeping him close.

Levi never looked away. Not when tiny cries of pleasure slipped from my mouth because Whip knew exactly what to do and how to move to get me off. And not when

I hit the maximum point of pleasure and fell straight into an orgasm that numbed my brain so beautifully I wanted to swim in it forever.

Whip seemed to know exactly that. When my eyes closed, he just kept going, prolonging the orgasm, milking out every second of the bliss while I spasmed around him. He came with a groan, saying my name, kissing my forehead like I was something special.

My entire body hummed. And for a good long minute, even though Whip got up to get rid of the condom, I lay there blissed-out enough that I thought I might even be able to sleep.

Until the orgasm ebbed away. And all I was left with was the aching hole inside me and thoughts I didn't want to have. The panic rose again, choking me painfully, the relief Whip had provided so sweet but not nearly long enough.

Levi got up from his chair and knelt at the edge of the bed, grabbing my hand. "Hey. Hey. Eyes on me, remember? You're here with us. You're safe."

Except I wasn't. I wasn't safe from the thoughts in my head.

Not unless one of them was touching me.

I pulled his hand to my naked breast.

His gaze flickered down at it in surprise and then back up to my eyes. "Vi..." There was a distinct tone of hesitation and wariness in his voice.

I pushed into his hand. "Please. I don't want to think."

Agony played out behind his eyes. He glanced toward the end of the bed, where I was aware of the other two men, even though I wasn't looking at them.

But I tugged his arm, drawing his attention back to

me. I knew what I wanted, and I needed him to see it. "Put your mouth on me."

He groaned hoarsely, his dick clearly hard beneath his towel. I tugged at it, and it came undone, exposing a thick cock nestled in a trim patch of dark hair at the base.

He was so damn beautiful, tattoos covering so much of his skin that I wanted to trace them and figure out what each one represented. They were beautiful pieces of art, and I wanted to take my time exploring each one.

But not now. Right now I needed more than that.

And so did he.

He maneuvered me onto my back, fitting his mouth over the tip of my breast and sucking my nipple. Warm, wet heat encased me once more, having the exact desired effect of keeping my brain from thinking of anything else but how it felt to have this man touch me after so many weeks and months of getting to know him via his letters.

The sheets did nothing to cover me. They'd slipped down, somewhere around my calves, but I didn't bother trying to hide. Whip sat in the chair Levi had vacated, but it was X's dark eyes, watching me silently from the end of the bed that drew my attention this time.

We'd been all over each other in the shower the other night. I'd been so sure he was going to be the one to take my virginity. I'd been so eager to give it to him. I'd wanted him. And even though he'd run out on me, for no reason I could explain, I still did.

"X."

His eyes focused on me.

I spread my legs.

It was brave and bold, but I no longer had any fucks left to give.

He sucked in a sharp breath, moving forward from the floor at the end of the bed. He was slimmer than the other two men, no less muscled, just not the thickly solid build of Levi, who had a bulk that came from working out, and Whip whose shoulders were naturally broad.

X was all long, sleek lines and fluid movements, including the one where he crawled up the bed, his gaze locked on mine, and wrapped his arms around my wide-spread thighs.

I didn't have to ask him. His mouth lowered to my pussy.

4

X

She could have asked me to run a marathon or fight a shark or climb a mountain bare-ass naked and covered in honey during lion breeding season, and I would have said yes.

Sinking my tongue into her sweet pussy was the easiest thing in the world and the last thing I deserved.

But she wanted this. Had asked me for it, and even though I was a piece of shit, who hadn't earned the right to be between her thighs, there was zero part of me who could say no to her.

Guilt sat heavy in my gut. Everything that had happened to her tonight was my fault. Why hadn't I gone after her the moment I'd seen her and Toby sneak away? I'd been so worried about scaring her again. Chasing after her down a darkened street while she ran away from me was almost as appealing as squeezing her throat, so I hadn't let myself do it. I'd thought I could be trusted, thought now I was older and had found a woman I didn't just want to fuck, but to hold and get to know, maybe those sick desires inside me would go away.

But they hadn't.

And so I'd let her run off into the night, even though I knew it wasn't safe.

And look what had happened.

This was all my fault, and I would spend the rest of my life trying to make up for what I'd caused. If that meant going down on her when she needed to switch her brain off then I would be at her beck and call, giving her the most mind-blowing orgasm I could.

But nothing about that felt like a punishment. She could ride my face, smother me in her juices, crush my head with her thick thighs, and none of it would ever feel like enough to make up for the mistakes I'd made.

Her fingers stroked through my hair, and my dick kicked painfully. I was so fucking hard. Watching Whip make her come had put a stranglehold on my cock that hadn't lifted when Levi had started sucking on her nipples. Jealousy burned through me, but I fueled it all into giving her what she needed.

Her clit was the most perfect little bud that rolled sweetly beneath my tongue. She was so wet, her pussy relaxed and seeping with arousal I couldn't get enough of. I stroked my tongue through it, licking her clit, her opening, and driving my tongue inside her, just to hear her moan.

I gazed up at her, memorizing the curves and rolls and dimples of her body, before locking on to her eyes.

I moaned against her flesh, because her watching me go down on her was the hottest thing I'd ever experienced. Way hotter than anything I'd seen at Psychos or Sinners.

Because it was her.

Her hips lifted, and her beautiful lips parted, breathy moans escaping.

She was close. I could feel it in the fluttering of her pussy when I drove my fingers inside her, pressing up so I was on her G-spot.

I knew this didn't forgive the way I'd run out on her. Or what I'd let happen to her tonight. Her letting me between her thighs had nothing to do with me and everything to do with her needing to disappear into some other place where the nightmares she'd lived didn't exist.

I worked her harder, faster, giving her that because it was all I could do right.

She came around my fingers, her eyes closing and her head pressing back on the pillows. Her pussy gripped me tightly, and with every ounce of my being, I wished it were my cock. I wanted her naked on my lap, riding me, our bodies pressed together and her lips on mine.

I wanted a connection I knew I didn't deserve and didn't get to have.

And Violet knew it too, because when she reached for someone to kiss, it wasn't me. She pulled down Levi's head, claiming his lips, kissing him so deeply I felt it in my fucking toes.

He kissed her back like he was starving for it, delving his fingers into her hair and cupping her face, deepening the kiss until they moved as one.

It was Violet who rolled him onto his back, and Violet who took control, lining herself up with his cock and then sinking down onto it.

His groan of approval filled the small room, but this wasn't about him, and we all knew it. This was Violet's show. She rocked her hips over his, taking what she needed, her thighs spread wide over his hips, her fingers on his chest for balance.

Her long blond hair fell down her back, dry and soft from the way Whip had taken care of her, but now sexily tousled from rolling around in the sheets. It was the most beautiful I'd ever seen her, her rounded ass bottoming down on Levi with each thrust.

She moved faster and faster, chasing down another orgasm, chasing away the night with sex that would get her through until the sun rose.

But she'd already had two orgasms, and I could see her frustrations rising as she fought to find another. Her fingers worked her clit furiously, but it wasn't as easy for her to find that next way out of her head.

I crawled farther up the bed, fitting myself in behind her. I wrapped my arms around her, grabbing a handful of her breast and tweaking the nipple between my fingers. The urge to drag my hand up her throat and squeeze was there, but with Whip and Levi in the room, there was safety for both of us. I knew they wouldn't let me hurt her.

"Lean forward while you ride him." I didn't want to make a thing out of her inexperience, but watching her struggle to get where she wanted to be was fucking killing me.

She did exactly what I said, dropping down to kiss Levi again like she needed him to breathe. Her tits rubbed on his chest, her clit against his pubic bone.

For long seconds, I stared at her pussy stretched

around his cock while she rocked back and forth on top of him, him thrusting up into her from the mattress. It was beautiful and mesmerizing and had me harder than I'd ever fucking been.

My cock ached to join them. To push inside her and watch her take both of us.

But her body wasn't ready for any of that.

But I could get her to come again.

I rubbed my hand over the tip of my cock, gathering up the precum sitting there, and then spread it over her asshole.

"Oh God!" Her shout echoed around the room.

I gripped her behind with one hand, not entering her, just showing her how good it could make her feel.

Her orgasm came with shouts of pleasure, both hers and Levi's, her pulsing pussy sending both of them into an orgasm.

She fell down onto his chest, taking every ounce of his cum, him whispering words in her ear I couldn't make out, nor did I want to, because the jealousy inside me would probably fucking kill me if I had to hear it.

She rested her head down on his chest, twisting it to one side to watch Whip while she caught her breath.

His voice was deep and gruff, strained with a need of his own. "You did good, sweetheart. Look at you, so fucking beautiful." He leaned in, kissing her again.

The possessive part of me wanted to scream and rip him away from her. To claim her lips for my own.

But that wasn't my right.

I'd done what she needed from me.

I didn't deserve more.

She and Levi breathed together, their chests rising

and falling, their bodies still joined as they came down. His arms held her tight, his palms stroking up and down her back soothingly, kissing her in between, like that was all he wanted to do for the rest of his life.

And I couldn't blame him. Her kisses looked drugging. Like a man could happily kiss her and no other for the rest of his days and never have a single ounce of regret.

It was an intimacy I knew I could never have, because I would always take it too far.

Violet shifted, lifting off Levi's cock but still lying on top of him like she didn't have the energy to move.

His cum leaked out of her pussy, and I couldn't stop staring at it.

The jealousy inside me demanded I take her too. Slam myself inside her and come so her body knew she wasn't his, but mine too.

I couldn't ask her for that.

But I couldn't stop myself either. With her still lying on top of him, I moved in closer, into the gap of his legs, and lifted her hips so her ass was in the air, her head still down on his chest.

My cock notched at her entrance, sliding through Levi's cum mixed with her arousal, and all I wanted to do was pound into her, replace all of him with all of me.

But that was as close as I would let myself get. I refused to drive inside her and let myself feel the sweet relief of her pussy wrapped around my cock.

It was Violet who pushed back. Violet who forced herself onto my cock.

And once the tip of me was inside her, there was no holding back.

I fucked her hard, slamming myself into her body, knowing she could take it because she was so warmed up from the other two. I held her hip with one hand, drawing her back to meet my thrusts, the other finding the star of her asshole once more and teasing it until her breathy moans of pleasure turned into screams of ecstasy.

She was so fucking loose and relaxed, exactly how I wanted my woman after fucking two other men. If she'd been tight, I would have been scared of hurting her, but there was no chance of that now, with how wet she was and how well her body took me.

I played her ass some more, lubing it up, still not entering her more than the barest hint while I rimmed her, teased her, built her up, until her pussy went from loose and relaxed to fluttering, to viselike pulses she couldn't control.

"Oh my God! X!"

My name on her lips was more than I could handle. I smacked my palm across her ass, and she squealed again, driving her hips back to meet me, fucking me as much as I was fucking her. The slaps of our bodies filled the room, and I drove inside her, faster and faster, milking her orgasm and holding on to mine for as long as I could until holding on a second longer felt impossible.

I slammed home, her soft ass too fucking sweet against my lower belly, her hips soft beneath my hands. I came in shudders, filling her, my cum mixing with Levi's, drowning it out, leaking from her pussy and across her inner thighs.

When I couldn't take it another second, I pulled out, watching white drip from her, and then giving in to my basic desires and pushing it back inside her with my cock that was barely hard anymore, needing me in for as long as possible.

She fell asleep like that on Levi's chest, Whip watching from the chair, and my cock still warm inside her.

5

———

VIOLET

The smell of fried bacon, and early morning sunlight that my broken blinds had never been able to keep out, woke me. And for the tiniest of moments, I thought the entire night before had been a dream.

But then I cracked open an eye, and the warm male bodies tucked around me reminded me otherwise.

I sat up quickly, tugging at the sheet, my eyes widening as I took in X and Levi both passed out in my bed, both still gloriously, one-hundred-percent naked.

Neither of them moved, but I couldn't stay there. I crept to the end of the bed, getting off it as quietly as I could because waking either of them up felt like a fate worse than death after everything we'd done last night.

I'd let three men fuck me, one after the other, until I'd passed out.

Shit, we hadn't even used a condom. The proof of that still coating my inner thighs. I slipped silently into the bathroom and cleaned myself up, but the smell of bacon was too good to ignore.

Whip worked his way around the kitchen like he'd cooked for me a hundred times. Gray sweats were tied tight around his muscled waist, showing off V lines either side of his hips that had no business looking that good on a man in his mid-forties.

He glanced up when he heard me and paused with his fingers around the frying pan handle. "Hey, sweetheart."

I gave him a small smile.

He watched me carefully for a second then pointed at one of the urban landscape photographs that decorated the walls of our living room. "I've been staring at those all morning. Did you take them?"

I gave a slight shake of my head. "No. I have no artistic talent. They're Toby's. He's really creative. Photography is his most recent obsession." I suddenly realized what I'd said. "Was...photography *was* his most recent obsession."

I fell silent.

Whip's expression filled with sympathy. "How you doing? Not about Toby. You don't have to talk about that right now. I meant about everything after..."

I hoisted myself up onto one of the breakfast barstools to watch him cook. "I don't know."

He shook the fry pan, making sure the eggs didn't stick. "You sore?"

A blush crept up the back of my neck. "Yes. But not in a bad way, exactly."

He nodded his approval. "Good. Last night was a lot. But you needed it."

I had. I'd wanted every second of their hands on me.

I'd wanted their tongues and fingers and cocks, and I'd had so many orgasms last night I'd lost track of them. "Do you think I'm a slut now?"

He let go of the fry pan so quickly it clattered against the stove top. "What? Of course not. Jesus, fuck, Violet. You went through something so traumatic last night that words can't even express how bad it was. And so you forgot about it for a little while with men you knew and felt safe with. Having sex to forget is probably the least destructive path you could have taken. Other people would have used alcohol or drugs. Or worse."

I supposed that was fair. Whip said it all so matter-of-factly that even my doubts flittered away. My gaze strayed toward the dish strainer where Toby's favorite coffee mug sat, waiting to be put back in the cupboard. I looked away quickly, not wanting to think about the fact he was never going to use that mug again.

"How many people have you slept with?" I asked Whip instead.

He glanced over his shoulder at me and raised an eyebrow. "You asking me if I'm a slut now?" His mouth lifted into a cute grin that was contagious and felt a whole lot better than thinking about Toby.

"Maybe."

He shook his head. "I don't know. A lot. It kinda comes with the job." He switched off the gas and scooped an egg onto a plate. He added bacon and plucked two slices of toast from a stack he'd made by the toaster and placed them in front of me.

I reached over the countertop and pushed open the top drawer to grab a knife and fork. "Okay then. How many of them were actually women you wanted to sleep with? Like, ones you'd taken out for a meal and were actually attracted to and weren't getting paid to be with."

He stiffened.

I instantly knew I'd asked the wrong question, though I wasn't really sure why. I shoved a piece of bacon in my mouth to cover how uncomfortable I suddenly was. "Sorry."

"No, it's fine." He picked up a piece of toast for himself. "Two."

"Two?"

"Two women. I've only slept with two I actually cared about."

"Oh." I crunched my bacon, wishing I hadn't brought it up, because I was suddenly so jealous of those women my bacon tasted sour. I washed it down with a glass of orange juice.

Whip watched me, but he didn't elaborate. "Listen. My guys were here last night, after you and Levi and X fell asleep. They took everything we were wearing last night, as well as my car. They've cleaned the scene as well, so there shouldn't be anything there at the warehouse to implicate you in Toby's death."

I froze. "Toby's murder, you mean."

Whip watched me carefully. "Do you want to tell me what happened?"

I didn't, but I knew I had to. I owed them that much after what they'd done for me. They had no real reason to help me, and yet they were anyway.

"Is that bacon?" Levi came into the room from the hallway.

I avoided his gaze; sure my cheeks were pink again.

Whip answered for me, "Bacon and eggs and toast.

Clean clothes in the bag by the door if you want to wear something other than a towel…" He glanced up and then laughed at X emerging from the hallway. "Or a robe that's way too short." He squeezed his eyes shut. "Dude, I can see your balls."

X might have been unusually subdued last night, but there was no sign of that this morning. There was indeed sign of his balls peeping out beneath a silky robe I'd bought online twelve months ago that had claimed to be an extra-large but had turned out to be more like a small. I hadn't had a hope in hell of fitting into it, but I'd been too embarrassed to return it and ask for a bigger size, even though the sizing had clearly been way off standard.

I'd kept it with my foster mom's words ringing in my ears about how I should always have a goal outfit, and that's how she had kept herself so trim over the years.

I fucking hated that robe. It had made me feel like shit about myself every day for the past year, and I didn't know why I hadn't thrown it out.

But maybe this was why.

Because seeing it stretched around X was hilarious. Balls hanging out and all.

Levi winced at him. "Seriously, go put some pants on. Nobody ordered sausage for breakfast.

X raised an eyebrow at him. "Says the man whose balls I had a bird's-eye view of last night. Tit for tat." But he moved toward the bag Whip had pointed out, giving me a small smile as he passed. "Hey, Omelet."

The weird nickname he was so fond of barely registered. All I could think about was the way he'd fucked me doggy style last night, plunging into me after Levi had already used me so well.

I was going to be reliving that night in my dreams for a long time. At least I hoped I would be.

It was much more pleasant than the alternative nightmares I also knew I would be capable of.

X pulled on an identical pair of sweats to Whip and tossed a third pair at Levi.

I pointed at the white T-shirts still sitting in the clear plastic bag. "Any of you going to put a shirt on?"

Levi held up the sandwich he'd made with two pieces of toast and filled with the runny eggs and crispy bacon. "It's a lot easier to wipe egg off my chest than off a white shirt."

"I need a shower first," Whip added.

X nodded in agreement. "Same."

I wasn't going to complain. Having three attractive men in nothing but matching gray sweats wandering around my kitchen and making me food was something out of one of my romance books. I couldn't wait to tell Toby all about it.

My heart sank when I remembered I was never going to get to do that. The image of his body lying cold in that warehouse had me regretting all the bacon I'd just eaten.

"It wasn't me who murdered anyone last night," I said quietly.

The three of them fell silent, each of them looking in my direction.

Levi's elbows rested on the countertop across from me, and he set his breakfast sandwich back down on his plate. "Nobody thought you did."

I nodded stiffly, avoiding his gaze, and instead glancing over at the letter that had made its way onto the coffee table at some point I couldn't remember.

"Someone made me think that letter was from you. But when we got there, the door locked, and it was Dickson inside."

Levi's mouth flattened into a hard line. "Then he deserved everything he got."

"No, he didn't. He was just as confused as we were about why he was there." I forced myself to look him in the eye. "I know you didn't like him, but I really don't think he wanted to start anything with you. Everything that happened last night...the booby trap that killed Dickson...the countdown...Dickson was just as much a victim as Toby and I were."

Whip's warm hand found the back of my neck and squeezed it reassuringly. "We need to know everything, Vi. I know it's hard, but we need to know it all."

I'd spent the last few hours forcing all thoughts out of my head but now I found them all tumbling out, that burden needing to be shared with someone, so it lightened the load that was too heavy for my shoulders alone.

I told them every gruesome, horrifying detail.

And when I was done with word vomiting my trauma, I waited for a reaction from them.

But it didn't come. I squinted at them. "Why don't any of you seem surprised?"

I knew they'd all seen their fair share of dead bodies, but surely men being decapitated in booby-trapped windows and death countdowns weren't part of their everyday any more than they were part of mine?

Whip sighed heavily. "We need to tell you something now. They aren't just targeting you. They're targeting all of us. We've been getting letters from them, similar to the one you got last night, for the last few weeks."

It took a moment for that to sink in fully. But when it did, it brought a cold flush with it that sent goosebumps across my skin. "You knew? You knew there was some psycho out there targeting me and you didn't think that was information I should know?"

Whip's gaze dropped to the floor.

Levi cleared his throat uncomfortably. "We didn't actually know they were targeting you too—"

I held up my hand, not interested in being fed bullshit, and a whole lot of other things fitting together. "But you suspected, didn't you? Even if they hadn't directly threatened me, you suspected. That's why the three of you haven't left me alone for a second for the past few weeks. One of you has always been with me or sitting out in front of my apartment."

I suddenly felt so stupid I couldn't believe I hadn't realized any of this before. I barked out a bitter laugh. "Wow. And here I was, thinking you were hanging around just because you liked me."

"I would just like it noted I was hanging around you long before Grayson told us to watch you," X mumbled cheerfully around a mouthful of toast, clearly not picking up on the vibe in the room.

I just stared at him. "Grayson told you to watch me?"

Levi groaned, "Seriously, X. Shut up."

I whirled on him. "No, you don't get to tell him to shut up. At least he's being honest, unlike the two of you. You knew I was in danger and instead of telling me, you three went all freaking macho and decided you knew best. That I was too weak and pathetic to take care of myself and I needed the three of you to do it for me."

Levi reached for my hand, but I snatched it away before he could touch me.

He sighed, dropping it back to the countertop. "It wasn't like that. We didn't have any direct proof they would target you too, and we didn't want you to live your life in fear, always looking over your shoulder. That's a shit way to live, and you'd already been through enough, what with everything that happened at that house on Olympic Drive..."

I closed my eyes, remembering the way the owner of that house, Paul Jeddersen, had drugged me, stripped my clothes, and would have done so much worse if X hadn't been there to stop him.

Suddenly, I could understand why they didn't think I could take care of myself.

But the fact they'd judged me and formed opinions of my capabilities over that one event sent rage through me. I was more than the terrified, half-naked woman Paul Jeddersen had turned me into. I was also the woman who'd pitched anything in reach at X and Scythe when I'd thought they would hurt me. I was the woman who'd put herself together, alone in her room so I didn't have to burden anyone else with my troubles. I was the woman who just last night had asked three men to fuck her because I'd needed something and made it happen.

I wasn't always strong, but the three of them hadn't seen any of that. And in underestimating me, they'd caused my best friend's death.

"Get out."

Whip winced at the ice in my voice. "Sweetheart, we can't. Not after what happened last night."

I narrowed my eyes at him. "You can't? This is my

goddamn home, and I'm telling you to leave. So get out."
My gaze switched to the other two. "All of you."

"Vi, he's right. We can't leave you here alone. We need
to work out what we're doing next." Levi's mouth formed
a tight line.

Rage rose inside me, and my voice rose right along
with it. "I said, get out!"

All three of them stared at me, guilt riddled all over
their faces, but refusing to budge.

I couldn't believe them. My stool scraped along the
kitchen tiles as I jerked it back and got off, leaving my
half-eaten bacon and eggs behind. "If you won't leave,
then I will."

I stormed to my bedroom, slamming the door
behind me.

My anger with them only increased when I heard
them reassuring each other I couldn't go anywhere. We
were on the third floor, and the fire escape was outside
the living room, not my bedroom.

Oh, fuck them. I picked up my phone, made a single
call, and then started shoving clothes into a bag. I didn't
even know what I put in there, I was too blinded by rage
and hurt and embarrassment, and an ache that wanted to
consume me if I let go of any of those other feelings. I jerked
on clothes, yanking a hoodie over my head so roughly it
caught on my earring and ripped at my lobe painfully.

But the pain only spurred me on. And when I got a
text, I was ready.

Bag over my shoulder, I stormed back into the living
area.

X was the first to notice me. His gaze darted to the

overflowing bag of clothes shoved over my shoulder. "Uh-oh. I think someone is staging a jail break..." He glanced over at Levi. "You probably have experience with that, right?"

Levi made a face at him.

Whip sighed, taking in the bag. "We're sorry. You're right, we should have told you. We thought we were doing the right thing—"

"Well, you weren't."

Levi nodded. "We know. We fucked up."

"Yeah, you did."

X threw me his most charming smile. "But you think we're really cute, and we gave you really good orgasms, so we're forgiven?"

I glared at him. "Not a fucking chance. The three of you can go to hell."

I stormed to the door, but Levi grabbed my arm. "Vi, stop."

I stared down at his grip around my wrist. "Let go of me."

"You'll leave if I do."

"Damn fucking right I will. I said let go of me." I didn't care my traitorous body loved having his hands on me. I didn't care that all I could think about was him gripping both wrists that tightly, raising them above my head, and pinning me to a wall so he could touch places a whole lot more intimate than my arms.

But if he didn't let me go, I was going to use my free hand to punch him in the face.

My apartment door opened behind me, which was the first time I realized the lock was broken. But I didn't have long to dwell on that as the six-foot-five man I'd called for backup strode into the apartment.

Fang took one glimpse of Levi's fingers wrapped around my wrist and his voice dropped to a growl. "Get your fucking hands off my sister before I rip them from your body."

Levi didn't let go. "Fang...fucking hell. Hold up, I'm not hurting her."

Fang glowered at him. "Do I look like I care about your excuses? She said let her go. Even I heard that and I was out in the damn hallway. So you have exactly three seconds to do that before I make you. Don't think for a second I won't fucking end you right here, right now, Reaper. You might have been my mentor, but you've been out of the game a long fucking time, and you have no fucking idea how pissed off I am right now."

Levi's fingers reluctantly unraveled from around my wrist.

Stupidly, I instantly missed his touch. But the anger inside me would have to keep me warm instead. I didn't look back at the other two, just stormed to the door, Fang hot at my heels. Anger propelled me down the stairs and out onto the front lawn of the apartment building. Rebel was waiting behind the wheel of an SUV, knuckle-dusters around her fingers.

I slid into the back seat and glanced at them pointedly. "Were you expecting a fight?"

She shrugged, but there was a bit of disappointment in her expression. "More like was hoping for one. I don't get to use these enough these days." She threw a few air punches at the space above the steering wheel while Fang slid into the seat beside her.

The three men I'd spent the night in bed with had followed us down the stairs and were now standing helplessly on the lawn, watching us.

Rebel hit the power button that opened Fang's window and yelled across him, "Well, you three fucked up, didn't you? Dumbasses! Next time I see you, each of you is going to get a taste of these! A solid punch right to the dick!"

Each of them could have picked her up and tossed her across the room, but she was fearless. I had no doubt, if I'd asked her to, she would have been running across that lawn, aiming those knuckle-dusters at someone's junk.

Fang clicked his seat belt into place. "Pix, the getaway driver is supposed to actually drive the car. Not antagonize the targets with threats on their reproductive organs."

She grinned at him. "Oh, right. Sorry." She shook her metal-decorated knuckles at my men one last time and then put her foot on the gas.

X, Whip, and Levi disappeared behind us and I breathed a sigh of relief.

Fang twisted to glance back at me. "Are you okay?"

I wasn't. I was mortified, filled with embarrassment that I'd been stupid enough to think they actually wanted me and I wasn't just some job Grayson was making them do. I'd been a desperate, easy lay. But above all that, I was heartbroken. I'd opened myself up and had gotten stomped down in the most painful way I could imagine. But I forced myself to smile at Fang because he didn't need me trauma dumping all over him too.

"I will be. Thank you for picking me up." And then I added on, "Brother."

He smiled at that, just a little, the small upward flicker of his mouth at least the closest I'd seen Fang come to smiling.

"You're welcome. Sister."

6

WHIP

"So does anyone want to take bets on how Fang is going to kill Levi?" X flopped down onto Violet's couch like he didn't have a care in the world. "I'm thinking poison dart, administered via a blowgun disguised as a vape."

Levi side-eyed him from where he paced beside the sliding glass doors that led onto the balcony. "He's not going to kill me."

I raised an eyebrow. "Were we not looking at the same guy? Huge, blond motherfucker who was pretty pissed off you were touching his little sister?" I fought to keep the amusement off my face and leaned my elbows back against the kitchen countertop. "And he doesn't even know you had her naked and riding your cock just a few hours earlier. How do you think he's going to react when he finds out about that?"

Levi groaned and scrubbed his hands over his face. "Shit. This is fucked."

I glanced at X. "I'm putting a hundred on an old-fashioned classic. Sharpened toothbrush shiv, straight to the kidney."

X nodded. "Very prison chic. I like it."

Levi glared at both of us.

But all his annoyance did was light up the green in his eyes that was already impossible to miss, even from across the room. I couldn't get the image of Violet riding his cock out of my head, which was exactly why I had been so quick to bring it up. Her thick thighs snug around his waist. His abs flexing every time he pressed his hips upward to pump into her. His expression when he'd come, buried deep inside her.

I'd been so hard watching them. It had taken all my willpower to keep my ass on the chair in her room and my hands to myself.

Not that I was about to tell him that. One foursome did not make us friends.

A sharp knock at the door interrupted the conversation.

X glanced over at it. "Did she come back?"

I pushed off the stool and moved toward the door. "Yeah, she came back and now she's knocking on the door to her apartment, ready to ask for another round of kinky three-man sex."

X's expression turned hopeful. "You think?"

"No, X. I don't think. And clearly, neither do you."

I peered through the peephole, any humor I might have been feeling disintegrating at the sight of the men on the other side of the door. "Cops," I muttered to the other two before I pulled it open.

One of the uniformed officers on the other side of the door flashed his badge at me. "Morning, sir. Is this the home of..." He stared down at his notepad. "Violet Garrisen?"

I nodded, mentally assessing how much of a threat the two of them could be and how quickly the three of us on this side of the doorway could handle them if the need arose. But my assessment came back as low risk. These looked like beat cops, most likely sent here to inform her of Toby's death. "Yes. This is her place."

"Can I speak to her, please?"

"She's not here right now." I wasn't going to give them any more information than they directly asked for. Anyone who lived in this area knew better than to tell them more than you absolutely had to. The cops were well known to twist your words to suit their narrative, so the less you told them, the better.

"Do you know where she is?"

"At her brother's place."

The cop nodded, jotting something down on his pad of paper. "We'll need his details, if you have them."

"We don't." I wasn't lying. I had no idea where Fang lived, but even if I had, I wouldn't have said anything. They could do the math themselves. It would buy us some time to let Violet know they were coming, and that she should be ready with an alibi and cover story. One that matched ours.

The cop eyed me, clearly getting irritated with my lack of cooperation. "And who are you exactly?"

"A friend."

He glanced past me to the other guys standing behind me. "And you two are *friends* as well, I assume?"

I didn't like his tone.

X narrowed his eyes at him. "Are you insinuating Violet can't have more than one friend?"

The cop crossed his arms over his chest. "I'm not insinuating anything. But I do need to know who was in this apartment last night."

"We were," Levi answered. "Violet too."

"But not her roommate?"

Levi played it cool. "Toby? No, he was here earlier in the night but he went out somewhere. Hasn't come home as far as I know."

"As far as you know? It's a small apartment, I think you'd know if he had returned, don't you?"

Levi shrugged. "We were busy."

"Doing what?"

X answered before Levi or I could. "Having sex."

I squeezed my eyes shut. He was so painfully, brutally honest at times. It kinda made me want to choke him.

Both police officers' eyes had widened.

"You were...having sex." He squinted. "All three of you."

"Yep!" X said proudly. "All three of us."

The cops' gazes bounced around us.

There was a hint of laughter on the older cop's rounded face. "Together?"

Levi stiffened, his voice harsh when he spoke, clearly no love lost between him and law enforcement. "Do you really need the blow-by-blow playbook? You want to know who touched who? Who sucked and licked and fucked the others? You want to write that down in your notebook so you can share it with your pervy friends back at the station?"

"Levi," I said quietly, a warning in my tone. He was

getting carried away, and the last thing I had patience for this morning was him getting arrested and us having to work out how the hell to get him out, along with everything else.

The cop stared at him. "No, but the woman will need an alibi, so if she was involved in all the sex, then we'll need to know."

My irritation with the two officers bubbled up. "That's none of your—"

X cut me off, not picking up on my or Levi's vibe at all, as usual. "Oh yeah, she was definitely involved. She was kind of the star of the show, if you know what I mean. And it really was a show. Whip over there was a total perv, just sitting in the armchair watching her bounce on Levi—"

"X!" I snapped.

"What?"

I gave him a look, but he clearly didn't get the meaning of it because he turned back to the officers.

"Have you spoken to the neighbors yet? Did they report screaming? Because if they did, don't worry. I think that was just me. Sometimes I scream when I come."

Levi dropped his head back on his shoulders, tilting his face to the ceiling. "Someone kill me now."

I shared the sentiment.

The cops stared at X for a long moment, clearly never having experienced anyone with quite as much verbal diarrhea that it was taking their brains a moment to catch up. So long, in fact, X leaned in and pointed at the notepad.

"Did you want to write that down? Screams when he comes…"

At this point, I realized X was messing with them just for his own amusement, and I moved to his side so I could dig my elbow sharply into his ribs. "If there's nothing else you need right now, Officers, we have things to do."

"Like more sex," X stage-whispered to them. "He can't get enough. I think it's the age gap thing that's got him so horny, you know? All the Viagra—"

I shoved X out the door so sharply he stumbled, and the cops had to catch him. I slammed the door behind him and leaned my back against it.

Levi battled to keep the laughter off his face. "Should I get a chair to shove beneath the door handle so he can't get back in? You know the lock is broken."

"Please!"

But I needn't have bothered. X's voice trailed back as he and the officers descended the stairs. "Do either of you like ice cream? My van is right out front. I can make you anything you want. Banana split? Milkshake?"

I shook my head at Levi, their voices drifting away. "I'm going to kill him."

Levi leaned back on the glass balcony doors. "Could you maybe give it a minute? We've got enough murders to deal with right now."

I strode across the room and slumped down onto the well-worn couch. "We need to talk to Violet."

He sat next to me, the cushions dipping beneath his weight. "Don't see that happening anytime soon. I just texted her to let her know the cops had been here and got this back in return from an unknown number."

He held his phone up to show me the GIF of someone smashing a set of dusters into a banana. The soft fruit had no chance against the brass knuckles. I squinted at it as it played over, and then up at Levi.

"Rebel," both of us said in unison.

I nudged his phone back toward him. "She's like a tiny mean chihuahua, that one."

Levi shoved me with his foot. "Don't speak bad of chihuahuas. I used to have one. They're great dogs."

I glanced over at him. "Did you carry it in your purse too?"

He made a face at me. "Hilarious. My point was, they aren't all mean. And I don't even blame Rebel for being pissed at us. She's just protecting Violet, and I can respect that."

I nodded, leaning back on the soft cushions of the couch, trying not to notice Levi was still shirtless and his arm and shoulders were just inches away from touching mine. His warmth radiated through the tiny gap between us, enticing me to inch closer, though I refused to give in to the desire.

So the guy was hot. Who fucking cared? I'd seen a ton of hot guys naked. I worked with couples just as much as I worked with women, it didn't matter to me if I was sucking and licking a pussy or a cock. I was just there to do a job.

But I was never attracted to them the way I was with Levi.

It was fucking annoying, noticing every little thing about him, especially when he was so clearly straight. He'd gotten all stiff and weird when X had let those cops think the three of us had been having sex together. It didn't matter that none of us had touched each other and the entire night had been all about Violet.

Levi was as straight as a rod, and I had zero interest in trying to change his mind. I was too old for that shit.

But then he shifted on the couch that was really too small to accommodate two big men, and his warm skin brushed mine.

He didn't glance my way, just stared at the TV that neither of us had turned on, his arm still pressed to mine.

Suddenly, all I could think about was dragging him back into that bedroom, just the two of us, and seeing what happened.

My arm burned where it touched his, electricity sizzling between us so hot I was sure it had to be leaving a mark, but Levi didn't seem bothered at all. He just sighed and drummed his fingers on his thigh.

"We fucked up so bad. Everything she said, she was right. We shouldn't have kept any of it from her. We could have gotten her killed last night." He swore under his breath. "Dickson's and Toby's deaths are on us, aren't they?"

I was so lost in the attraction it took me a second to register what he was talking about. I could have used one of Rebel's knuckle-dusters to the junk just to get my head screwed on right. "I don't know about Dickson, but Toby's death is a hundred percent on us."

Levi dropped forward, resting his elbows on his knees. "She's never going to forgive us. And I don't even blame her."

I sighed heavily, that guilt rushing back in thick and fast. "All we can do is try to make it up to her." I swallowed thickly, the words on my tongue turning sour. "Or respect that she doesn't want anything to do with us."

Levi glanced over at me sharply. "I can't do that. I can't

just walk away. That's not an option." There was something hot in his eyes that told me he meant every word. "I'm fucking in love with her."

I let out a long breath. Of course he was.

But Levi's gaze didn't let up. It burned through me. "Can you? Can you just walk away from her like that and pretend none of this...last night...can you pretend all of that didn't happen?"

I felt my shields going up. The ones I kept tall around my heart to protect what was left of it.

I'd let them drop when I'd met Violet. And that had left room for my attraction to Levi.

Both of which were dangerous.

He was in love with her. And there was zero doubt in my mind she was in love with him too. I'd seen it time and time again in the way she looked at him. She might have been mad at him, but there was a connection there I couldn't compete with, nor did I want to try.

She deserved a man who would love her as wholeheartedly as Levi did.

I couldn't give her that. My heart was too fucking broken to give her anything more than sex.

And it always would be.

7

X

My truck was about as depleted of sweet treats as one would expect, given I'd allowed an entire underprivileged neighborhood free rein in it. There were candy bar wrappers and sticky puddles of melted ice cream from one end of the truck to the other.

But the thing still started, and I thanked whichever gods watched over Saint View that the little hoodlums hadn't stripped the entire thing for parts.

I needed to get my baby cleaned and restocked but instead found myself parked out in front of Scythe's house in Providence. He opened the door before I was even halfway down the path. His gaze skated over me, and without even asking why I was barefoot and shirtless, he just ducked back inside, emerging with a pair of sneakers and a hoodie.

He tossed them at me, closing the door behind me. "Come on. I've got to do school pickup. It's the girls' early release day, and I'm the only one here to do it. You can talk on the way."

I trailed along after him, hoisting myself up into the passenger seat of his SUV that had two baby seats in the back. I pulled on the hoodie before drawing the seat belt across my chest and clicking it into place.

Scythe put the car in reverse and then with his hand on the back of my seat, he twisted so he could look over his shoulder.

He winked at me. "Don't go falling in love with me."

I frowned at him. "Why would I?"

He shrugged. "Bliss always gets giggly when I put my hand here to reverse. Apparently, it's a thing."

I frowned at him. "But your hand is just on the back of my seat. And reversing a car isn't a big deal. I don't get it."

"Me neither. But it has resulted in head while I drive before, so I just wanted to be sure you weren't getting any ideas."

I raised an eyebrow. "No shit? She likes it that much?" I tucked that little tidbit away for future reference. Then sighed when I remembered Violet wouldn't be giggling at me, let alone anything else anytime soon. And being alone in a car with her was now completely off-limits, after what I'd done.

I sighed again, making it as dramatic as possible.

Scythe rolled his eyes. "Talk, X. And make it quick, because in about five minutes, we're going to be surrounded by minivans playing Taylor Swift and teachers trying to herd swarms of kids into them."

I grinned. "That sounds like a vibe. Do you have an entrance song? You know, like one you always play as you slide on in through the school gates, with it blaring out the window?"

"This isn't a wrestling match."

I shrugged, fiddling with the music switches on his dashboard, flipping through the playlist to find some Tay Tay I could crank up loud.

Scythe glanced over at me, a frown crinkling between his eyebrows. "It's bad, huh?"

"Taylor's stuff is never bad! Wash your mouth out."

"I meant whatever you've done, and you know it. I've never seen anyone procrastinate so hard on spilling his guts."

I breathed out heavily, forcing every bit of air out of my lungs until they ached. "I choked Violet, then her best friend died, and then we had a foursome."

He spun the steering wheel, taking a corner. He peeked at me once he had the car straightened again. "That's a lot for one sentence."

"You said to stop procrastinating!"

"Well, I can see why you were, if that's what you've been up to! Just to clarify, when you said you choked Violet, then had sex with her, she was still alive during the sex? Or no?"

"What? Of course she was!"

"Okay, okay! I was just checking we weren't dealing with some sort of 'fucking dead people' kink. I'm not one to judge."

"I'm kinda judging you for not judging! That's not a kink, that's messed up."

"Agreed. What were we talking about again?"

"Me choking Violet. And the fact I'm never going to be alone with her ever again."

Scythe stopped in the car pickup line. "Right. Gotcha."

"You ever do that to Bliss?"

Scythe shook his head fast. "No. Never."

I slumped in my seat. "Great. I'm a monster even among monsters."

Scythe let the car roll forward a few feet as someone farther ahead of us in the line drove their kid away. "You stopped though, right? You didn't actually kill her. That's a good thing."

"I put my fingers around her throat and squeezed. And liked it."

Scythe shrugged. "So you have a choking kink."

"What if it's more than a kink?" I asked, voicing the fear that had plagued me ever since I'd done it.

He didn't say anything for a long moment. He didn't need to. We both knew the answer.

Scythe tapped his fingers on the steering wheel and crept us forward a few more inches. "What if she liked it?"

"She didn't," I said quickly. "I scared her."

"Do you know that for sure or are you just projecting your fears onto her? You said you had sex with her last night. She wanted that, right? I know you didn't fucking force her. You might be a monster, but you aren't that sort of man."

I nodded quickly, remembering the way Violet had opened her thighs for me, showing me how wet her pussy was and inviting me into it.

Scythe pushed further. "If she was scared of you, do you really think she would have done that?"

He had a point.

But it was kind of moot, considering she'd stormed off this morning, after she'd realized what we'd kept from her. "Bliss ever get so mad at you she ran off to her brother's place and swore she never wanted to see you again?"

"Bliss's only living brother is about thirteen...so no."

"Violet's brother is Fang."

Scythe snorted on a laugh. "You're so fucked."

Didn't I know it.

We reached the top of the car line, and two dark-haired little girls ran over. Scythe got out of the car and rounded the hood to the sidewalk, scooping both of them up in a hug.

He opened the back door, setting down the oldest to wriggle over to her seat, and helping the younger one into hers, strapping her in tightly.

The older one looked at me curiously and then held her hand out to me. "Hello. I'm Lexa."

I took her little fingers in mine and shook them seriously. "X."

She nodded at that. "X is a weird name. But so is Scythe. And that's one of my dad's names."

Scythe chuckled beneath his breath. "Hey, Lex? X likes Taylor Swift too."

Her eyes widened. "You do?"

I nodded. "Sure do. What's your favorite song?"

Lexa launched into a detailed description of all of her favorite songs, which turned out to be pretty much every song on every album Taylor had ever recorded.

Scythe got back behind the wheel and got us onto the road again. He glanced over at her proudly.

"You love her, huh?" I asked him, watching him stare at his daughter.

He grinned and nodded. "Mila too. And Ridge, our son. They're the best kids."

I envied him, and the family he'd created for himself. He and I were similar in a lot of ways, but I couldn't see me ever getting to where he was. He had Vincent, his other personality, to offset his crazy and keep him in line.

What I wouldn't give for a second personality I could just trade out with. One who wasn't as messed up in the head as I was.

A saner personality would have been able to stay away from Violet. But I knew I couldn't.

I didn't want to share her. It had been fucking torture watching her with Whip and Levi last night.

But it had kept her safe. Their presence had been the only reason I could be with her at all. Because I'd known and trusted neither of them would let me hurt her.

I wanted what Scythe had with Bliss. I wanted to be alone in a car with her, and to have her watch me reverse it and find it so sexy she couldn't wait to have me and had to blow me right there.

I couldn't have that without Levi and Whip.

But right now, none of us had her.

Which was a problem we really needed to fix.

8

VIOLET

My brother's house was pure chaos. There were toys strewn across the floor, sippy cups and bottles on every available surface, and a stack of brightly colored plastic plates waiting to be piled into the dishwasher.

But there were also four gorgeous kids running around, and a baby who was barely old enough to smile but who lit up the moment Vaughn placed her in her mother's arms.

Rebel brought the baby's head to her lips and inhaled her scent, smiling down at her youngest daughter before thrusting her in my direction. "Smell her head. It's like crack. So good."

"Uh…" I was pretty sure I'd never smelled a baby's head before and it felt a bit weird to do it now, but Rebel was dangling the kid beneath my nose like a carrot, so I leaned in and took a whiff.

Surprisingly, she did smell quite good. Somehow sweet. Rebel practically tossed her into my arms, and I only minorly freaked out about dropping my youngest niece. I settled on the couch with her and took another sniff of her head to calm myself.

Rebel wrangled a little boy who had launched himself at her as soon as her arms were free, and a younger girl trailed with a blanket dragging behind her.

Fang sat across from me in an armchair that seemed too small for his huge frame, but then he picked up the tiny dark-haired girl who immediately curled up on his lap and stuck her thumb in her mouth, while she watched me with big eyes from the safety of his lap.

He smoothed her tousled hair back from her face. "This is Lavender. LaLa, this is your aunt, Violet."

I gave her a wave, and she turned shyly into my brother's shirt. She didn't look anything like my hulking, Viking-ish brother, and I suspected she was not his biological child, but that clearly didn't matter to him.

The boy climbing all over my sister-in-law was now upside down, swinging from her arms like a monkey but peeking at me curiously. Rebel twisted so I could see his cute face. "And this is Wolf. The big two who ran through earlier were Remi and Madden. The one you're holding is the newest recruit. Her name is Snow, but she probably doesn't know that because everyone just calls her baby or bubba."

I stared down at her and felt my ovaries clench at her happy little face. "I can't believe you guys have five kids."

Rebel laughed. "Trust me, we can't either."

Another man swept down from the stairs carrying an armload of laundry. I recognized Kian from when we'd met at Psychos, and he grinned at me. "Wondered when you'd end up over here." He leaned down and kissed my cheek. "Welcome to the madhouse, sis."

"Aunt Violet!" a little voice called from the top of the stairs. "Do you want to see my monster trucks?"

I twisted to see the two older kids, who still really weren't very old at all, maybe six or seven. The blonde-haired girl, Remi I assumed, whispered something to her brother.

Madden called back down, "Remi wants to know if you want to see her monster truck too. Hers is pink though, so it's not as cool as mine."

I opened my mouth to tell them I'd love to, but Rebel cut me off. "Give Aunt Violet a minute, okay, guys? Take Wolf upstairs with you and get a track set up."

Wolf twisted, trying to get down fast, and Rebel set him on his feet so he could sprint up the stairs after his older siblings.

Lavender had fallen asleep on Fang's lap, though how that had happened with all the shouting was beyond me, but I guessed she was used to it.

Fang's phone buzzed, and he took it out of his pocket, frowning at it, and then glancing over at me.

I sighed. "Which one is it?"

"Reaper. Says they just had the cops over at your place. They know you're here, but they don't know where here is, so we probably have some time."

I pressed my teeth into my bottom lip. "I don't know what to say to them." I'd filled them both in on the drive over here, so they knew everything that had happened the night before.

Well, almost everything. I hadn't told them about the orgy.

"Not the truth," Rebel said quietly, sinking down into the seat beside me. "You were the only person who walked out of that building alive last night, and you're a woman from Saint View who grew up in foster care. The lazy pieces of shit at the Providence Police Department will take one look at that and instantly make you the number one suspect."

A shudder ran through her slight frame, and Vaughn, standing behind us, squeezed her shoulders. "Hey. Don't go there. This isn't the same as when your mom died."

I glanced questioningly between Rebel and Vaughn, but she'd closed her eyes, leaning into his touch, and he was fully concentrated on her.

Fang pulled Lavender closer on his lap. "Rebel was the prime suspect in her mom's murder about six or seven years ago, despite there being zero proof she had anything to do with it."

"Which of course, I didn't," she muttered angrily, still clearly holding a grudge I couldn't blame her for. She turned her dark eyes on me. "Don't ever think they'll help you. The police in this town are as corrupt and useless as they come."

I stroked the baby's head, understanding what she meant. "I know. I've had my own run-ins with them in the past." I would never forget how they'd treated Toby and me after his attack. Never.

Fang's phone buzzed again, and his cheeks went pink.

Rebel squinted at him. "What is it?"

Fang just passed her the phone. She read it, snorted on a laugh, and held it out so I could read it as well.

My face instantly flamed with embarrassment.

Rebel's laughter filled the room. "Want to tell us why

the guys told the cops you were having sex with them all night, little sis?"

The tiny five-foot-nothing woman calling me little was hilarious, but that was the second time someone in this house had called me sis, and they weren't even the ones who were blood related to me. I barely knew these people, and yet with one phone call they'd dropped everything to come get me. Their kids were calling me Aunt, and a warmth settled over me that went a small way toward filling the gaping void inside me that had always craved family.

My brother and I had never had it with our biological parents or siblings.

But he'd found it here, with Rebel and Vaughn and Kian, in the most unconventional way.

Fang groaned. "I don't think I want to hear this."

I glanced at him. "You really probably don't."

He nodded. "I'm going to take LaLa upstairs to bed then."

Vaughn followed, but Kian dropped down into the seat Fang had vacated and grinned at me like an overexcited golden retriever. "Tell us all the juicy hot details."

Rebel sniggered. "He wants the tea as much as I do. So spill it."

So I did, because I needed someone to talk to, and I no longer had the one person who'd always been my go-to. Eventually the police showed up, and I put on the show of my life, acting shocked when they told me about Toby's death, though the numb feeling that spread through me at hearing it on their lips was real.

They asked where I was, and I told them the alibi the guys had given me. If they questioned the neighbors,

Cassy in particular, they might have found out that alibi had holes in it, but for now, at least, it satisfied them.

They left, telling me they may need to contact me again.

My fingers shook the moment the door closed.

Kian took them and squeezed them. "You did good."

I nodded up at him, and he let me go.

"What now?" Rebel asked. "You've got a shift at Psychos tonight, but I can tell Bliss you won't make it in if you just want to lie low."

But that reminded me what day it was, and I fumbled with my phone to check the time. "Shit. No, I'll do the shift tonight. I need the money. And the distraction. But I have a job for Clean Sweep this afternoon. I can't miss it or Francine will fire me. I'm already skating on thin ice with her."

Fang picked up a set of car keys. "I can drive you."

"Thank you." I paused. "Can you do something else for me?"

He nodded solemnly. "Anything."

"I need you to convince Grayson to tell me when the next meeting of his group is."

Rebel quirked an eyebrow. "Because you're feeling the urge to kill and need to be counseled out of it?"

Fang ground his molars. "If its Reaper or X or Whip you're thinking of offing, don't worry about it. I've already got that covered."

I waited for someone to make a joke out of that, but it didn't come, and I realized he was dead serious. "Okay, don't do that, please."

He let out a *humph* of acceptance. Or maybe of disappointment, I couldn't quite tell.

"Then why do you want to know about Grayson's meetings?" Rebel asked.

I stared her dead in the eye. "Because I'm sick of being on the sidelines of my own life. Somebody tried to kill me last night, and in the process, they murdered my best friend. I can't just let that go."

She pressed her lips together. "Vi, those guys in Grayson's group, they aren't...normal."

Like I didn't already know that.

She carried on, but her expression was full of worry. "I'm really happy for you, that they were there when you needed a three-way railing—"

Fang let out a groan that sounded like it was full of pain.

Rebel ignored him. "But those guys aren't men you want to be hanging out with."

I appreciated her concern. I really did. But I was so far past this point. I'd already had this argument with myself, with Toby, and I kept coming back to the fact I couldn't just walk away.

Now more than ever, I was all in.

Not in bed with them. That had been a step too far.

But they were the only ones who were going to be able to help me work out who had killed my best friend.

Because I wasn't safe until we worked that out.

And neither was anyone I cared about.

Including the three of them, even though if anyone had asked me to admit it right then, I would have preferred to stick a fork in my eye than admit I cared about them.

Rebel sighed heavily at the determination in my gaze. "You aren't going to let this go, are you?"

"No. Would you have walked away when your mother was murdered?"

She shook her head. "I couldn't have."

And neither could I.

"I'll talk to Grayson and have him text you about the next meeting."

I nodded.

I might not have been a psychopath, but I was joining their murder squad. Whether they liked it or not.

Francine texted me thirty minutes before my shift that afternoon was supposed to start and asked me to come to the office instead. I screwed up my face at my phone but redirected Fang anyway.

When he pulled up out in front of Clean Sweep headquarters, right across the road from Psychos, a low growl rattled from his chest.

Or maybe it came from mine, I wasn't quite sure.

"Want me to deal with them?" He cracked his knuckles and gripped the steering wheel tighter, as if he needed it to keep himself from launching out of the car and clobbering the three men who stood waiting outside my place of employment, apologetic expressions firmly fixed in place.

"No. I can. You go home."

"I'll sit at Psychos. I'll be close by if you need a ride." He glared at his old best friend through the glass. "Or someone to punch Reaper in his stupid face."

But I was so mad at all three of them, if anyone was going to be doing the punching, it was me.

I slid out of the SUV, slamming the door behind me, even though the car had done nothing to warrant my frustrations.

"Violet," Whip started.

I stepped up onto the sidewalk and held my hand up in a stop motion in front of his face. "Save your breath. I'm not interested in anything any of you have to say."

Levi tried next. "Baby, just let us explain."

I glared at him. "Call me baby again, and you'll wish you hadn't."

"Can I still call you Omelet?" X asked hopefully.

The death stare told him it probably wasn't a good idea if he wanted to keep his balls intact.

All three of them fell into silence as I stormed past them and stomped up the stairs to Francine's place.

She glanced up from behind her desk, and I forced a smile for my boss.

"Afternoon. I got your text. You wanted to see me?"

It suddenly occurred to me I should have been nervous about this meeting. There was every chance I was getting fired. I'd been so worked up and distracted about Toby and the guys, it was only now I had even considered this meeting might be about more than just cleaning supplies or a new client.

But Francine smiled widely at me, clearly in a much better mood than the last time I'd been here. Her eyes were no longer bloodshot from her allergies, and she wasn't scowling at me, so I guessed I was forgiven for calling in sick and her picking up my shift.

"Yes! Violet, thank you for coming in. I want you to meet Nyah."

She pointed behind me, and I whirled around.

A dark-haired woman sat there, her leg bouncing nervously.

I blinked. "I'm so sorry! I didn't even notice you there. I didn't mean to be rude…" I caught sight of X's head popping up in the window behind the woman. Oh my God. Was he jumping up and down in order to be able to see in? I was actually going to kill him. I was probably going to end up in jail for Toby's murder anyway, so I might as well commit a real one so the crime actually fit the sentence.

I tried to rein my temper in by reminding myself X was not actually a bad man; despite the fact he'd done bad things. My time in foster care had taught me all about truly bad people. My foster dad. Mother. The boy who'd called himself my brother but had never acted like one.

I swallowed hard, pushing away the thoughts of the shitty house I'd grown up in after my birth family had abandoned me.

Nyah stood and held a hand out to me. "It's really nice to meet you…"

"Violet," I supplied.

Francine interrupted our meeting and thankfully gave me a reason to look away from X's stupid grinning face popping up in the window every few seconds. "Nyah's new, so I'd like you to train her for your next couple of shifts, please."

My smile fell. Francine was putting on someone new? She barely had enough work for the three of us she already had employed. It was why I'd had to pick up extra shifts at Psychos, because she couldn't give me the full-time hours I needed.

It was a kick in the guts to realize she had the work; she just didn't want to give it to me.

But I couldn't say that to her. I didn't have it in me to cause a scene. I was probably overreacting anyway. For all I knew, Francine had a big new job coming in I didn't know about.

And I wasn't training my replacement because she was still mad about me losing her a client.

A client who had attacked me and who had been lost not because he didn't like my work, but because X had gutted him. Not that Francine knew any of that, nor could I tell her.

Frustration swirled inside me. I needed this job more than ever now I didn't have Toby. The rent on my apartment was solely my responsibility. I didn't get a chance to grieve and wallow in my guilt over his death, because I had to be here, training some woman to replace me.

I was bound and gagged in so many ways, and angry tears of frustration and guilt and grief all welled behind my eyes.

But I blinked them back and forced a smile for my employer. "Of course I can train her. No problem at all. I just need to top up a few products in my cleaning caddy, and then we can get out of here."

Francine gave me a pleased smile. "Thank you, Violet. You and Nyah have a great afternoon. Don't forget to get a copy of your schedule for the week before you leave."

I nodded, picking up the products I needed and not bothering to spare a glance at the schedule because I'd already checked the online version and knew there wasn't much on it for me.

But none of that was Nyah's fault, and I refused to take it out on her. We walked out, side by side.

"The job isn't too far from here, so I was just going to walk. Is that okay with you?"

She nodded. "Of course. No problem at all. It's a nice day."

It was.

Until I pushed open the door and realized Whip, X, and Levi were all still out there waiting for me.

Nyah stiffened behind me as all three of them moved toward us.

"Ignore them," I told her. "Just walk right on by like they aren't even there."

Nyah took in the three huge men who towered over her, her eyes going big. She wasn't super short, but Levi in particular made even me feel small, so I could only imagine how intimidating he seemed to her. His biker jacket and tattoos, including the little one just below his eye, probably didn't help matters any.

I tucked my free arm into hers, my cleaning products clutched in my other. I caught sight of Fang watching me from behind a glass window at Psychos, and he raised an eyebrow in my direction, a single silent question on his lips.

I shook my head, letting him know I had it under control.

Because I did. Levi, Whip, and X didn't approach me again, but the three of them tailed us the entire way.

Nyah kept shooting nervous glances at them, but the looks I threw back were more like murderous glares. We reached Mrs. Sinterro's cottage-style house and knocked on the door, calling out to her, but when she didn't answer, I let us in with the keys she had provided to Francine. The guys all followed us up the path, like they were the third, fourth, and fifth members of our cleaning crew.

I shut the door in their faces and locked it.

Nyah relaxed just a bit with the locks engaged, us on the inside of the house, the men on the other. "I know you said to ignore them, but who the hell are they?"

I moved to Mrs. Sinterro's laundry closet and pulled out her Hoover and mop bucket. I didn't even know how to answer that. Were they my friends? My boyfriends? My merry little band of psychopaths?

Okay, I definitely couldn't call them that without terrifying Nyah further. She probably already thought they were my stalkers, since that was exactly what they were acting like. She would likely report this to Francine, which would be the nail in my coffin with her, I was sure.

I tried to distract her with cleaning instead. "They're harmless, I promise. They'll get bored and go away. In the meantime, we have cleaning to do. So the routine I was taught is kitchen and bathrooms first so the cleaning products can soak in if needed. Dust, vacuum, mop, and then we're out the door. And we need to move fast because Francine doesn't like if we take longer than two hours per job. An hour for smaller houses like this one."

Nyah rolled up the sleeves of her work shirt. "Got it. I like a challenge. I can start with the bathroom if you like."

I blinked, surprised she would offer to take a bathroom. Most wouldn't. But then, I'd done exactly the same thing when I'd had my training day. I'd desperately wanted to make a good impression on Josie, the cleaner who had trained me. I'd really wanted her to report back to Francine that I was good at my job, and a team player, so I'd get a lot of shifts.

That clearly hadn't worked out too well for me. Maybe I hadn't made the good impression I'd been hoping for. I'd never gotten a chance to ask Josie since she'd quit a few days after I'd started. Had I talked too much? I'd tried to be friendly, but maybe she'd found that annoying? I sighed, hating that I was always so concerned with what other people thought of me, even months after it had taken place. I wished I could just not care, but that had never been something I could do.

I smiled at Nyah. "That would be great. I'll start in the kitchen, and we'll meet somewhere in the middle."

She popped an earbud in and went off to the bathroom with her supplies, while I made my way into the kitchen. Mrs. Sinterro was a little old lady who liked to cook. She cleaned up after herself to the best of her ability, but there were always spaghetti sauce stains on the stove top and breadcrumbs all over the countertop. I moved a couple of dirty plates to the kitchen sink and got the hot water running.

It wasn't part of my job to do her dishes, but I always did. And I didn't tell Francine, because she would have charged her more.

Mrs. Sinterro's kitchen overlooked her backyard, with overgrown grass growing up around old bits of junk that had been left out there to rust, and a broken wood picket fence that wouldn't keep out bunnies, let alone anything else. The thing was hanging on for dear life, and a stiff breeze probably could have knocked it down.

I frowned at it, lost in thought of how I wished I could get it fixed for the sweet old lady who always left me cookies wrapped in plastic as a thank you for helping her keep up with her place. But with no money and even less handyman skills, all I could really do was what I was already doing.

It sucked, because I knew Mrs. Sinterro didn't have any children to help her. She'd been single all her life, and now she was closing in toward the end of it, there was nobody to support her.

This would probably be me one day, I realized with a start. I'd always pictured Toby by my side in our old age, even if he ended up with someone. But now that was never going to happen. God, did Devin even know? Did Toby's parents? Was it on me to tell them all?

I didn't want to think about that. I didn't think I could.

Something popped up on the other side of the window, and I stumbled back a step in shock.

X's stupidly handsome face beamed at me, all white teeth and wide grin.

I put my hand to my heart, then groaned when I realized I was getting soap suds all over my shirt. "Oh my God, X! Go away!"

He cupped a hand around his ear, acting like he couldn't hear me.

Though I doubted that was true. Mrs. Sinterro's crappy old cottage was probably made of the cheapest, thinnest materials you could build a house from, and it was old and run-down enough that there were plenty of gaps and cracks for sound to travel through.

I opened my mouth to complain, but he held up a finger, telling me to wait. I frowned, but did, washing dishes while he pulled a notepad and a black Sharpie from behind his back and scribbled something on it, before turning it around to show me.

It read, *I'm sorry.*

I sighed.

He held his finger up again and then scribbled some more.

The second time, his note said: *You're awesome.*

I just stared at him, because what was I supposed to say to that?

His third note was: *I suck. And not only in the good way.*

My cheeks went pink, remembering the way he'd sucked me throughout the night. That had definitely been in the good way. It had been so good, in fact, my pussy got wet just thinking about it, and I knew as soon as I got home, once I'd finished all my shifts for the day, I would very probably need to whip out my vibrator.

Which would be a poor substitution for his tongue.

He stared at me hopefully, but when I didn't say anything, he screwed up his face and scribbled a fourth note.

When he turned it around, I couldn't help but snigger.

Please don't shank me. My duck needs me.

A smile spread across his face, not the smug or stupid one I wanted to slap off him at times, but a genuine smile. One that made me realize he actually found true pleasure in making me laugh.

And it was hard not to, when he was cute and silly and didn't give a shit what anyone thought about him.

I envied that so much. I could guarantee X had never worried about a bad impression he may or may not have made on a coworker months ago.

I leaned forward and lifted the window with a sharp tug that made a piercing screech of protest. "Was this your grand apology plan? To write me silent note cards, *Love Actually* style? Where did you even get that paper and pen from?"

"I broke into the house next door and stole it."

I widened my eyes at him. "Are you serious?"

He laughed. "Of course not." Then he glanced at the house next door. "But just so you know, that window was definitely already broken when we got here. That was definitely not because I threw a brick through it."

I groaned. "You can't just do things like that!"

"You wouldn't listen to my apology."

"Yeah, because I was mad at you!"

He raised an eyebrow. "Was?"

"Am. Still am mad at you."

"No, you said was. You can't take that back. My apology worked. You forgive me. You said it yourself."

"Mmm, no, I definitely never said that."

He eyed me, being really stupidly cute. Then he sighed, leaning his arms on the windowsill and ducking his head so he could peer through it.

I took a spoon from the soapy water and placed it in the drying rack. "What?"

"I really want to kiss you right now."

I picked up a butter knife and ran my sponge over it.

It caught X's eye. "If that's supposed to be threatening, it's not. It's just making me want to kiss you more."

I leaned in, so our faces lined up better, his lips just a few inches away from mine. "Is it?"

His gaze flickered to my mouth. He closed his eyes, and waited for the kiss he knew was coming.

It would have been so easy to meet in the middle. To kiss him through the open window. Every part of me demanded I do exactly that.

But my body was a traitorous, horny bitch who couldn't be trusted.

And X, Whip, and Levi were all liars.

I slammed the window down, just barely missing his puckered lips.

He blinked in surprise.

I smiled at him smugly and then gave him the middle finger.

He pressed his lips to the glass instead. And then winked at me.

All the smugness I'd had a minute ago at getting the upper hand melted away.

Because we both knew I couldn't keep this up. And for the rest of the day, I would be thinking about that kiss I'd just let slip away, when all I had wanted was to let it happen.

9

VIOLET

Nyah and I finished the rest of the houses booked for that afternoon without my entourage following us around. I had no idea where they'd disappeared to after I'd shut X down, but instead of feeling relief they had done as I'd said, all I felt was disappointment.

And a low dose of fear.

I'd gotten used to at least one of them being with me at all times, even if they were just watching my apartment from the street. Without that, I suddenly felt very alone and very vulnerable.

I hated that they were right. Hated that having them watch over me had made me feel safe.

Hated I'd realized it too late.

At least I had Nyah. She was sweet and chatty, and she'd worked hard all afternoon. She was a couple of years younger than me and completely opposite in terms of appearance. Where I was tall and fair, she was shorter and dark. Her long hair was almost black, and her eyes matched. We'd talked about all sorts of things as we'd worked, none of it very deep or personal, and she hadn't pushed me to talk about why I'd had three men following me around, which I'd appreciated because I didn't know what I'd say if she did.

She didn't realize it, but she'd been the one thing to get me through a day I would have otherwise just spent lying in bed, crying over Toby.

I didn't want that. Not yet. I didn't have the luxury of falling apart, and I knew if I let myself start down that road of grief, I might never be able to pull myself out of it.

No, it was much better to focus on work.

Or the way I couldn't stop thinking about how close I'd come to kissing X, or where all three guys had disappeared to.

I walked Nyah back to Clean Sweep and happily reported to Francine that Nyah was amazing. I knew it might cost me shifts, but it was the truth, and I wouldn't play down how great she'd been just to save my own skin. If Francine was still harboring grudges over me losing clients, then there was nothing I could do to change her mind. None of that was Nyah's fault.

But Francine was in a great mood, and she smiled at both of us before shooing us out the door and telling us to "go be young and have fun."

I eyed the door suspiciously as it closed behind us. "She was oddly chirpy."

Nyah glanced back through the glass door at Francine, who was smiling at something on her computer screen. "Maybe she has a hot date tonight."

I smiled at the thought, Mrs. Sinterro on my mind. "I hope so. Francine can be a grump at times, but nobody deserves to grow old alone. I hope she finds someone who makes her happy."

I suspected I was talking about myself as much as my boss.

Nyah nudged me with her elbow. "You see that place across the road? I hear it's a secret sex club."

I chuckled. "It is. I just started working there. Actually, I have a shift tonight."

Nyah's mouth dropped open. "Get the fuck out. Are the rumors true?"

I nodded. "Yep."

"Holy shit. I really thought that was an urban legend." She stared at the creepy clown mural like it was some sort of gateway to Narnia.

"You want to go? I'm sure I can get you in tonight if you want to," I offered.

She clutched my arm. "Shut up. You cannot. I would die."

I laughed. "I'll be working so I might not be able to hang out with you all night or anything, but you can sit at the bar...or mingle...if you prefer."

She raised an eyebrow. "Mingle as in..."

"Get naked and fuck a stranger?" I grinned. "Sure, if you want to."

She shook her head fast. "I think that might be a bit much for me, but I definitely want to come and sit at the bar and watch..." She cringed. "Wait, that sounded bad, didn't it? I don't want you to think I'm some sort of perv..."

I gave her a quick hug. "I don't think that. I get being curious. It's definitely an experience. Go home and get changed. My shift doesn't start 'til ten, and the place will be in full swing by then so we can make an entrance together. Meet me out front five minutes early?"

Nyah nodded, excitement dancing in her eyes. "I'll be there."

We parted ways, but instead of calling Fang for a pickup, like I'd promised I would, I caught a taxi back to my apartment.

The road in front was empty of ice cream vans, motorbikes, or silver sedans, and that sense of loneliness deepened. I'd been stupid to get so mad at them when they'd only been trying to protect me.

Because the alternative was this. Peering into the shadows nervously. Looking over my shoulder as I collected my mail from the box in the foyer and climbed the dingy stairs to my apartment.

I was completely alone, and if someone dragged me off to some new house of horrors, there would be nobody to hear my screams.

At my apartment, I paused, realizing something was different.

It took me a good moment to realize it was the lock. It was brand-new and shiny, a dead bolt that was a big upgrade on the flimsy thing that had been there earlier.

A piece of my heart squeezed, knowing it was Levi or Whip who had installed it. I couldn't see X knowing one end of a toolbox from the other, but this had Levi and Whip written all over it.

Only problem was, I had no key to open it, but a quick search through my mail solved that problem. A yellow envelope had my name in the center, written in Levi's messy scrawl that I loved so much.

I opened it, and a key fell into my palm.

But there was no letter. No note.

I fought off the disappointment and let myself into the apartment. I wouldn't stay here long. I couldn't even let myself look in the direction of Toby's bedroom. I just needed the outfit I'd bought to wear at Psychos, since my dowdy black pants and blouse hadn't really been the vibe last time. In my rush to get out of the apartment that morning, I hadn't even thought to pack it.

I yanked open the drawers in my bedroom and pulled it out, still not sure I would have the guts to wear it, but Toby's voice was loud in my head.

You better put that on and wear it with pride, girly pop. Slay like the queen you are.

Emotion threatened to overwhelm me, so I rushed out, closing the door behind me.

Unshed tears blinded my eyes, so I didn't even see Devin in the hallway until I walked right into him. He caught me, steadying me, his voice gravelly when he said my name. "Violet."

One glance up at him told me he already knew. That my worrying over whether I would have to be the one to tell him had been in vain.

His expression was full of pain, and he swallowed thickly. "Is it true?"

I barely knew Devin. He and Toby had only been dating a short while, but the anguish on his face cut deep.

All I could do was nod and whisper, "I'm so sorry."

He nodded, looking numb. Then he glanced down at me. "I'm so sorry, I can see you're on your way out, but I left some things in his room I'd like to get..."

I nodded, quickly opening up the lock again for him.

"Of course. Go ahead. I need to get to work, but just close the door on your way out, okay?"

I was sure he could use a moment to grieve alone and in private. He certainly seemed like he was battling to keep it together there in the hallway.

He nodded. "Thank you."

He seemed so utterly broken I couldn't help myself. I stepped in and wrapped my arms around him, squeezing him tight.

Then walked away, because his grief was so thick that if I stayed a second longer, I knew it would consume me.

* * *

I put on my outfit and did my makeup in the guest bathroom at my brother's place. At nine, I called an Uber and started making my way downstairs to wait for it.

But Fang, asleep with his head on Wolf's mattress, the rest of him sitting on the floor, caught my eye from the doorway of the little boy's bedroom.

I stifled a laugh when Wolf waved his chubby hand at me.

"Go to sleep now, okay?" I whispered to him.

He squeezed his eyes shut and made an overexaggerated snoring sound.

I swallowed down my giggle so as to not wake my brother. He clearly needed the sleep, and with so many kids, I couldn't blame him for getting some wherever he could. Wolf seemed quite happy to have one of his dads there with him, even if he was sleeping on the job.

Downstairs, I found Rebel, Vaughn, and Kian all

curled up on the couch together, a movie flickering in the darkness, but all three of them gazing down at the baby in Rebel's arms.

My heart gave a tiny squeeze, though I wasn't one-hundred-percent sure why. I didn't want babies right now. Hell, I had nobody to have babies with. I barely knew Whip, I was mad at Levi because we could just not get our shit together at all, and X was completely insane... though he would make the prettiest babies.

I gave myself a shake. I was missing a whole bunch of steps I needed to take before I could get myself from where I was right now, to snuggled on a couch with a baby and three men who loved me as much as Rebel's guys loved her.

Vaughn was the first to notice me. "Going to your shift at Psychos? You need me to drive you?"

"I've got an Uber on the way. I'll be fine. But thank you."

He nodded and went back to stroking his youngest daughter's soft hair while she fed.

Rebel glanced up at me. All the hard edges she'd had in the car earlier that day when she'd been fired up and ready to fight on my behalf had melted away, and all that was left was the mom and partner who loved her family more than anything else. "Have a good shift. I hear Dax from the tattoo shop is down there tonight, doing flash pieces." She grinned, a little of her sass breaking through the mom routine. "Do not come home with a tattoo on your pussy."

I choked on that. "What?"

Kian couldn't keep his amusement off his face. "At least get a good one if you do. Something pretty."

"Not a guy's name," Rebel added.

Kian glanced at her. "You did—"

"And I think that's my cue to leave. Pretty sure I hear my Uber outside. Have a good night, you guys." I scuttled out of the room before I could hear any more about how Rebel may or may not have my brother's name tattooed on her vag.

Outside, my Uber had arrived, so I got inside and texted Nyah that I was on my way. I checked a few other notifications, but by the time I looked up from my phone, I realized I wasn't sure where we were. I peered out the window, but nothing outside was familiar, just dark houses in a suburban neighborhood.

I leaned forward to speak to the driver. "I'm going to Psychos in Saint View. I'm not sure we're going the right way."

"We are," came back a deep voice. "This is a shortcut. There's traffic on the main roads."

A tiny alarm bell went off in the back of my head. "There's traffic at this time of night?"

"Road work."

I supposed that could be true, but a shiver ran down my spine anyway. I checked the driver information on the app and then tried to catch a glimpse of his face from the back seat, but he had a baseball cap sitting low on his brow, and it cast shadows across the top half of his face, leaving me only his lips to identify him with.

I couldn't tell if this guy was the registered driver or not.

And I really did not recognize this part of town.

It quickly dawned on me it didn't matter. If this guy

wasn't going to Psychos, then he was taking me somewhere else.

Everything that had happened last night in that warehouse came rushing back in bright, vivid color, and my stomach churned in sick panic.

"Pull over please. Just here is fine."

The man shook his head. "Relax. I'll get you to your destination."

I was pretty sure telling me to relax was the absolute least relaxing thing he could have said in that moment. "No, please, let me out."

I hated that I was being so polite, but it was what had been drummed into me my entire life. To never rock the boat. To just be a good girl and go along with whatever I was told because otherwise my foster parents might send me back.

Now I just felt jammed up with fear.

My brain rolled through every fact I knew about kidnappings and abductions, the main one sticking in my head that you could never let them take you to a second location.

And here I was, willingly getting in the car so they could drive me wherever the hell they wanted.

I reached for the door handle, doing the mental math about how fast we were going and whether I could truly throw myself out of a moving vehicle. The point quickly became moot, since the door was locked, and no amount of flicking at the lock opened it. The child locks had been engaged.

With shaking fingers, I took out my phone again, praying that this time, unlike when I'd been locked in that warehouse, I would have enough signal to make a call.

My finger pressed down on X's number.

"Here you go," the driver announced as we made a turn out of a side street and onto the main road. "See? Your club is just up there."

I'd never been so relieved to see a freaky, sharp-toothed clown in my entire life.

I quickly cancelled the call, hoping I had been quick enough it wouldn't register on X's end.

"This is close enough," I told the man. "The parking lot will be busy, and I can walk the rest of the way."

He nodded, steering the car over. "You have a good night." The child locks clicked off.

I tried to thank him as I stumbled out into the darkness, just half a block away from the club. The cool night air was the relief I needed to cool my hot cheeks. The car drove away, and I closed my eyes for the tiniest of seconds, just melting into the relief that none of that had been what I'd thought it was.

But closing my eyes was a mistake.

Because it meant I didn't see the man step out of the Saint View shadows.

I just felt his fingers wrap around my wrist and the sharp tug as he dragged me into the alley.

10

LEVI

I was early to Psychos, getting there well before the doors opened, and only let in because Vincent, guarding the door, recognized me.

I found Bliss and Nash and War inside, along with a bunch of their staff members, all getting the club ready for the party that night. War looked up and waved me over.

He dragged a heavy leather bench along the floor, and I immediately picked up the other end without being asked.

He nodded at me gratefully, guiding us through the club to the new spot where the bench was to be placed. "Thanks. These are heavy fucking things. You're early."

I nodded, setting the bench down where he indicated with a nod. "Yeah, sorry."

War studied the bench placement then nudged it with his knee into a slightly different spot. "We never mind when friends get here early. Just means we have extra hands to help set up. So if you didn't want to help,

you might want to run straight outta here before Bliss
sees you—"

"Too late! Bliss has already seen you and has a to-do
list a mile long." She grinned at me from behind an
armful of boxes. "Hi, Levi."

I plucked a box from her arms, lightening her load.
"I just came down to talk to Violet, but I'm happy to
help."

"She's on second shift, because she'll be cleaning
afterward. So she's starting a bit later."

My shoulders fell. "I didn't realize that."

Bliss smiled sympathetically at me. "You don't really
have to stick around if you want to come back when she's
on shift. We don't actually make all our friends volunteer
here."

But I shook my head. "No, it's fine. I'm happy to help.
Just tell me what you want me to do."

Bliss jerked her head toward the hallway that led
down to the private rooms Violet and I had cleaned the
other day. "We just had a huge delivery come in this afternoon. We got the boxes back to the storeroom, but we
desperately need to unpack them because we need a lot
of the stuff to stock the private rooms for tonight. The
front doors open soon, but we can't open the private
rooms until we restock them. They all need condoms,
lube, new toys. I know it's really unsexy, but there is actually a checklist on the back of the storeroom door that
will tell you what needs to go where."

I put my box down on the bar top for her so it was
easy for her to unpack. "Sounds easy enough. I'll get
on it."

She blew me a kiss and disappeared beneath the

countertop, presumably putting drinks in fridges or maybe ice buckets.

I didn't concern myself with what sort of cooling system they had, my brain was too full of everything I needed to talk to Violet about tonight. The fact she wasn't here yet was probably a good thing. It gave me more time to calm my stupid nerves and think about what I was actually going to say.

Trying to talk to her outside Clean Sweep this afternoon hadn't gone well at all. I had doubts that trying to talk to her during a different shift was going to go any better, but what else was I supposed to do? I couldn't just sit around at the clubhouse, waiting for her to forgive me.

I wanted her.

I wasn't going to get her by sitting around at home, whining about how she was the one who got away like some of the older guys liked to do. They were full of heartbreak stories now that they were too old to be fucking around with the club women.

I didn't want to be a sixty-year-old biker with nothing to his name but the fucking Harley he rode. I loved my brothers at the club, and hell, I even loved my bike, but I loved Violet a hell of a lot more than either of them.

And the fact she didn't know that was killing me.

Everything I'd done was because I loved her so damn much.

And because I knew I didn't deserve her.

But God, I fucking wanted to. And I would do whatever it took for her to see that.

I easily found the storeroom Bliss had mentioned, right at the very end of the hallway, and clearly marked as staff only. I ignored the sign and turned the doorknob.

On the other side, the room was fully lit up with ugly fluorescent overhead lights that had none of the vibe the club had. I blinked in the brightness, and then again at the man standing on the other side.

"What are you doing here?" I asked Whip. And then squinted at his hand. "And what are you holding?"

Whip held up the combination of leather and latex. "I think it's a ball gag with a dildo attachment? Not entirely sure. Which is a bit of a shock because I thought I'd seen it all."

We both cocked our heads, staring at it.

I agreed his assumption did seem to be correct. "That doesn't explain why you're here though. Are you working with one of your clients?"

"No. I came to see Violet."

My mouth flattened into a line. "Same. And she's not here so Bliss put you to work?"

He put the ball gag/dildo contraption back on a shelf. "You too?"

I nodded.

He shrugged. "We're going to need to unpack all these boxes before we can distribute them anywhere. Seems like they were really low on stock until this stuff came in."

I shrugged out of my jacket, dropping it onto an empty shelf.

I turned around, only to catch Whip's gaze wandering all over my chest, clad in a tight white T-shirt that clung to my pecs and abs, with sleeves that curved with my biceps.

I didn't miss the flush of heat his gaze sent through my body.

Fuck. Why did he have to look at me like that? Or

more to the point, why did he have to look the way he did in a suit? He was always in those fucking things, all damn fancy and completely out of place in a town like Saint View.

I ripped open a box that turned out to be full of smaller boxes of condoms, and started stacking them on the shelf.

Whip did the same a few feet away, his box full of floggers. I'd already seen the room those went in. I guessed the club let patrons take home the toys they used. Which I could appreciate because some things shouldn't be shared, no matter how often they were cleaned.

I picked up a box of strawberry-flavored condoms and shook them in Whip's direction. "You reckon these actually taste like strawberry?"

Whip raised an eyebrow.

Instantly, I realized I'd brought up him giving head without even thinking about it. Heat flamed up the back of my neck, and I turned away quickly. "Sorry. I didn't mean..."

Whip snorted on a laugh. "Didn't mean to ask if I suck dick?"

Ah, fucking hell. I'd just made this so awkward. I didn't know what I'd meant. Or why I'd said it. And I'd thought it was X with no brain-to-mouth filter. But apparently I was just as bad.

At least when it came to Whip.

I had no idea why he had me so fucking rattled. One minute I hated his guts. Then next we were watching each other fuck. And now I was asking him about what condoms tasted like when they were wrapped around another man's cock?

When I ripped open the next box and found it was filled with bottles of bourbon, I didn't think twice about opening one up and taking a long swallow of the dark-brown liquid inside.

I could feel Whip's gaze on me, and I held the bottle out in his direction without looking at him.

He took it, his fingers brushing mine, electricity zapping between what I was sure as fuck putting down to the static in the room. Even though it felt identical to the pulse of something unnameable that happened when I touched Violet too.

"Should probably move this box back up to the bar. Guessing it's not meant to be back here," I mumbled uselessly, because I made zero move to actually pick it up and take it where it belonged.

Whip eyed me as he took a swig from the bottle. "They don't taste like strawberry."

I lifted my gaze to meet his.

His eyes held a challenge. "And yeah, I know that because I've sucked off guys wearing them."

Images of Whip down on his knees, his fingers wrapped around a cock, taking it into his mouth while someone held the back of his head, encouraging him to take it deep, had my dick stirring behind my pants.

Because it wasn't just some random guy he was sucking off in my head.

It was me.

I needed another fucking drink.

And he knew it. He had a smug fucking grin on his

stupidly attractive face, the bottle of bourbon dangling from a loose, two-finger grip.

I took the bottle, needing the deep swallow of alcohol. I wasn't fucking doing this with him. This stupid flirting thing. We weren't friends. We'd gone through a thing together in finding Violet and then giving her what she needed afterward.

But we weren't bonding. I didn't need any more friends.

I just needed Violet to forgive me, and that had to be my sole focus.

I went back to shoving boxes of condoms onto the shelf, but it had been years since I'd drunk hard alcohol. And the half a dozen pulls I'd taken on the bottle were already warming through my body and loosening my lips. "You been here before?"

Whip glanced over at me. "In the closet with a straight man?" He snorted on a laugh. "Yeah, been here, done that."

I scowled at him. "I meant have you been to this club before?" But before he could answer, I shrugged. "Stupid question. You probably come here all the time, considering the line of work you're in."

He glanced over at me. "What is it, exactly, you think I do?"

I shrugged. "Fuck strangers for money."

It came out harsher and more judgmental than I'd really meant it to.

He stopped what he was doing, his hands resting on the edge of a shelf. "So you just think I'm some sort of cheap hooker?"

"Aren't you?"

His grip tightened around the metal, and he shook his head. "You're a prick, you know that?"

I dropped a pile of condoms back into the box. "What? You are? Why act like you're not?"

An awkward silence filled the room, and he turned to face off with me. "I'm not acting like I'm not. Yeah, I'm a sex worker. I'll happily own that all day, every day, and sleep just fine at night. Because at least I'm not standing over there, casting holier-than-thou judgments. Which is pretty fucking rich coming from a man who spent the last six years in prison, has no job, and is living in a glorified version of a frat house."

I rolled my eyes, playing down the fact I knew every word was true. "Oh, fuck you. You don't know shit about me, Whip."

"And yet you think you know me? You don't." He swore under his breath.

Irritation had me clenching my fingers into fists. No small part of it based on jealousy over the way Violet had taken him straight into her bed, needing him to comfort her before she'd even looked at me.

It was him she'd had first. Him who'd been her safe place.

She'd let me and X fuck her, but only after she'd had Whip. She'd only come to us to numb herself.

And that was the thing I couldn't let go. That jealousy that he had something with her I didn't.

"Tell me something real then," I challenged. "You want to fling accusations at me. Make out like I'm the shallow one. You ever think that maybe all I know about you is that you sleep around because you're so closed off that's all you give people to form an opinion on? I don't know a single thing about you, Whip, other than you like to fuck around and that taking a life doesn't bother you. Not a single other fucking thing."

Anger flashed in his eyes. "What do you want to know?" He threw his hands up in the air. "You want me to open up my diary and read you the last twenty years' worth of entries? You want me to tell you I like baseball, and I run most mornings, and I drink red wine every time I put on a suit because it's part of this whole fucking schtick? But what I'd always prefer to drink is the cheap bourbon in that bottle you're chugging down like its water because I make you uncomfortable?"

The bourbon sloshed in my hand, and I realized he was right. Between the two of us, we'd polished off half of it in a very short space of time.

I didn't know about him, but I was feeling it.

So it was easy to blame the alcohol when I glared at him and said, "Tell me about the woman and kids in the photo."

He froze.

I instantly knew I'd gone too far.

I'd only been to his place once, and the photo on his bookshelf was clearly one he hadn't wanted me to see. He'd snatched it up from under my nose and hidden it away so fast I'd barely caught a glimpse of it.

But it had been stuck in my mind ever since.

Whip. A woman. And two little kids, all grinning at the camera on a sunny summer day, a big white house in the background.

Pain flashed behind his eyes. Not the fleeting, surface kind that came from a minor inconvenience.

But the deep-rooted kind of agony that destroyed a

man, one cell at a time, until his entire body was engulfed in flame and there was nobody around to help put it out.

The shock wore off, and Whip moved in so fast I stumbled back against the shelves to avoid a full-on collision with his face.

But he just kept coming, until we were chest to chest, eye to eye.

His warm breath coasted over my lips, just barely an inch from mine.

It would have been so fucking easy to close that gap. To put my lips on his and kiss him.

And for the tiniest of heartbeats, I held my breath, every nerve ending in my body coming to life and wanting him to do it.

But his mouth twisted in a cruel line. And his words came out harsh. "Don't ever fucking ask me about that photo again. Forget you ever saw it, forget you know anything about it." His angry gaze flickered all over my face. "They might call you Reaper, but if you so much as mention that photo again, it'll be me sending your soul to fucking Hades. You hear me?"

He shoved off me before I could even answer and stormed out of the room.

I blinked at the door slamming behind him.

And then did the stupidest thing I could have possibly imagined.

I went after him.

11

VIOLET

I opened my mouth to scream in the man's face.

Only to realize it was X's brown eyes I was staring into.

The scream disappeared instantly, the fear replaced by relief it was him and not someone I needed to be afraid of.

Before I knew what I was doing, I had my arms around his neck and my lips against his. I fell into his warm arms, pressed myself against the strength of his chest, and let myself be devoured by the safety he represented in my terrified brain.

Except he didn't kiss me back.

He pulled back, his brows drawn together in confusion. "Violet?"

I just needed him to kiss me. I tried again, forcing my lips to his, but he backed off once more. "Hang on. Something's wrong. Talk to me."

Hot embarrassment slammed through me, and I jerked away from him. It wasn't a good combination, mixing with the fear and grief. All of it was too much. And the last thing I wanted to do was admit to him I was so damn weak I couldn't take care of myself. That I was now scared of every man. Of every shadow.

That I was so jumpy I'd thought I was being kidnapped when a simple look at a map would have told me my fears were running off with my brain and I was actually perfectly safe.

I didn't feel safe. It felt like danger lurked everywhere I went, and I could no longer trust anyone.

Except him.

But now I was throwing myself at him like a desperate maiden, and I couldn't take the embarrassment of yet another rejection. I spun on my heel, storming away, out of the alley and toward the lineup of people waiting to get inside Psychos.

"Violet."

I kept going. I just had to get inside, and then I could lose him in the crowd. Or at least pretend I was working. The club probably actually wasn't big enough to lose anyone, especially not someone like X, who seemed to have the nose of a bloodhound when it came to tracking me down.

"Violet."

I kept going.

"Dammit, Violet!"

He grabbed my wrist, spinning me around so we were face-to-face.

I glared up at him, my fear and embarrassment turning into anger because the alternative was tears, and I had too much pride for that.

His mouth slammed down on mine.

For a long moment I didn't move. It took that long to register he was kissing me.

But once my body realized what was going on, there was no stopping it.

I wrapped my arms around his neck again, drawing him close. He deepened the kiss, slanting his head, his lips soft but demanding, his tongue licking his way into my mouth.

I moaned unashamedly as he pushed me up against the wall of the club, his big body crushing mine onto the bricks. Every inch of him was hard, from his leanly muscled arms to his abs, to his dick, instantly alert and nudging into the softness of my lower belly.

He brought one hand up to the side of my face, cupping me there, holding me in place, while the other caged me in, palm pressed to the wall.

I was well aware there was a line of people just feet ahead of us, and Scythe or Vincent would be at the head of it, letting people in or turning them away.

But all I could feel was X. All I could see and taste and smell was this man who I had wanted to kiss me like this for the longest time, even if my brain knew better.

Screw my brain. Screw everything rational it knew about him.

When I'd been trapped in the back of the car, it was him I'd called. Him I'd wanted.

Him I'd needed.

X kissed me like I was the air fueling his lungs. His tongue swept away any reservation I might have had, and his body on mine lit up every pleasurable part of me, each one demanding I do a whole lot more than just kiss this man.

His lips trailed off my mouth and down my neck. He fumbled with my knee-length jacket, unbuttoning the top of it with one hand to give himself better access to my throat and cleavage.

He caught a glimpse of the lacy corset-style top I'd bought, and he groaned, licking and kissing his way across the swell of my tits until he dragged his mouth back up to mine.

"Fucking hell, Violet. What the hell are you wearing under that jacket?"

Except he didn't give me a chance to answer him. Because his mouth was back on mine, claiming me, branding me, his kisses spinning my head until I had no idea where we were.

His hand slid from the side of my face to my throat, and wetness pooled between my thighs. My knees went weak, pleasure exploding all through my body at every touch.

With a sharp groan of need, he stepped back, his eyes unfocused, his expression tortured.

And then he was dragging me past the waiting line of people and inside the club. He didn't even stop to acknowledge Scythe or Vincent on the door, I wasn't sure which because X didn't slow even for a second. He towed me inside, people instantly surrounding us.

Performers had already taken to the cages, the gold glittering beneath spotlights that lit up the bronzed, sweaty bodies of the people dancing, kissing, or fucking inside them.

I didn't get a chance to take it all in though, because X knew exactly what he wanted.

From the corner of my eye, I caught sight of Whip

and Levi moving toward us but then I was being led down a hallway, private rooms behind closed doors, though that didn't stop a crowd from forming around them.

Some of the rooms had glass viewing windows. Some people just used the hallway as a dark, quieter place to have sex.

The scent of it was already thick in the air, the club barely open, but everyone here for one thing, and nobody was wasting any time.

X was one of them. He ushered me into an empty room, closing the door behind us.

For a long moment, I couldn't work out why this room was here. The other ones I'd seen when Levi and I had been here cleaning were full of kink equipment and toys or had peepholes so you could fuck while being watched.

This room had none of that. It seemed completely private.

I couldn't work it out, but then X pushed me up against a wall, his fingers around my throat once more, his lips at my ears. "I want to fuck you, Violet. I want you naked, riding my cock, and screaming my name when you come."

Oh God. This man. He was so goofy and silly and ridiculous...until it came to sex.

Then it was like a different side of him showed up. One that was a whole lot darker than anything I'd ever experienced.

One that scared me, just a little.

But there was no denying the effect he had on my body. A few words from him, and I was already undoing the rest of the buttons on my jacket, the one he'd already started taking off outside. My clit tingled with anticipation, and my core clenched, desperate with need for him because my body remembered how good it felt when he was inside me.

"I want you," I mumbled to him, my jacket hitting the floor at my feet so he could see the outfit I'd bought for him.

No, not for him. I'd bought it for myself. So I could try to fit in with the other women who worked here, all of them owning their sexuality and their bodies, no matter the size of them.

And it was working. Because standing there in a corset and panties with X staring at me like I'd just unwrapped a present tailor-made for him, was the biggest confidence boost I'd ever had.

His gaze burned a trail across my skin, and the way he grabbed the back of my neck, hauling me in so he could claim my mouth would live rent-free in my head for the rest of my life.

He devoured my lips like he wanted to own them, only pulling back to tongue my ear, his stubbled jaw scratching perfectly across the sensitive skin there. "You have no idea what you're doing to me right now, Violet. No fucking idea how bad I want my dick inside you."

"Do it," I panted. "I want it."

"I'm going to. But you need to know there's people watching us. This is a camera room."

I paused, peeping over his shoulder.

There were indeed cameras in the corners of the room, a tiny red light blinking from each of them, telling me they were on.

Every doubt I'd ever had about my body rushed back

in. It was one thing for X to stare at me like I was a meal on a plate that he wanted to eat every night for the rest of his life, but it was another thing altogether to realize there were any number of strangers watching us.

I wanted him so badly.

But I wasn't sure I could do this.

His fingers found my chin, and he grasped it, tilting my head so I was focused on him again. "I need them. I can't be alone with you." He kissed me again. "I'm scared I'll hurt you."

I shook my head. "You won't."

But his eyes were full of a fear I'd never seen in them. Not when he'd killed a man in cold blood. Not when he'd found me sitting in a pool of it.

I'd never seen him scared.

Until now.

No, that wasn't true. I'd seen it one other time. When we'd been in the shower and he'd run out.

I suddenly understood that night a whole lot better.

His tongue trailed up my neck. "You've barely seen glimpses of the monster I am, Violet. You want them watching us."

His voice somehow managed to send chills of both fear and pleasure through my body all at once.

My brain said to say no.

Said to walk right out of this room and not look back, because clearly this man was dangerous.

And yet I couldn't force my feet to budge.

Because even though he was warning me away, all I saw was the man who'd killed my attacker. The man who'd caught a duck for me just because I'd said I'd liked them. A man who would only touch me in public because his need to keep me safe outweighed everything else.

I reached behind me and tugged at the ribbon on my corset.

It didn't undo easily. X turned me around so I was facing the wall. He brushed my fingers aside, taking over the job of tugging the laces free one at a time, while he kissed my neck in alternating sucks and gentle bites.

Pleasure coursed through me, starting from every place he touched me. His lips and tongue burned a hot trail across my skin, which was only heightened by the glide of his fingers and the silky corset ribbon that danced along with them.

It loosened, and relief rushed in that I could breathe properly again.

He pulled the last bit of ribbon free, and the corset fell away.

I didn't dare move. I was facing the wall, so the cameras would only see my back, and I was entirely too scared to turn around.

But X didn't push me. He just trailed his fingers down my naked back and over my side rolls and the curve of my hips.

A low growl came from deep within his chest that took me by surprise.

I glanced over my shoulder at him. "What's wrong?"

"That thing you were wearing...it left marks all over your body."

"It was a bit tight."

His thumbs traced over an indent the corset bones had left on the back of my hip. It wasn't really sore, I hadn't been wearing it long enough for it to do any real damage, but I could feel the marks he saw.

His voice was deep and possessive when he said, "You're not putting that back on. Your clothing isn't supposed to hurt you."

"You've clearly never been a woman," I said quietly. "I'd never have clothes on if I never wore things that hurt."

Ninety percent of my clothes hurt. From underwire bras that jabbed beneath my arms, to boots that rubbed at my calves, and dresses that were too tight around my belly... Finding anything that fit properly when you were bigger than a size ten was nearly impossible.

Clothes were often just not made with bigger women in mind. We were always an afterthought, never the main target for fashion.

He dipped his head to kiss the back of my neck and then worked his way down my spine, his lips delivering soft kisses over every lump and bump and angry red mark until he was on his knees.

His hands found my ass cheeks, still clad in a pair of panties way skimpier than I normally wore. His fingers slid beneath the elastic, until he had two full handfuls. His thumbs stroked me there, kneading and massaging, inching closer and closer with every pass to the crease between my thighs.

My heart beat with anticipation.

He didn't leave me waiting for long.

He dragged my panties down over my ample ass, then lower, over my cellulite-dimpled thighs until I was standing in nothing but the low heels I'd decided to try to wear tonight since the corset outfit hadn't looked very good with a pair of sneakers or dowdy, though more func-tional, orthopedic work shoes.

X groaned. "Fuck, Violet. This is what you wear whenever we're together. Not those fucking clothes that hurt you. You wear nothing but those heels. God, you're beautiful."

A smile played across my lips. "Actually, the heels hurt a bit too."

His playful side came out. "Then give them to me."

I laughed. "You gonna wear them?"

He grinned as he rose to his feet and then leaned in, whispering in my ear so only I would hear, "No, but I can always use an extra murder weapon. And the spike on those heels will look better in the jugular of the man who scared you tonight than it does in your closet."

A shiver ran over me.

"You're going to tell me his name and I'm going to take care of it."

It was sick I found that hot.

And later, I would set him straight on what had really happened because I didn't want my poor Uber driver, who had done nothing wrong other than getting me to my destination quicker, to pay the ultimate price for good service.

But I didn't want to talk about that now.

Not when his hands were all over me.

He pressed his body against me again from behind, this time reaching around, his arm resting on my belly, his fingers skating over my mound and then lower, until he found the nub of my clit.

One touch brought it to life with a pulsing pleasure that had me gasping.

He rubbed it slowly, in circles that got smaller and faster with each pass.

I held on to the wall, bracing myself with my fingertips so I wasn't smushed by his weight.

I got wetter and wetter with every stroke he made of my clit. He sucked the side of my neck while he worked me up, and I twisted my head so I could kiss him.

He tasted of salt and lime and tequila, and it was as delicious as the way he touched me.

I couldn't stop thinking about the people watching us though. "Do you think there's a lot of them?"

The idea was terrifying. I was judged just walking down the street in broad daylight. How much harsher would those judgments be when I was completely naked and having sex in front of them? I could barely stand the thought of it. Their whispers would be all I would hear. I had to work here for the rest of the night. After half the patrons had watched X rail me.

Doubts crashed in.

X wiped them all out with a single sentence. "I think every man up there watching has their cock in their hand, jerking off, and wishing they were me right now."

It was the confidence in his voice that really sold it.

There wasn't a hint of doubt.

And it left no room for mine.

So when he said, "Turn around, Violet. And let them see what they're missing." I did.

X backed up a few steps, unbuttoning his shirt.

He was no longer blocking my body from the cameras.

Every man watching would see exactly what I looked like.

Before I had a chance to panic, X caught my eye. "Fuck your fingers for them."

My mouth dropped open. "I..."

He undid the button on his pants and dragged down his underwear, just enough to free his cock. He stroked it slowly, his fingers wrapped around himself.

He was something right out of one of my books. Sitting on a leather couch, leaning on one hand, shirt undone, perfect cock, thick and hard.

Because he was staring at me.

It was me getting that reaction out of him.

And all I was doing was existing.

How many times and in how many ways did he have to tell me I did it for him? Hadn't he been telling me that since the day we'd met?

So it wasn't for any other man that I put my fingers to my slit, even though I knew they were watching and the idea sent waves of heat through my entire body.

It was for him.

Because he deserved my full attention.

My pussy was hot and wet. My fingers slid through my arousal so easily it would have been embarrassing if I hadn't been in the middle of a sex club, where getting off was the entire aim of the night.

X groaned, his fingers around his cock moving at the same pace mine plunged inside my body.

I brought my free hand up to my breast, squeezing it, finding the nipple with my fingers and tweaking it in just the way I liked. The way that sent pleasure shooting straight back down between my legs.

X's cock leaked precum, and he spread it across his tip, coating himself in it.

It shined in the dim light of the room, and I ached for it to be inside me. I needed the thickness of him. Needed to stretch around him in a way I couldn't achieve with my fingers alone.

"X," I moaned.

"I know, baby. Get over here and ride me."

I moved across the room, following his directions, turned on by them, and wanting to please him in any way I could.

Because everything about him pleased me. From his tattoos that snaked across his skin, to the scar through his eyebrow, to the singular focus I had from him every time we were together.

I was always the woman he saw. Even in a club full of beautiful women, all ready and raring to have sex with him, it was me he looked at.

I went to straddle him, but he grabbed my thighs. "Turn around so they can see you too."

I had no idea what I was doing, but I followed his instructions. I faced the cameras, not looking at them directly, but hot enough now I would have done anything this man asked of me.

With me facing away from him, he adjusted me to stand with my legs either side of his and then guided me down onto his cock.

I sank onto him, and we both groaned at the angle and deep penetration of the position.

I used my legs to lift myself up his shaft, before lowering back down, and he swore from behind me.

"Jesus fuck, that feels good."

It did for me too. I was still tender from the sex we'd had the night before, but I was so wet it didn't even register that I might have wanted to take a little more time in between. All I could think about was having him inside me, taking him deep, making him feel as good as I felt when his eyes and hands and lips were on me.

He wrapped his arms around me from behind, one cupping a handful of my breast, the other finding his favorite spot, fingers splayed out around my throat.

He didn't squeeze. The cameras kept him in check, but having his hand there, so damn possessive and needy, had me desperate for more.

We experimented with the angle, both of us moving slowly, until he was lying back on the bench and I was leaning forward, supporting my weight on his thighs while I rode him. I found myself missing the light pressure of his hand on my throat, but then they were trailing down my spine and over the globes of my ass.

He stroked his finger in between, rubbing it over my tight rear opening.

The moan I let out was completely indecent, but there was no stopping it.

"If you keep making noises like that when I touch your ass, Violet, I swear to God I'm not going to be able to stop myself from fucking you there right now, right here."

I bit down on my lip, knowing I wasn't ready to take his cock there.

But the idea didn't scare me.

Because I already knew he would never do anything to hurt me. He'd proven that time and time again, even if he didn't believe it himself.

Just like he had the night before, when he'd fucked me doggy style, he played with my ass while I rode him. I reached between my legs to battle with my clit, an aching need there that couldn't be satiated in any other way in this position.

It gave the camera a bird's-eye view.

I instinctively knew Levi and Whip would be watching.

But when I came, it was the man beneath me whose name I shouted.

12

WHIP

Ten minutes earlier...

I couldn't fucking breathe. My chest felt like it was caving in, each rib cracking painfully, both lungs desperate for air I couldn't get.

The crowd of people in the club swarmed around me, too hot, too close.

Levi shouted my name behind me, but he was the last fucking person I wanted to see. I pushed my way around people dancing, people kissing, people fucking, just searching for a break in the room where I could get some fucking space.

But I knew in my gut I wasn't going to find it. Because what I was really searching for was a break in the never-ending grief I kept locked tight, that Levi's question had set free.

I could look at that photo on my shelf and be okay.

But I couldn't fucking talk about it.

I needed out. Out of this club, out of this town, out of

my fucking head that insisted on playing memories over and over in a never-ending loop I couldn't hit stop on.

I needed to spill some fucking blood.

It was one of only two things that had ever helped ease the desperate ache inside me that opened up like a gaping, mortal wound, trying to end me whenever I thought about the people in that photo.

I didn't see anything. Just stumbled blindly, needing to get out and find a knife and someone off that fucking list that I could plunge it into.

Levi's hand clamped down on my shoulder, and I whipped around, shoving him up against the wall, my forearm across his throat.

His eyes went wide, his hands coming up in surrender.

But he didn't try to fight me off. Just stood there, gaze connected with mine, taking in the deep heaves of my chest as I fought to get enough air.

People around us gasped and backed away. They reminded me of where I was, and that even though, in that moment, I might have happily taken Levi's blood to calm the storm inside me, that I couldn't do it here, in my friends' club, with a hundred fucking witnesses.

I dropped my arm from his throat, shaking out the fists I'd bunched my fingers into.

Levi took a deep breath now that I wasn't cutting off his oxygen supply, and I braced myself for him to come at me, fists flying.

But he just eyed me. "You good?"

I was so fucking far from good I couldn't even comprehend what good was. "No."

His mouth flattened into a grim line. "Too bad.

Because whatever the fuck is going on with you is going to have to wait a minute."

I shook my head. "Can't. I can't be here." I backed up a couple steps, but that was as far as I got.

Levi grabbed my arm and snapped his fingers in front of my face. "I get you're having a mental breakdown right now, and I'm sorry I set that off, but can you put a fucking pin in it for a minute? Did you miss the way X just dragged Violet into a private room?"

I blinked. "What?"

He breathed out an exasperated sigh. "You heard me."

Fear curled in my gut. "And you just let him? He can't be alone with her, Levi! Jesus fucking Christ. Where are they?"

Levi muttered something that sounded like a "fuck you" but pointed down the darkened hallway I'd just stormed out of.

Un-fuckin'-believable. I hauled ass back in that direction, shooting Levi a dirty look as I went. "Seriously, you didn't for one second think, oh, there goes Violet with a madman who has a fucking choking kink. Maybe I should stop them?"

Levi glared at me, matching my pace so we were side by side. "Oh, I'm sorry. I was too busy chasing after you, making sure you weren't going to draw a gun in a crowded club and take out half the room!"

"I wasn't going to do that!"

"Well, how the fuck was I supposed to know? You were acting like you wanted to murder an entire stadium full of people, and if you'd been anyone else, I would have just let it go, but because it was you, I had to consider you might actually do it!"

I grabbed his arm and hauled him in close. "Would you stop fucking shouting at me? Everyone can hear you yelling about guns and murder! You want all these people panicking and running out of here to call the cops?"

"Oh, for fuck's sake, Whip! Just say thank you!"

"Thank you? Why would I say thank you to you, of all people? Are you that much of a narcissist?" Was he for fucking real?

"A narciss—" He shook his head. "God, you're such an asshole. Whatever. Are we going to find X before he murders Violet or what?"

I shot him a dirty look 'cause that was a fucking shitty thing to say, even if he didn't mean it.

To his credit, he averted his eyes, like maybe he realized he'd gone too far as well.

I stormed down the hallway, moving through the crowd, checking each peephole and glass window to see if Violet and X were behind any of them.

Bliss passed us, coming from the supply room Levi and I had been restocking earlier, and I grabbed her hand. "Have you seen Violet and X?"

She had a small grin on her mouth. "I have. But I think they're kind of busy."

"Where are they?"

She raised an eyebrow. "When I say busy, Whip, I mean they're in a private room."

My stomach churned with the knowledge of what X could be doing to her right now behind a closed door. "But which one?"

She glanced between me and Levi, both of us towering over her, both of us desperate for her to tell us where Violet was. She finally registered our serious expressions, and her smile slipped away. "They're in the camera room."

Levi barely waited until she had the words out. He charged down the hallway, and I had to run to keep up with him.

At the door marked cam room, he turned the knob, but unsurprisingly, X had locked it.

He reared back, lifting his leg, one heavy, booted foot aiming for the door.

"Stop," I hissed at him. "You can't kick it down."

He put his foot down but spun to glare at me. "You're the one who said he could be killing her in there!"

Jesus, Levi had no control on his volume. I gave the couple next to me a reassuring smile and dragged Levi in closer. "It's a camera room. He's not going to fucking kill her while there's a live feed rolling. He's impulsive—"

"And completely insane, Whip!"

I continued like he hadn't spoken. "But he's not stupid. He hasn't gone this long without getting caught, just to do something rash in the middle of a club full of people with cameras watching him." I eyed the rise and fall of Levi's chest that was so rapid he might have been verging on a panic attack. I glared at him. "Take a fucking breath."

He did.

But it didn't settle him much. His gaze flicked to the next door that had a plaque marking it as a viewing room.

Both of us moved toward it in unison, and I found myself in a darkened room full of people, some sitting, some standing, all of them touching themselves or each other.

A big screen TV on the opposite wall.

On it was an image of Violet in nothing but a corset and panties, X kissing her senseless. When he pulled away from her mouth, his voice was clear as day when he said, "You have no idea what you're doing to me right now, Violet. No fucking idea how bad I want my dick inside you."

"Get out," Levi and I said in unison.

I glanced over at him, surprised but the deeply guttural, demanding tone in his voice, all while knowing it matched mine.

The people in the room all stopped what they were doing and swiveled in our direction. One couple stood, picking up the clothes they'd taken off, and scurried out. But the remaining men, three of them who'd had their cocks out, jerking off while watching the free show X and Violet were putting on, turned and scowled at us.

Levi glared at them. "I said, get out."

One guy frowned in our direction, only half giving us his attention, the rest of it on Violet's body, tits perfectly spilling out over the top of that corset in a way that had me instantly hard. Again.

"It's a cam room," the man complained. "You don't fucking own it."

Levi opened his mouth, but I was just as done as he was. These assholes with their dicks out, getting off watching Violet was sending a rage through me I couldn't control. "He said, get. The fuck. Out. Go find somewhere else to jack off. This room isn't for you."

The warning in my tone wasn't missed this time. The guy who was drunk enough to want to pick a fight finally thought better of it. He shoved to his feet, dick still half out of his pants, and stumbled toward us. "Whatever. She's a fat bitch anyway."

I moved so fast the guy didn't even see me coming. Within an instant, I had him by the throat, slammed up against the wall, his head bouncing off the plasterboard. "What did you say?"

It wasn't that he'd called her fat. Violet wasn't a tiny woman. She wasn't slim. By anyone's definition, she would be classified as fat.

That was just a statement of fact.

But it was the fucking disrespect this prick had said it with that had me wanting to strangle him until his eyes rolled back. It was the way he'd used it as a slur, to put her down, just to make himself feel big.

Rage coursed through me.

That woman had been through hell and back and had still somehow managed to remain beautiful, both inside and out.

That was what I'd seen, watching her in bed with the three of us. That was what I saw now, staring at her image on the screen, her curvy body not seen as beautiful by that man.

It was to me.

And it clearly was to Levi and X too.

"Let him go," Levi said quietly in my ear. "He's not worth it."

It was only his voice that cut through the red haze in my head that begged to be sated with a life. It calmed something inside me, just enough for me to uncurl my fingers from the man's throat.

He slumped back against the wall, coughing painfully, his eyes now wide with the fear he should have had all along. "You're fucking crazy!" he shouted, staggering away, his friends by his side. "You could have killed me!"

"Could have," I agreed. "But I didn't. So get the fuck out of this club before I change my mind."

His eyes were filled with fear and the men disappeared out of the room.

Levi kicked the door shut behind them and shoved a chair beneath it, since it didn't have a lock.

Both of us stared up at the screen.

X had her naked, facing the camera. "Fuck your fingers for them."

I groaned and sank down onto the couch. "Shit."

Levi sat on the other end of it and glanced over at me. "I know you don't want me up in your business, but are you all right?"

"I'm sitting here and watching X fuck Violet to make sure he doesn't kill her in the process. I'm just fine and fucking dandy," I spit out between grinding teeth.

Levi looked up at the screen, and Violet's fingers skimming her body, and then pressing up inside herself. She darted peeks at the cameras, and each one felt like it was directed solely at me.

God, I wanted to touch her. I wanted so much more than just sitting in this room babysitting while X got to have her.

Because the only other thing that calmed a storm inside me was sex. Losing myself in someone else so I didn't have to feel the crushing pressure of what I'd lost.

It was why I'd gotten into sex work in the first place. Because it was safer and easier to lose myself in the body of another person, rather than taking the life of one.

Whatever let me forget.

The silence in the room drew out, both Levi and I staring up at the screen watching every little thing X did to her.

I didn't know about Levi, but I was dying inside watching it.

But it wasn't my place to want anything more than what I'd already had. My job was done. That woman up on the screen was a million miles away from the timid woman who'd first called me up, who blushed and shook at just the mention of taking off her panties.

She might not have been fully confident in her own skin yet, but that wasn't my job. X or Levi, whoever the fuck she chose to be with, they would take her the rest of the way.

I was supposed to be walking away. Moving on to the next client.

Yet not one part of me could do that. Every cell in my body was cemented to this seat, unable to turn away from the way her body moved, searching for a pleasure I was so desperate to give her.

"If he doesn't make her come in a minute, I swear I'm gonna bust down that door and do it myself," Levi practically growled.

I glanced over at him.

His dick was hard behind his pants, the sizeable bulge straining at his fly.

Mine matched. I was so damn hard it hurt.

Almost as much as the raw wound inside me that had opened up tonight.

I undid the button on my pants. Unzipped them. Pushed my hand inside and let my cock free.

I needed release. If it wasn't going to be blood, it was going to be cum.

Deliberately ignoring Levi, I watched Violet on the screen, my breaths increasing as she and X moved around the room, and he positioned her to ride his cock cowgirl style so she was facing the cameras, nowhere to hide.

Moisture beaded at my tip, a silky slick arousal building there at the sight of her lowering herself down, inch by inch onto another man, and then riding him, her fingers digging into his thighs while she bounced up and down.

Her tits were full and perfect, bobbing with each rock of her wide hips.

She lost herself in the rhythm, and I lost myself in the vision, pleasure shooting from deep in my balls and right through the rest of my body.

"If you keep making noises like that when I touch your ass, Violet, I swear to God, I'm not going to be able to stop myself from fucking you there. Right here, right now."

Levi groaned beside me, and I snuck a glance over at him, already knowing that in the darkened shadows at his end of the couch, he was doing the same thing I was.

If X took Violet's ass, I was going to come instantly. There was no way I could watch him fuck her there, in that tight little hole I wanted so desperately around my dick.

It was bad enough watching the slide of her pussy, stretched out around him, his dick glistening with how wet she'd made him.

I needed more. More than just my fucking hand around my cock. It wasn't enough.

I needed someone else's touch.

"Levi," I groaned, pumping my cock slowly.

It took me a good second to realize I'd said his name out loud.

I looked over at him.

And all I got was heat in return.

Fuck.

But he was planted to his seat. His dick hard in his hand, his gaze on me, watching every move I made with a fire in his eyes I couldn't deny.

But he was stiff as a fucking board. Frozen in place by his name on my tongue while we watched porn together and tried to pretend there wasn't something more in the air between us.

How quickly the urge to kill became the urge to fuck.

I shifted across the bench, drawn to him like a magnet, one I couldn't fight and didn't want to.

He didn't move away. Didn't stop me.

I inched in, my gaze on the screen, watching X finger fuck Violet's ass while she rode his cock, each slap of their bodies meeting only pushing me closer to the other man in the room.

Levi's heavy breaths matched mine. The two of us sitting side by side, so close now our arms brushed, both of us jerking off, our rhythms finding a matching pace, even though neither of us were looking at each other.

My balls tightened, a need to come burning inside me but unable to escape.

Violet panted on the screen, her moans filling my ears.

I wanted to touch her so fucking bad.

But it was Levi I reached for instead, wrapping my hand around his cock, his hand beneath mine.

He hissed, "What are you doing?"

But he didn't stop me. We jerked his cock together a few times, before his hand dropped and he tipped his head back on the couch, letting me take control. "Fuck."

I pumped his cock with my right hand, working my own with my left.

I waited for him to shove me away. But he didn't.

I fell into a familiar rhythm, pushing him toward a climax, letting his fast breaths fill my ears until it was all I could hear, and my hand on my cock was all I could feel.

There was no room for anything else.

No memories. No reminders of what I'd lost. No urge to kill just to make myself feel better.

I had a job to do, and I was doing it.

Working my own cock while I had his in my hand was new, I'd never done that with a client, it was always all about them.

I couldn't stop though. I stroked us both, taking us closer and closer to the edge, matching the pace to what X and Violet were doing on the other side of the wall, all four of our moans and breaths joining until the room was filled with the sound of pleasure.

"Fuck," Levi groaned again. His eyes opened, his cock kicking in my hand, me as close to orgasm as he was.

A few more pumps and we'd both be there. I'd have used him for what I needed.

I closed my eyes, hating myself for what I was doing. This man was as straight as they fucking came, and I was just using him to get off. To feel something other than the gut-churning pain of losing people.

His fingers gripped the back of my neck, hauling me in, forcing me to face him.

He didn't speak. Didn't say my name.

Our gazes collided, and he pressed his mouth to mine.

The kiss was hot and hard, both of us groaning, him taking control and kissing me deep, his tongue finding its way into my mouth.

His bourbon-and-mint taste lit up on my tongue, and I gripped both of us harder when he moaned against my lips, the kiss connecting us more than just my hand on his cock had.

He came first, his dick erupting, cum coating my fingers. He tensed, muscles going tight, but his mouth never slacking off.

When he was finally shaking and spent, I used his cum to finish me off. My balls tightened, and there was no stopping the orgasm that ripped through me, white coating my lower stomach, while Levi's tongue was in my mouth and he was kissing me like he really fucking liked it.

And for as long as it took for my orgasm to ebb, I let myself like it too.

But when it faded, I pulled away.

I got up, finding some wipes to clean up with, avoiding his gaze until I was done. I threw the wipes at him.

"Whip…"

I didn't want to hear whatever he was going to say. Whether it was lame excuses that he wasn't into guys. Or maybe worse, an admittance there was something between us he couldn't deny.

I didn't care. Violet was safe.

And whatever the hell had happened in here tonight had only been a Band-Aid for the parts of me that were so fucking broken I was sure they'd never heal.

13

VIOLET

I came out of the women's bathrooms, right as Nyah walked into them. She grabbed me, clutching my arm.

I had to blink at her for a long moment to mentally place why she was even here.

I was pretty sure X had scrambled my brain, and it was no longer working properly. It was too blissed-out on the lingering tingles of the orgasm X had given me in that camera room to function right.

But when I came to, I realized with sharp shock that I'd completely forgotten about meeting her.

Instant regret filled me. "Oh my God, Nyah. I'm so sorry! I was supposed to meet you outside and—"

She shook her head, the widest grin I could have imagined all over her face. "No, don't apologize. It worked out perfectly." She checked to see who was within earshot, then leaned in. "I just had sex in the middle of the club!"

I widened my eyes at her. "Seriously? With who?"

She swiveled, pointing through the crowd. "See over there? The tattoo guy?"

My mouth dropped open when I spotted the man she was talking about. "Holy shit, I know him. That's Dax."

She pretty much hopped from one foot to the other. "I think I'm in love. That was the biggest rush of my life. I want to do it again. Vi, there was just this...I don't know, chemistry between us. One minute I was helping him inside with his equipment and we were joking about me being his assistant. The next he's got my tits out, sucking on them, and then my skirt up and he's fucking me right there in the middle of the club while everyone around us watched." She blew out a long breath that lifted her bangs.

I laughed at her. Her eyes were all sparkly, and her skin was glowing. She looked alive in a way she hadn't earlier that day. I grinned at her. "You want to go for round two with Dax or hit up someone new?"

Her gaze slid back to him, and she grinned when she realized he was watching her. "Him. Definitely him. But I don't want to seem desperate. Maybe I should play it cool...?" She reached for my hand and squeezed it. "I really need to go clean up. And you probably need to get to work. Your shift starts in a few minutes, doesn't it?"

It did, so I sent her on her way, promising I'd catch up with her later, if she wasn't too busy bouncing on Dax's cock.

I raised an eyebrow at him as I passed and hid a laugh at the way he blushed and busied himself with his work.

I found Bliss behind the bar, serving up drinks with the prettiest of smiles on her face. Another sexy piece of lingerie clung to her curvy figure, this time a black number that plunged low between her breasts and was cut high around her thighs.

She didn't seem to care one iota that her cellulite-dimpled thighs were on display, and I basked in her aura for a moment while she was busy with a customer. I wanted her confidence. I wanted to just drop the jacket I'd put back on over my corset after X had finished with me.

If I could get naked and have sex with him while a roomful of people watched us, then surely I could pour a few drinks in underwear that covered almost as much as regular clothes did.

Bliss did a double take when she caught sight of me. "Violet! What are you doing here?"

I blinked. "I have a shift tonight...don't I?"

Bliss left her customers with their drinks and tugged me to the side of the bar. She was a good few inches shorter than me, and I would have guessed we were about the same age, but she stared up at me with a mothering expression of concern. "I heard about what happened—"

I shook my head quickly. "I'm fine. I don't want to talk about that."

Her full lips straightened into a concerned line. "I can imagine. And I've been in your shoes. I've had my fair share of traumatic events, so I know how numb you probably feel right now—"

"I'm fine," I insisted.

It felt like Bliss's eyes saw right through me.

But her voice was gentle when she spoke. "You're not. You're in shock and you're doing whatever you can to not think about it. I get it. Trust me, I really do. But sooner or later, you're going to crash down from the safety tower you've built for yourself. I've been there and seen it happen to my guys, and to Rebel, and when it comes, if you aren't ready for it, it hits hard and swift and can be dangerous." She took my hand and squeezed my fingers. "Don't do that to yourself. Go home. Let yourself grieve and process your loss. You can work again tomorrow, or next week or the week after. Whenever you feel up to it."

I really liked Bliss, but she had no idea what she was talking about. She hadn't been there, in that empty warehouse, locked in with a dangerous man, watching people die in the most violent of ways.

I didn't want to go home and think about that. That was the absolute last thing I wanted to do.

But I could see, even though she was being gentle with me, she wasn't going to back down. "You aren't going to change your mind, are you?"

"I can't make you go home. But you aren't working tonight."

I shoved my hands into my jacket so she wouldn't notice the irritated clench of my fingers. I knew she meant well, but she wasn't helping.

I forced myself to stay polite. "Okay. I understand." I spun on my heel and walked away.

But I had nowhere to go. If I went back to Fang's place, they'd all be crashed out with their kids by this hour. If I went home, there'd be nobody there.

I didn't want to be alone with my thoughts.

I didn't want to close my eyes.

I was utterly terrified of not having a distraction. Of having to relive it all in my head, over and over.

I was still so mad at Whip and Levi and even X. I hated that they'd kept me in the dark.

But last night they'd been the only reason I could sleep.

And tonight, they were all I had.

14

X

*E*nergy buzzed through my body like a blow fly on crack. It shot through every vein, my blood pumping too fast, heart pounding, muscles primed.

All I could smell was her. Her hair. Her skin. Her sweet pussy, slick with arousal. It all floated around me, in a cloud of heaven.

I was never taking a shower again. Washing away the scent of her would be a fate worse than death.

I put my clothes back on, taking my time even though Violet had rushed out of the room like her ass had been on fire. It definitely hadn't been though, because I'd been watching it as she'd left, and it was nothing but sweet perfection, swaying enticingly as she'd hurried out the door.

I finally followed, emerging into the dark hallway and finding myself surrounded by people again.

The door to my left opened, the one with a plaque marking it as a viewing room, and Levi and Whip walked out of it. Both of them were flushed in the face and adjusting their clothes.

They both froze when they noticed me standing there.

I grinned and waved a finger between the two of them. "Well, hey there, Brokeback Mountain. Blink once if there was tongue. Blink twice if Whip cried after."

Whip gave me the middle finger.

But I didn't miss the way he couldn't even look at Levi. Or the way Levi's lips were swollen. I chuckled beneath my breath and slung an arm around both their shoulders, drawing them in. "You know what I like to do after a good round of sex club shenanigans?"

Whip glanced over at me warily. "Shower? Fucking hell, X, you reek of sex."

"Glorious, isn't it? But no." I squeezed them tighter. "Murder, boys. I'm emotionally unstable, sexually satisfied, and lightly caffeinated. Let's go commit a felony."

Levi struggled his way out from under my arm. "Not a chance. No one is killing tonight."

I rolled my eyes at him. "Boring! Whip?"

I didn't hold out much hope. Whip was the most in-control psychopath I'd ever met. Sex probably didn't hype him up the way it did for me. But I was absolutely buzzing. I had been ever since our little four-way last night, and I'd kept it in check all day, but getting inside Violet twice in the space of twenty-four hours? That was way too much for me.

I needed a knife in my hand. Blood needed to spill. I could practically feel it running over my fingers, hot and wet, just like her pussy had been.

I had to stop thinking about that or I was gonna get

hard all over again, and I didn't think she would appreciate me bending her over a table and taking her hard and fast from behind while she was holding a tray of drinks or trying to take an order.

I was on a Violet high I couldn't get off, and that energy needed to go somewhere.

Whip was gonna say no too, I could see it on his face.

I threw up my hands. "One blowie and the two of you turn into pumpkins. It's barely ten. We aren't going home."

Levi glared at me. "There was no 'blowie.'"

I raised an eyebrow. "Really? No bob on the knob?"

Whip rolled his eyes. "Seriously?"

"No slurpin' the gherkin?"

Levi made a face. "What?"

I pushed my tongue into my cheek a couple of times, making it bulge, and winked at him. "You know what I'm talking about."

"I wish I didn't." Whip strode toward the main room of the club. "I need way more alcohol to deal with you in this mood."

But alcohol wasn't going to touch the need I had curling around inside me. "No alcohol, and no going home. Someone has to supervise me before I go on a stabbing spree. You don't want me on the morning news, do you?"

Whip groaned. "Isn't this why you have parents?"

I grinned at him. "Are you asking me to call you Daddy?" I glanced at Levi. "Is that what you call him?"

Levi threw up his hands. "For fuck's sake, X. Fine! We're going killing. Jesus, I've never been so annoyed at the thought of taking someone out. But anything to shut you up."

I kissed his cheek, and he shoved me off.

I couldn't control my laughter. "You only like kisses from Whip, then, huh?"

The instant flush of pink in his cheeks told me there had definitely been some saliva swapping when the two of them had been in that viewing room.

That was kinda hot.

Whip gave me a look. "If we take you killing, will you shut up about it?"

"Yes, Daddy."

He pinched the bridge of his nose. "Just call me your first victim of the night, because you are killing me. Go. Please. For the love of all things fucking holy, go get a knife before I turn my gun on myself."

We moved for the door, but someone calling my name stopped me.

I drank in the sight of Violet weaving through the crowd toward us.

She stopped in front of me, glancing at Whip and Levi before turning back to me. There was the tiniest hint of a pout on her lips. "Where are you guys going?"

Whip and Levi both opened their mouths to answer, but I got in first. "Killin'."

Whip elbowed me. "Shut up. She doesn't need to hear that, after...everything."

Seriously, the Dad title really did fit him. He was such an old grump. "Would you prefer I lied to her again? Have we learned nothing from the last twenty-four hours? Violet doesn't want us lying to her. So I'm not. Get on board the truth train with me, Whip."

"Is it possible for that truth train to just run you right on over? Like, I can tie you to the tracks if it helps?"

I made a face at him.

Violet narrowed her eyes at him. "Don't give him shit. He's right. I'm so sick of you three keeping stuff from me."

Levi sighed. "We aren't doing it to hurt you. We just want to keep you safe."

"They're very boring," I whispered to her. "But don't worry, once you marry me and we run off to Barbados to live happily ever after, with our two children and a pet enchilada, they will be nothing but a memory."

All three of them stared at me.

Whip pinched the bridge of his nose. "A pet enchilada?"

I nodded. "Yeah, you know those furry gray things with the big ears? Kinda like cuter, cuddly rats? Wikipedia says they make great but unusual pets."

Levi squinted at me. "Do you mean a chinchilla?"

I waved my hand around dismissively. "Chinchilla, enchilada, same-same."

"Not even remotely the same, X," Whip muttered.

I clapped my hands. "So, while Violet is working, we're all going stabbing." I kissed the top of her head. "Have a great shift, chinchilla mama. I'll be back to pick you up when you're finished."

"Take me with you."

Now all three of us stared at her.

And one syllable came out of all three of our mouths. "No."

Something flashed in Violet's eyes. "What do you mean, no? My best friend was murdered last night. We all know the cops aren't going to do anything about that.

They don't care about anyone who lives this side of the Saint View-Providence border. You think I can just work and go home and act like nothing happened?"

Whip brushed the back of his hand beneath her chin, tilting her head so she was looking up at him. "Hey. Nobody is asking you to act like nothing happened. But, Violet, you cannot come with us. We're hunting targets from the list, and one of those people murdered Toby and could have just as easily killed you too."

"All the more reason for me to come with you. I'm the one who was personally singled out by this guy. I need to be involved."

Levi wore regret all over his face. "Vi, it's dangerous."

"So is having sex with X, but the two of you were happy to sit around and watch that happen."

I choked on a laugh that only doubled when Whip and Levi both appeared suitably chagrined. Levi shot me a look that clearly said: "Do you want to help us out here?"

He was right. Violet most definitely could not come hunting with us. "You have a shift. I know you don't just want to leave Bliss and the others shorthanded. We'll take you out to play another day." Then I mouthed, "No, we won't," to the other guys.

Violet glared at me. "You know I can see you doing that, right?"

I cringed. "Oops. I was trying to be subtle."

"You're about as subtle as a steamroller," Whip said.

"Or a bull in a china shop," Levi added.

"Or a stripper at a church picnic." Violet's fingers had clenched into fists by her sides.

My mouth dropped open. "Hey! You're supposed to be on my side!"

"Take me out with you tonight and I will be. Put a knife in my hand and point me at whoever took my best friend from me."

All the jokes died.

Because all three of us knew it wasn't that simple. Taking a life, even one you felt you were owed, came with a lifetime of baggage. Fear. Regrets.

Ones you couldn't outrun. Couldn't get away from. Ones you saw at night when you closed your eyes.

I couldn't stop the urge to kill any more than Levi or Whip could.

But that didn't mean I didn't regret my actions. That they didn't keep me up at night.

I didn't want that for Violet. No matter how much she wanted it right now.

I snaked my hand to the back of her neck, twisting my fingers in the long lengths of her hair.

I waited until her pretty gaze locked on mine. And even though I knew it was going to undo any favor I might have won with her that day, and I would be right back to where I started, with her hating my guts, I knew I had to say it anyway.

"No."

She jerked herself out of my touch, and I let her go, unwilling to hold her there against her will.

But I wasn't budging on my answer. And I knew Whip and Levi wouldn't either.

She didn't know what true darkness felt like. And she didn't want to know.

She stormed away, disappearing into the crowd of people in the club.

I looked at the other two. "Do we go after her?"

Levi sighed. "No. Let her go. She has every right to be angry at us. I don't blame her. But she can't ever…"

Whip nodded. "I think we're all agreed on that. I'd rather her hate me and never know what it feels like to kill a man than let her do it and live with the consequences."

"I'm going to kill every person on that list so she doesn't have to. I'll kill every man in this whole damn world if it means she never has to get blood on her hands," I said quietly.

Levi watched her through the crowd. "One of us should stay and keep an eye on her."

Violet's death stares were like daggers, shooting in the air between us.

"Or maybe we should give her some space tonight. Her shift finishes at five, we can come back then and make sure she gets back to Fang's safely. But she'll be okay here until then. Nothing is going to happen with her surrounded by people."

Whip and Levi both seemed a little uneasy by the idea, but it was the best solution. We couldn't watch her twenty-four seven and hunt down the targets on the list. When she was with other people, that was our best chance to leave her.

And right now, judging by the expression on her face, we were the last people she wanted to see.

15

VIOLET

All three of them could go to hell.

I watched as they slunk away toward the door, all three looking like misbehaving dogs with their tails between their legs, having just been yelled at by their owner.

And yet I knew they weren't going to change their minds.

Chauvinistic pigs.

If men could kill, then how fucking hard could it be? Everything inside me blazed with anger and grief and loss. There wasn't a single muscle in my body that wasn't currently primed for a fight, for violence, or for blood to spill.

Screw them for thinking I wasn't up to the challenge.

Screw Bliss for thinking I wasn't up to working tonight.

Screw everyone. I wasn't a fucking child who needed coddling. I'd watched my best friend bleed out in my lap last night. I'd fucked three men, and then gone another round in a sex club while people watched. If I wanted to go on a killing spree then I would.

The sensible part of my brain warned that despite everything I'd been through, we both knew I wasn't going to do that, but I wasn't in the mood for rational, well-thought-out plans.

I was running on emotion and sadness and anger and I wasn't in the mood to be told I couldn't fucking do something.

I grabbed Nyah's arm as she walked past me with a drink. "Will you come somewhere with me?"

She cocked her head. "Where?"

I screwed up my face then decided to just tell her the truth. "Stalking."

Her eyes went wide. "Seriously? Like a police stakeout?"

Oh God, she was more innocent than I was. And dragging her into this was probably insane. But following the guys alone felt too dangerous. I needed her. "Yeah, I guess like a stakeout. You in?"

She glanced over at Dax.

The chemistry between them was so palpable I could practically touch it.

I squeezed her arm. "Sorry, no. Never mind. You should go get your freak on with him again. There's clearly something between you two."

But Nyah shook her head. "No, he has a line of people to tattoo anyway, and I really don't want to be a desperate fool." She grinned. "Better to leave him wanting more, you know? Then when I casually drop in at the tattoo shop during the week, he can be pleasantly surprised." She set her drink down. "Let's go do some stalking!" She tucked her arm into mine. "This night is the best night of my life. Have I told you that? You live a wild life, Violet Garrisen. I'm just happy to be invited to tag along."

It took me a good long moment to process that. That she thought I, Miss Queen of Spending Weekends on the Couch with Fictional Doctors, lived a wild life was so laughable. I'd spent my whole life being vanilla.

But the girl I'd been before that night I'd met X in the most horrible of situations felt like someone I didn't even know anymore.

Suddenly, I realized I couldn't drag Nyah into all of this without explaining to her what she was getting into. I'd been thrown into this world without a choice in it. But it wasn't fair to do that to her.

With one eye watching the guys talking to Vincent at the door, I pulled Nyah into a corner. "Listen, you need to know something before we go out there. The guys that were following me around at work today? That's who we're stalking."

Her eyes lit up with excitement. "Oooh, eye candy. They were hot."

A flicker of jealousy lit up inside me at cute, little Nyah thinking my men were attractive.

I had to do a double take at the possessive "my men." They weren't mine.

Except they felt like they were. And that was something I was going to have to get over. Because them being mine would make me theirs. And that was a thought I couldn't comprehend, even though the idea left me warm on the inside.

I couldn't belong to three men.

I couldn't belong to three *murderers*.

What the hell was I doing?

"Don't be fooled by pretty faces. They aren't good guys and they are involved with bad people. Coming with me tonight will be dangerous." I blew out a long breath, realizing I'd made a huge mistake in even asking her to come. "You know what? Just forget I said anything. Stay here with Dax. He's a good guy. And this club is safe."

X shook Vincent's hand, the two of them nodding, and I narrowed my eyes, catching X's gaze.

He gave me the widest smile and then pointed at Vincent, then shook his finger with an overexaggerated frown.

Nyah squinted at him. "His charades game is weak. I have no idea what he's trying to say."

But I did. He was telling me Vincent wasn't letting me out.

He was telling me I was stuck here for the night.

Un-fucking-believable.

But also stupid, especially of Levi, because I knew where the back door was. I'd seen it when he and I were cleaning.

As if I wasn't going to use it.

I moved through the club, beelining for that back door, hoping it didn't have an alarm on it.

Nyah jogged along beside me in her glittery heels, taking two steps to match each of my longer strides. "Wait for me. I'm coming."

"You shouldn't. It's dangerous."

Her dark brows furrowed. "All the more reason for me to come. You need someone to have your back."

I sighed at the couple fucking standing up against the emergency exit. How was I supposed to get out now?

They were fully into it, eyes closed, tongues and lips and hands all over each other, slow pumps into the woman's body while her head hit the door.

I couldn't just tap her on the shoulder and ask her to delay her orgasm so I could get by.

"Excuse us," Nyah announced. "We need to get by, please. You're blocking the exit."

The couple didn't pay us any attention. They were too lost in grinding on each other, the scent of alcohol and sweat and sex wafting off them, wrinkling my nose.

Nyah reached around me pushed down on the handle, sending it flying open.

Without the door to lean on, the couple staggered out into the dark parking lot, completely naked, his dick still buried deep inside the woman.

That got their attention. He shouted at us, and my immediate reaction was to start apologizing, but Nyah grabbed my arm and dragged me past them, her middle finger up.

"We asked you politely!"

Vincent turned our way, his attention caught by the commotion.

Ah shit, my babysitter was on to us.

"Run," I said, grabbing Nyah's arm. "We're about to get busted."

My heart pounded, even though I knew Vincent wouldn't hurt me. But the thought of him forcing me to stay here was just as bad. Getting locked in Psychos suddenly felt as claustrophobic as the warehouse a madman had locked me in. My skin crawled at the thought of it, my chest tightening like a vise.

Nobody was locking me in anywhere.

I scanned the parking lot, noting X's van and Levi's bike, but Whip's car was noticeably missing. I caught a glimpse of taillights turning out onto the road and the silver sedan he drove. "Shit! They've already left."

"We can catch them. My car is right here."

And that's when I realized that Nyah was wearing nothing more than her tiny skirt and barely-there top. We hadn't stopped to get her coat or her purse.

"Your keys..." I watched, frustrated, as Whip's car disappeared around the corner.

Nyah opened the door of her car. "Girl, please. I'm from farming country where everyone leaves their doors unlocked and their keys inside." She flipped down the visor, and the keys dropped into her open palm.

I winced. "You know, around here, that's a recipe to get your car stolen, right?" But I wasn't going to look a gift horse in the mouth. I slid into the passenger seat and Nyah got in behind the steering wheel.

She grinned, her eyes flashing with excitement. "From what I hear, if someone wants to steal your car in Saint View, they'll do it with or without the keys."

She had a point. A locked car had never been a deterrent in this town.

Nyah gunned the engine like she was an F1 driver on the starting line and then slammed her foot down on the accelerator. Vincent, halfway across the lot to where we were, had to jump out of the way to avoid getting mowed down.

"Yeah!" Nyah fist pumped the air. "Ain't nobody holding us down! Not even you, scary, brooding, bouncer dude!"

I cringed and waved an apologetic hand in Vincent's direction.

Seemed smart to be polite to the psychopath.

But Nyah was hopped up on an adrenaline high and took the corner out of the lot in a screech of tires. I gripped the holy shit bar so tightly my knuckles went white and fought to keep my head from smashing into the window with the g-force she was creating.

"Don't worry, Vi. I'm an awesome driver. I'll catch up in no time."

I widened my eyes at the speedometer, clicking up to the speed limit in seconds, until we were flying down the main strip of Saint View at about twenty over.

"Oh, I'm going to die," I muttered, bracing myself against the dashboard.

Honestly, dying in a flipped car or one that had crashed into a pole had not been on my bingo card for the week.

How on earth could I have survived the warehouse, and the psychopaths who had all come out of the wood-work, only to be killed by the cute little brunette who looked like she should have been a school teacher?

Nyah ran a red light, and I squeezed my eyes shut, praying not to hear a horn blast or the wail of police sirens.

But neither happened. We straightened up after taking a corner at a pace that rolled my stomach, and I finally dared to peel open my eyes.

Nyah backed right off the pace and pointed at the car ahead of us. "Found them."

I breathed out a sigh of relief. Then glanced over at her. "Where the hell did you learn to drive like that?"

"Uh, Oklahoma?"

"Why did you say that like it was a question?"

She sighed. "Fine! You busted me. I didn't grow up in the country. I grew up in New York."

I had no idea how that related to the way she'd just driven the car.

She glanced over at me. "I might have spent my teens stealing cars and running from the police. It's no big deal."

I widened my eyes at her, remembering something she'd said at work earlier that day. "You said you didn't have a car…"

She gave me a sheepish smile. "I don't."

I gazed around the interior of the car like maybe I'd dreamed it. But no, we were very definitely in one. "Then what the hell are we driving?"

She gave a laugh that clearly told me she was on a high she couldn't get down from. "I saw this couple park their car and put the keys in the visor while I was standing in line."

"You're driving a stolen car?"

She shrugged. "Only until we ditch it."

I stared at her. "Is it me? Am I just the magnet for all people with no respect for the law?"

She laughed. "It's fine, Vi. Seriously. The people who own this car will be in the club for hours yet, getting their freak on. You wanted to stalk, let's stalk."

I didn't have it in me to argue. At this point, I'd been exposed to so many illegal things that stealing a crappy old car and taking it on a joyride through town seemed almost innocent.

She peeped little looks at me as we followed Whip's

car from a distance, letting several other cars sit between ours and his. "You want to tell me what's going on?"

I sighed. "I wish I could. But honestly, all of it is insane and illegal, and I've already implicated you in too much of it just by bringing you tonight. I don't want to make it worse."

She waved her hand dismissively. "I can guarantee that whatever it is, I've been there, done or seen that." She gave me a half-smile. "Let's just say my parents aren't very nice people, and I grew up surrounded by their friends, who are also not very nice people. So there's really nothing you can tell me that is going to shock me. I've seen it all before, and probably worse."

I bit my tongue, knowing that stealing a few cars had nothing on murdering a few people.

Was "few" even accurate? How many people had the three of them taken out between them? Five? Ten? A hundred?

I was suddenly reminded that getting involved with any of them was completely insane.

And yet here I was, chasing them around town, because I couldn't fucking quit any of them.

Nyah tapped the brakes, slowing us down for a red light, and we both ducked in our seats, closer to Whip's car than we'd been yet. I could see X's head through the back window, him sitting in the center of the back seat while Levi and Whip rode up front.

Nyah swiveled to face me. "My dad is in the Mafia. He kills people with a click of his fingers. And so do my brothers and my uncles and my cousins, and pretty much everyone I know."

My mouth dropped open. "Holy shit." I blinked at her.

"You're an honest-to-God Mafia princess? Do they actually exist outside of TV shows and books?"

She shrugged. "I've been trying to get out of that life for years. I've been lucky so far. My dad hasn't tried to marry me off to anyone. But I know he's been saving that drawcard for when it best suits him. That's all I'm good for to him. I'm just a bargaining piece to play when he needs a new alliance."

"That's...a lot." I didn't know what else to say.

She nodded. "But I'm out, at least for now. They'll come after me eventually, I'm not stupid enough to think otherwise, but right now I'm free." She raised a shoulder. "But whatever your guys are into, whatever you've found yourself in, I've probably seen and done worse." Her laughter filled the car. "I just need a friend. I don't know anyone here, and I've never been alone in my whole life." She sniffed. "Wow. Sorry. I just really dumped all that in your lap, and now you probably think I'm a desperate loser who needs therapy for her family issues."

I shook my head. "I could really use a friend too." I took a deep breath then let out the words in a rush. "I watched a man get decapitated, and then I watched my best friend bleed out in front of me, and those three guys we're following? They all murder people 'cause they like it."

I waited for Nyah to admit my story was worse than hers. For her to be shocked or worse, fearful. I waited for her to slam her foot down on the brakes and demand I get out of her car.

Her stolen car, but I guessed it was still hers more than mine.

But she just gripped the wheel tighter. "Sorry about your friend."

Out of everything she could have said, that was probably the most normal response I could have imagined.

I burst out into uncontrollable laughter.

Nyah's expression morphed to concern, but just as quickly turned into laughter of her own. "Did we just become best friends?"

I was pretty sure we had.

16

WHIP

"Murder crew, murder crew. Whatcha gonna do? Whatcha gonna do when we come for you?"

I pressed my fingers to my temples, trying to fight off the pounding pain building behind my eyes that seemed to always be present when X was around.

Levi groaned as X repeated his little singsong mantra for about the hundredth time since we'd left Psychos. "Please. For the love of all things holy. Would you pick a different song?"

Ah, fuck. That was the absolute worst thing he could have said. I knew what was coming.

X warbled loudly and off-key. "Ninety-nine bottles of beer on the wall, ninety-nine bottles of beer…"

I groaned, scrubbing my hand through my hair.

Levi grimaced. "I made a mistake there, didn't I?"

"Ninety-nine bottles is his default. The murder crew ditty was definitely preferable. He'll go right down to one bottle and then he'll start over."

"We could kill him instead?" Levi offered.

X snorted from the back seat. "You could try. But you would fail."

I think both Levi and I realized there was a high possibility that could be true. Levi and I could probably go head-to-head in a fight and I would have a fifty-fifty chance of coming out on top.

But neither he nor I had a screw quite as loose as X did. We might have been bigger than he was, but he had unpredictability on his side.

I wasn't stupid enough to mess with that. Maybe we were something that resembled friends, but that didn't mean I forgot to keep a healthy dose of fear in my heart when it came to him. It would be stupid not to, and I tried not to make a habit out of being stupid.

X quit singing, only to say, "If you prefer, we can talk some more about how you two got all up and intimate with each other in that viewing room. I still don't have any details on that. Was it just a bit of friendly sucky-sucky between friends? Or did someone take a ride on the Hershey Highway?"

"Hey, X?" I called to him in the back seat.

"Yeah?"

"You wearing your seat belt?"

"No. Why?"

I slammed my foot on the brake hard, sending him flying forward. He hit the back of my and Levi's seats with a groan.

I shrugged at Levi. "Damn. Was kinda hoping he'd sail right through the windshield."

"Hey! I heard that!" X muttered from behind us, pushing himself back onto his seat. Though it was a bit late now, since we were nearly there, he put his seat belt on and glared at me in the rearview mirror.

"Sorry," I called back to him. "There was a duck on the road."

"Reginald!"

I rolled my eyes, my irritation with X only feeding the desire in me to stab something. I stopped outside the destination Levi had given me. We were well out of Saint View, after taking the road that led to the city. We hadn't quite hit the city center, but we were in a shitty part of the outskirts. It wasn't terribly different than Saint View, other than the fact the apartment buildings were a lot taller than the ones we had at home.

I cringed at a rat running across the alley in front of us, disappearing into a crack in the outer walls of the building we were watching. "This place is a hole."

Levi nodded. "Did you really expect a man who was involved in a trafficking ring to live somewhere fancy?"

I peered out through the windshield at the people walking by on the street ahead of us, despite the fact it was after midnight. "I don't expect anything. Ever. I've known violent men who were poor as dirt and ones who were richer than I could ever dream of. And everything in between. Expectations are what get you killed. And I prefer to remain breathing."

Levi let out a long breath. "Fair enough."

X finally dared to unclick his seat belt, even though we'd been stationary for more than a few minutes. "And where exactly do you fall on that scale, Whip?"

"On the scale of violent men? When you're singing, pretty high."

"I meant where do you fall on the richer or poorer

scale? Because you live in that shitty little house in Saint View. But yet you drive this really nice car...are these leather seats?" He ran his palms all over them, then leaned in, loudly sniffing into the air. "What's that I smell?"

"If you farted..."

X ignored me. "It's the smell of someone who owns more than three matching forks." He grinned. "You're rich, aren't you? Let me guess. Old-school money, but you wanted to prove to Daddy you could make it on your own. So you took the shitty house, but you couldn't give up the car." He patted me on the shoulder. "You're doing it, Whip! You're sticking it to the man!"

I pressed my lips together. "I liked it a whole lot better when we didn't question each other's personal lives. Let's go back to that. Okay?"

"Sure."

There was a beat of silence before X said, "Okay, I'm bored with silence. Tell me how many numbers were on the closing balance of your last bank statement?"

I groaned.

Levi twisted to look at me front-on. "We could be sitting here for a while before anything happens. We might as well talk."

I glared at him, irritated by all the attention on me and the fact I was still sitting here in this fucking car, instead of finding out who was targeting us and putting a bullet through their brains.

And that was before I even started thinking about what Levi and I had done in the darkness of that room. My fingers wrapped around his cock had been...whatever. You could put that down to a heat-of-the-moment need to get off that had gotten out of control. I'd initiated it. I'd wanted it, and he hadn't stopped it, but I wasn't about to start questioning what we were over a quick rub and tug.

It was the way he'd grabbed the back of my neck that I couldn't stop thinking about. The way he'd hauled me in with a groan and pressed his mouth on mine.

I didn't know what that kiss meant. And I couldn't stop thinking about it.

The fact he was acting like it hadn't even happened was pissing me off.

"Sure. We can talk," I agreed. "About you. How about you tell us why you haven't told Violet you love her yet? Why don't we talk about how you're scared she's going to reject you, in favor of X, and so you haven't said a word like a gutless coward?"

I didn't care that I was being cruel.

I didn't fucking want to talk about myself. Or where I lived. Or who the people in that photo were.

I just wanted to fucking put a knife or a bullet into someone so that pain was out of me and into someone else.

But of course, I had to get stuck with these two jack-asses, who suddenly wanted to have deep and meaningful conversations about things that were none of their damn business.

Levi glared at me. "How about we talk about the way you just jerked my cock until we both came?"

Oh, fuck him. He couldn't act like that was all one-sided. "How about we talk about the way you kissed me like you loved me?"

Levi said nothing, just stared at me in the dark interior of the car, his broad chest heaving with fast breaths of anger and irritation that I was sure I mirrored.

X's head popped through the seats between us, and he stage-whispered, "Just so you know, if you two start hate-fucking, I'm not getting out of this car. There's a really big rat out there." He shuddered.

I yanked open the door. "No problem. I'll leave instead." I got out and slammed the door shut, stalking off down the alley. The night air did absolutely nothing to cool my heated skin.

One of them opened their door.

"What the hell is your problem?" Levi shouted. "Why are you being such a fucking asshole?"

I spun to glare at him. "Me? Why are you? What the fuck was kissing me like that?"

"You had your hand on my fucking cock! What else was I supposed to do?"

I blinked. His words felt like a slap in the face.

I'd never felt like more of a two-dollar hooker in my life. I'd always convinced myself the work I did didn't affect me. That it was just a job and it didn't have any consequences.

But apparently the consequence was Levi saw me as nothing but someone to get him off.

At least I knew where I stood. That kiss had clearly meant more to me than him. And I'd been stupid to think otherwise.

"Is the rat still out there?" X called from the safety of the car.

"Yeah, it is." I didn't know if I meant Levi or myself, but the furry kind had scuttled away, scared off by our shouts.

I wanted to join it. Because standing here, this close to Levi, didn't feel good.

He reached for me. "Whip...I didn't mean..."

But he did. And we both knew it. His hand dropped before he could make contact with my skin.

I turned away, not wanting to look into his eyes for a second longer.

And instead found myself looking square into Violet's. "What the fuck?"

Her eyes widened, and she ducked down beneath the car window. Another woman, in the driver's seat next to her, did the same.

Oh hell fucking no. They had not followed us out here, right into the heart of the gang-owned city streets. I stepped off the curb, beelining for her, because dealing with her ignoring us telling her to stay put was a whole lot easier than dealing with Levi and his bullshit.

Headlights lit up the street.

I stopped in place, shielding my eyes, blinded by the bright lights.

A roar of an engine blocked out all other sounds as the vehicle zoomed up the street, cutting me off from getting to Violet. It headed right toward me and Levi.

There was nothing for me to do but dive out of the way or get mowed down. Levi hit the deck beside me.

My heart stopped, knowing I couldn't get to Violet.

Tires squealed.

Glass shattered.

Violet's screams filled the night air.

17

LEVI

’d twisted something in my ankle when I’d jumped out of the way, but the sharp pain disappeared the instant Violet’s panicked screams ripped through the night.

All I could see in the back of my mind was her covered in blood. It had been Toby’s blood last time, but I was terrified when I opened my eyes, it would be hers.

“Violet!”

That was Whip’s shout, but it echoed the one in my head. Both of us staggered to our feet, the van disappearing around a corner, already forgotten because getting to Violet was all that mattered.

Glass covered the road, sparkling in the moonlight like jagged diamonds. It would have been pretty if it hadn’t been accompanied by shouts of terror.

Whip and I both reached her at the same time. My gaze raked over her in a panic through the broken windshield. There was blood in her hair and trickling down the side of her face, but it didn’t seem too bad. The woman I'd seen with her at work earlier that day was in the driver's seat, her eyes wide, and she had herself braced up against her door, as far away from the broken glass as she could get.

A brick sat on the center console between them, a white note wrapped around it, held in place by thick elastic bands.

Dread pooled in my stomach at the sight of it.

I already knew what it was.

But Violet had to be my first priority.

Whip beat me to it. He grabbed her chin between his fingers, twisting her face so she was looking at him. "Hey, sweetheart. You're okay. Breathe."

She instantly calmed down at the sound of his voice. He held her frightened gaze, and he breathed deeply and evenly, until her breaths matched his.

Something passed in the air between them. An understanding. A comfort. One he seemed so good at giving her.

Jealousy curdled inside me, and I shoved it away, knowing I had no right to it.

But then it was replaced with anger. And I couldn't stop the words spewing out of my mouth. "What the hell are you doing here? We told you to stay at the club!"

It wasn't the first thing I wanted to say to her. It wasn't even the last thing I should have said, but my heart pounded at the sight of her blood and the realization of how lucky she was the brick had landed between the two women and not right in one of their faces.

She dragged her gaze away from Whip and narrowed her eyes at me. "Last I checked, I wasn't a dog you could tell to sit and stay. And you weren't my registered owner."

I ground my teeth at how reckless she'd been. I fully understood she'd gone through something traumatic, and she'd been acting out of character, but following us, when she knew we were going hunting, was straight-up dangerous.

"You could have been killed," I grit out.

Her eyes blazed. "Seems like I could be killed at any moment, anywhere, so what difference does it make if it's at Psychos or here?" Her eyes filled with unshed tears. "There's someone trying to kill me, Levi. What part of that don't you understand?"

The problem was I understood every part of it.

And that's what terrified me.

I was so stupidly in love with her, all I could think about was losing her.

Not that I'd ever really had her. But at least she was alive. The thought of her hurt, or worse, left me feeling so sick I could barely breathe.

X's footsteps thumped down the alley behind us, and we all swiveled in his direction. He pulled up short a foot or two in front of me, then leaned over, resting his hands on his knees, breathing hard, like the short sprint he'd just done from the car hidden in the alley to where we stood now on the street had been a marathon.

He even squeezed out a wheeze. "Sorry. Would have been here earlier, but that rat had me holed up in the car and was eyeing me like I was a snack." His gaze shifted to Violet. "Omelet? What are you doing here?" His eyes darkened when he noticed the blood and all the glass.

"They followed us," I said dryly.

X winked at her. "I know that orgasm I gave you in the

camera room was good, but you could have just called me if you wanted another. No need to follow me."

Nyah let out a little snicker of nervous laughter.

Violet just glared at him. "Thank you for broadcasting that to everyone—"

"Actually, we already did that back in the camera room."

"X!"

He cringed. "Right. Sorry. Not the point." He reached across Violet, offering Nyah his hand. "I'm so sorry. We haven't officially met. I'm X. Licker of Violet's pussy."

"Oh my God, I can't even with you." Violet's face was beet red as she turned to the other woman. "I'm so sorry. We're seeking intervention for his lack of brain-to-mouth filter. Are you okay?"

Nyah brushed some glass off her lap. "I'm fine." She cringed at the gaping hole in the windshield. "This car we stole isn't though."

My mouth dropped open. "You stole a car?"

Violet shot me a glare. "Like you can talk! Mister Biker, Ex-crim, Probably Stolen Hundreds of Cars Not to Mention Murdering People in His Lifetime!"

I shot a glance at Nyah, and she waved a hand dismissively. "Oh, don't worry about me. Mafia kid. I'm down with all the killing. Nothing new to me."

X clucked his tongue and then leaned down to whisper to Violet. Though we all heard it because nothing about X was ever actually quiet. "Violet, I think you should probably reassess who you hang out with."

She shoved him away. "Oh, don't worry, I am. I'm currently very much reassessing the three psychopaths I've found myself in bed with!"

X winked at Nyah. "It was a foursome."

We all just stared at him.

But he clearly had zero realization that he was the world's biggest blabbermouth. When nobody filled the silence, he, of course, did. "So, uh, what were we talking about?"

Whip sighed. "How about we discuss the brick currently sitting in the middle of this apparently stolen car?"

Violet stared down at the brick on the center console. Her fingers trembled.

I wanted to grab them. Wrap my hands around them and rub them gently until the tremble disappeared.

But I couldn't, because I kept fucking things up with her. And she looked like she'd rather stab me than accept comfort from me.

Violet yanked on the handle and shoved the door open. "I can't do this right now. I need air."

She got out, and on the other side, Nyah did the same thing. They moved to check on each other, embracing at the front of the car, clutching each other close.

The three of us watched them in silence, until X murmured, "Anyone else really want to know what's written on that note?"

For once, I agreed with him.

I leaned through the open door and picked it up. Pulling off the rubber bands, I unwrapped the note. My gaze skimmed over it, and the churning, sick feeling in my gut intensified. "Fuck."

Violet's head snapped up. She took one glimpse of my expression, and I could tell she knew that what was written on that page wasn't good.

Not that any of us thought it would be.

"Read it out loud," she demanded, her mouth pulled into a tight line, her fingers gripping Nyah's.

I really didn't want to be the one to voice the words written on that page. But I wouldn't make her read them either. I inhaled a jagged breath and recited the words that left me cold and dead inside.

"Tick-tock, boys. The countdown has started.
One by one, you'll all be departed.
She slipped through my trap, but only just barely.
Next time, I won't be playing so fairly.
Next time we play, she won't be so clever.
You'll beg for her life.
I'll end it forever."

The silence that dragged out after I read the last line felt like it lasted forever. Until Violet choked out a laugh. She coughed, but the laughter didn't stop. It turned hysterical while I watched her, just wanting to wrap her in my arms and hold her and tell her everything was okay.

Except she wouldn't welcome my touch.

And absolutely nothing was okay.

She laughed until tears streamed down her face. "Well, that's just great, isn't it? Just fucking fabulous."

She spun around in a circle, then tipped her head up to the sky. "Come get me then, you asshole! You're always watching me, aren't you? Stop playing these fucking games and just come get me if you want me that badly!"

None of us said anything

There was no comforting her. No reassuring words to say that weren't out-and-out lies.

None of us were safe.

Especially not her.

Whip drove back to Saint View in silence. I knew tomorrow we would have to return. To find shops or houses that might have some video surveillance we could watch. Something that might give us some sort of ID on who was driving that van, though I was already certain the license plates would come up as stolen.

And we still had our target to hunt down.

But the night was rapidly turning into day. None of us had slept. Violet was bleeding, though she wouldn't let anyone touch her to address the cut on her head. We dropped Nyah off at a shitty little house not far from Whip's place, and all four of us left in the car watched like hawks as she crossed the patchy lawn and let herself inside with a key that was hidden in a planter box.

I let out a grunt of disapproval at her lack of security, which only pissed Violet off more.

"Her things are still at Psychos. She left everything there to come help me. Sorry she doesn't have her keys on her."

"Doesn't change the fact, leaving a spare in the planter right next to her door is dangerous," I muttered.

She glared at me. "Anyone ever tell you you're as bad as a helicopter parent? Is there anything you don't find dangerous?"

Yeah. Her, tucked up in my bed at the clubhouse, with the door locked and my brothers on patrol, behind the imposing metal gates and the new security surveillance system that had been installed once the guys all started settling down with women and babies.

That was where I wanted Violet. And until she was there, safe and sound, I was gonna fucking hover.

Whip cleared his throat. "I've got to take Levi and X back to Psychos to get their vehicles anyway. I'll get her things and deliver them back to her in the morning." He glanced at the time, that read nearly 4:00 a.m. "Well, later in the morning anyway."

"Thank you," she told him sincerely. Offering him a half-smile.

Seriously? All I got was scowls and blazing anger, and he got smiles?

I was being a grump and I knew it, but this wasn't what I wanted. It wasn't the life I'd dreamed of having with her. I was supposed to get a job, a house on a quiet street, in a decent neighborhood where kids rode their bikes after school.

It wasn't going to be a fancy life, but it would be honest and sweet because she was next to me.

And somehow I seemed to have set the whole thing on fucking fire.

Whip pulled up outside Fang's place in Providence.

Violet dragged herself out of the front seat wearily. "I know we need to talk about this and work out what's next, but not tonight. I just can't."

Whip nodded before either X or I could speak. "It can wait. You're safe with your brother and the others. Just get some rest."

She nodded, closing the door.

I got out of the back seat. "I'll walk you to the door."

She raised a hand in a stop motion. "Don't. I'm fine. We'll talk tomorrow."

X and Whip sat in the car like obedient little dogs while she slowly shuffled to Fang's front door. I watched her fingers move across the electronic PIN pad, and the panel light up green before she pushed down on the door handle and let herself in.

She didn't look back.

My skin felt too tight. She was bleeding. Traumatized. And she was going to be up there in her bedroom alone. I already knew she wouldn't wake her brother or Rebel.

I couldn't stand the thought of it. It made me literally sick to my stomach to think of her curled up in the fetal position, crying, hurt, scared. She played a tough game, and she was angry, but beneath all that, I knew she was terrified.

Because I was too.

"Levi, get back in the car, would you?" Whip complained.

I glanced down at him behind the steering wheel, and X contorting himself into unnatural angles to climb over the center console from the back seat to the front.

I squinted at him, his big body half stuck somewhere in between. "Why the hell didn't you just open the door and walk around?"

He lifted his head. "I have impulsive thoughts, Levi. Sometimes they win."

He really didn't need to say more than that.

Whip just grunted and tried to avoid getting one of X's knees to the face.

I tapped the roof of the car. "You two go. I'm staying."

X was head down, ass up in the front, practically doing a handstand trying to turn himself around in the too-small space. "Hey, Whip, did you know you have a bunch of Skittles down here on the floorboard?"

Whip ignored him, shoving his flailing legs out of the way. He caught my gaze through the open window. "You sure about this? She's probably not going to be happy when she realizes you're hanging around."

But I didn't care.

I couldn't go home to the clubhouse and lie awake in my cold bed, just praying she was safe. Fang was a ruthless killer. I knew because I'd trained him myself, once upon a time.

But he was one man, and he had a family. A woman. Kids. Two other partners.

If something went down, his priority was going to be them.

But my priority would always be Violet. Whether she liked it or not.

"I'm staying," I confirmed to Whip.

He nodded. "Your funeral."

He put the car in reverse and zoomed backward down the driveway, with X hollering that he didn't have a seat belt on.

I watched the taillights disappear around the corner of the darkened road. The sun hadn't started its rise yet, the night sky still an inky black, though I knew from years of watching through grimy prison windows, that the sky would start lightening in the next thirty or so minutes as dawn approached, and not long after that, it would be streaked with gold and pink and orange.

I wasn't going to wait around out here to see it this morning though. I crept across the yard on silent feet, keeping to the grass to cover my footsteps. I took the stairs, eyeing the façade of the house Fang had found himself living in and swore under my breath. "Pretty damn fancy, brother. No wonder you don't sleep at the clubhouse anymore. I wouldn't either if my house was big enough to have wings."

It was a far cry from the days when the two of us had been the youngest in the club, him a prospect, sharing my shitty little bedroom with twin beds. It had been my first taste of fucking with an audience. Fang hadn't been big on bringing women into his room. He knew he scared most of them. Even as a teenager, he'd been huge. Intimidating, with a face only his mother could love. But that hadn't stopped the occasional club slut from wanting him. And what was a guy supposed to do when he woke up with a naked woman, getting him hard, begging to bounce on his cock?

I'd been older, living it up, out from under the nose of my parents for the first time in my life.

Sharing that room with Fang had been our version of college. Neither of us had finished high school, let alone thought about getting a degree, but those years sharing that room, enforcing for War's old man back when he'd been the prez, had been some of the best and wildest days of my life.

Until Army had thrown me under the bus, and I'd spent six years in prison for something I hadn't done. Away from the life I'd built. Away from my best friend.

I wasn't even sure I could still be mad at Army for it.

Because if it hadn't been for those years in a jail cell, I would have never met Violet.

And knowing her was worth every minute I'd lost in that hole.

At the door, I punched in the code I'd watched Violet enter earlier. It was easy, the numbers all spaced apart. When the sun rose, I'd get them to change it. And tell Violet she needed to cover her hand when entering a PIN. But for now, it worked in my favor. The locks disengaged with a quiet whirr, and I pushed down on the handle.

The entry foyer on the other side was as grand as any I'd ever seen. Though there was a toy truck and a doll with messy hair left on the tiled floor. I closed the door behind me, silently toeing off my shoes so I wouldn't be as noisy getting up the stairs.

I avoided some Lego, using the streetlight coming in through the large windows to make my way up the stairs.

The landing up there was darker, and I crept along the hallway, eyeing each closed door, trying to work out which room they would have put Violet in.

This house was insanely huge, the hallway wide, the ceilings high. The first couple of bedrooms were easily identified as kid rooms, their names on the doors, the girls in one room, the boys sharing the one across the hall.

In the next, a crib and change table gave away the baby's room, the soft glow of a monitor lighting up the bub's tiny, sleeping form.

All the doors beyond that were closed, but my gut instinct said, with a new baby in the house, the parents wouldn't want to be too far away.

That was confirmed when soft noises came from the two rooms next door.

Snoring from one.

A squeak of a bedframe from the other, mixing with deep, low, male voices and soft groans of pleasure.

Heat rushed down the back of my neck.

I didn't know the intimate details of Fang's relationship.

But I knew the sounds of two men fucking.

Because I'd been very close to making them myself not all that long ago.

I squeezed my eyes shut, thinking about Whip with his hand wrapped around my cock, and the way I'd grabbed his neck, hauling him in, claiming his mouth with my lips and my tongue.

I didn't even know why I'd done it. I'd never been into guys in the past. Sure, I'd watched my brothers at the clubhouse fuck women, and enjoyed watching the way their bodies moved, just as much as the women beneath them, but actually fucking a guy myself?

No. Army would have fucking crucified me.

That had never been an option. Even in prison, I would have never let myself be that vulnerable.

And yet with Whip, it had been impossible to resist. I'd wanted his hands on me.

Wanted so much more than that, if I was really being honest with myself.

Which was fucking annoying because then he had to go and be a dick about it.

I shoved all thoughts of Whip and fucking men out of my head, my face blazing. Down the hallway I paused at each room, but my gut told me that because of the probability of a crying baby, Violet's room would be the last one.

I took a chance and opened the door.

Violet looked up from her perch on the end of the big, four-poster bed and quickly wiped her eyes.

Her surprise quickly turned into annoyance. "Levi? What are you doing?"

I shushed her, which only made her eyes, still filled with unshed tears, blaze with anger. But I'd expected to piss her off. "Shh. Everyone is sleeping."

Well, almost everyone, but that detail wasn't important right now.

"What are you doing in here? Get out!" It was a whisper, but it was an angry one.

I closed the door behind me. "No."

She narrowed her eyes at me. "What do you mean, no? You can get out or I can scream for my brother."

"You aren't going to do that." I folded my arms across my chest and stared down at her. "I know you won't because you care more about other people than you care about yourself. You know they've probably been up half the night with the baby. And your screams are going to wake them all and that would be the last thing you want to do."

Her anger and irritation with me were practically palpable, even in the soft lamplight. But I didn't care. There was blood all matted in her hair, courtesy of the cuts she'd suffered from flying glass. They didn't seem to still be bleeding, but just the sight of her injuries had my fingers clenching into fists.

"You don't know anything about me, Levi." She shook

her head sadly, gazing down at her hands twisting in the quilt.

"Bullshit."

She glanced up at the harshness of my tone.

But I was so done with this fucking back-and-forth between us. I'd screwed up and I knew it. But I was over her pretending there wasn't a connection between us. Something that went so much deeper than anything I'd ever experienced before, and one I wasn't willing to give up.

I stalked toward her, but then kept going into the en suite connected to her room. I went straight to the bath and turned it on, running my fingers beneath the water, checking the temperature was warm enough.

Water flowed from the faucet, and while it was filling the freestanding, claw-foot tub, I hunted around what was clearly a guest bathroom, searching for something that smelled nice to put in the water.

"What are you doing?" Violet asked from the doorway.

"Running you a bath."

Her lips pursed together. "I can see that. But what I actually meant was, why are you running me a bath?"

The caveman inside me roared it was because I wanted X off her body. I'd watched him fuck her, her fuck him, her take him deep inside while he filled her.

And though it had gotten me hot, there was a base desire inside me that demanded I erase all traces of him and fill her with my own.

But the bigger part of me was more evolved than that.

"I'm taking care of you, because you're so determined to not take care of yourself."

She glared at me. "I'm perfectly capable of running myself a bath, Levi."

I spun around and moved in close, crowding her against the wall. "It's not about the fucking bath and you know it."

Her breath hitched.

But I just kept going, pressing right up on her because I couldn't fucking stop myself. I wanted to be all up in her space, so every breath she breathed was of my scent. I wanted that smell of her body permanently imprinted in my brain. I wanted to feel every rise and fall of her chest, her soft tits against me. "It's about the fact you could have gotten killed tonight because you were so hell-bent on avenging Toby's death that you didn't even stop to consider you could be walking straight toward your own."

Her bottom lip trembled, but her eyes remained hard. "I'm in danger all the time anyway. What the hell does it matter?"

I could see the fear behind the fury. Feel her terror behind the brave face she was putting on. I could practically hear the screams she was keeping inside.

"Oh, Vi."

She crumpled, her shoulders slumping forward, her head falling against my chest.

I had my arms around her in a heartbeat, her tears soaking my shirt while she sobbed in my arms.

I cradled the back of her head with one hand, my fingers in her matted, bloody hair. I stroked the other up and down her back, whispering words of comfort into her ear, holding her while she finally let out the sadness and grief she'd been keeping inside her for days.

I waited for her to stop, but when she didn't, I pulled back, undoing the buttons on her jacket.

She just stood there, head hanging, tears rolling down her face, and let me.

The corset and panties I'd seen her in at the club were beneath. I'd found them so damn sexy earlier in the night, but now they were just a barrier to taking care of her.

I edged around her, unlacing the corset and grimacing at the red marks it had left all over her body. I hated she was hurting herself, shoving herself into a garment that looked like torture. But I said nothing and let the corset fall to the tiled floor. Her panties were next, and then I scooped her up in my arms, holding her tight for a few long moments because that's how long it took me to convince myself I should put her down when everything inside me just wanted to hold her.

But I placed her down in the water anyway, sinking her to the bottom and reveling in the sound of her soft moan of pleasure as the water enveloped her.

"Tilt your head back. Wet your hair."

She did as I'd asked, bending her knees so she could sink right down deep, fully submerging her upper half.

"This bath is amazing," she said quietly when she resurfaced. "I never fit in regular bathtubs. I haven't had one since I was a kid."

It was definitely a rich person bathtub, not the shitty kind that was so small only a toddler could fit in. It was deep and wide and long enough for a woman who was almost six feet tall. She propped her arms up on the sides and tilted her head back, closing her eyes.

There were no bubbles to hide her body from me, and she didn't try.

God, that was so fucking sexy. The way she wasn't trying to shy away from me. The way she just lay there, so I could see every inch of her through the sparkling clear water.

I found a bottle of shampoo in the shower and grabbed a towel hanging on a rack. I tossed it onto the floor at the end of the bath and knelt behind her head.

The squirt of shampoo onto my palm left a fruity-smelling tang in the air, and I lathered up my hands before putting them into her hair.

"I'm sorry if it stings a little," I said into the quiet of the room, working the soap through the matted lengths and rubbing with extra vigor at the strands that were coated with red. "I'm trying to avoid the cuts on your scalp."

"Don't. I don't care about the pain. Your hands feel good." She swallowed thickly, her dark eyelashes fanned out across her cheeks. "Please, just don't stop."

I would do this all fucking day if that's what she wanted. There was a practical element of it, and that had been my only intention when I'd started, but she could ask me for the fucking moon, and somehow, someway, I would get it for her.

I didn't know when I'd fallen in love with her, but it had been long before I'd gotten to see or touch her. This was just an added bonus.

I rinsed her hair once, then lathered it up again. The water turned soapy, but she didn't seem to mind. Her body relaxed, inch by inch with every stroke of her hair, until it was glossy and her breathing had turned so soft and regular I thought maybe she was asleep.

"Levi," she whispered.

"Yeah?"

"I'm sorry."

I squeezed my eyes shut. "You have nothing to be sorry for."

She didn't argue, just sighed softly. "I don't know how I got here."

I didn't either. But a big part of me felt like the shit she'd gone through in the last few weeks was on my shoulders. I knew I couldn't take full blame. X and Whip were a part of it too, and her own decisions had brought us here as well.

But it didn't ease the guilt over my part in Toby's death. My part in the fact danger lurked outside these walls, just waiting for us in the shadows.

But here, she was safe and warm and taken care of.

Which was all I had ever wanted.

Maybe this wasn't the house with the picket fence I'd promised her. But it was safety. At least for now.

And with threats and danger knocking on our door every time we stepped out of it, right now was all we had.

The scalp massage morphed into a neck massage, my fingers digging into the tight muscles and forcing away the tension. Every finger had a different purpose, my thumbs getting in deep, forefingers soothing the sides of her neck, pinkies brushing the throat I so badly wanted to put my mouth to.

I worked my way across her shoulders, and then down her arms, pressing into her palms, kneading her biceps, stroking her skin.

Sliding back up to caress her chest. The gradual rise of her tits.

Her breath switched from slow and relaxed to something faster. Something needier.

I stroked lower, taking two handfuls of her breasts, cupping them, and groaning at the way they spilled over.

"That feels so good," she whispered. "Thank you."

"You don't have to thank me for something that is entirely my pleasure, Violet." I could barely get the words out. They were deep and guttural and laced with need that was directed all at her.

"I'm not even touching you."

"But you're naked and wet and letting me touch you."

She let out a sigh, her eyes fluttering open. She tilted her head back to look up at me.

My heart clenched so fucking tight I thought for a good long second I was having a heart attack.

But then I leaned down and planted my lips on hers, and the tightness in my chest ebbed away into something gentle and sweet.

Her arms lifted to hold each side of my face, and we kissed upside down, both of us soft and quiet, connecting in a way that was so different to the fast-and-hard fuck I'd given her the night before.

That had its place. It had been hot, and it had felt good.

But kissing her like this, intimately, with no audience...fuck. This shit owned my heart.

She twisted, flipping over onto her stomach, her rounded ass so fucking sweet peeking out of the soapy water. Her back arched so she could wrap her arms around my neck and continue kissing me, this time the right way up.

My lips parted, tongue seeking entrance, finding hers ready and willing. I grabbed the back of her head, unable to get enough of her taste, kissing her until my head spun, and all I could see and think and smell and feel was her.

"Need you," I murmured over her lips, knowing I had no right but wanting it all the same. "Fucking hell, Violet. I love you."

She drew back, but I didn't want to see the questions in her expression. Didn't want to give her the chance to tell me she didn't feel the same.

I wrapped my arms around her back, hauling her up out of the bath, kissing her mouth so fucking thoroughly she didn't have a chance to reject me.

I carried her to the bathroom vanity and settled her ass on the edge of it, her thick thighs spread out around me, banded around my waist like they had been made exactly for that purpose.

I couldn't remember ever feeling like a woman's body was made for mine. But every inch of Violet felt perfectly carved to fit the size of me.

I got straight back down on my knees and buried my face between her thighs.

Her pussy was the sweetest thing I'd ever had my tongue on. Her juices wept from her entrance, silky and smooth, showing me how turned on she already was. And I'd barely even started with her.

I licked her from entrance up to her clit and then set up camp there, worshipping that bud like it was a new god. Her pussy deserved a fucking cult of followers. I'd be the damn head of it for as long as she would let me.

She leaned back on the mirrored bathroom cabinet above the sink, and I drew her legs up so her feet rested on my shoulders, opening her up so I had full access to every inch of her slit and the tight little hole beneath.

She was all clean and delicious-smelling, and I just wanted to make her come for hours on end without sharing her with another soul.

I dragged my tongue all over her, kissing and nipping her inner thighs, loving the way they shook around my head whenever I got closer to her opening. I thrust first my tongue, and then my fingers into her channel, the fluttering beginnings of an orgasm sending straight-up pride through my system.

She liked this. Everything I was doing was what she needed. Her moans only confirmed it. She kept them quiet, bringing her arms up over her head to hang on to the top of the cabinet, and twisting her head so her mouth was muffled by her arm.

I fucked her with my tongue, my fingers joining in, stretching her wide so she could take two, then three.

I pulled back to stare at her, all pussy and tits and belly, head thrown back in pleasure and totally open to me, trusting me to keep her safe.

It was the sexiest gift she could have given me. I didn't need the lingerie she'd worn to the club that night. I didn't need her dancing for me or putting on a show. Her trusting me with her body was the hottest thing she could have done.

"Need you to come for me, baby," I mumbled against her belly, kissing all over it, then lower across her mound while I thrust into her with my fingers. "Need to feel that pussy squeeze."

She reached for me, and I let her because she was so hot and wet, I could tell she needed more. I let her unzip my jeans and drag my underwear down just enough to free my cock. And then we were both battling to get me inside her, her making desperate moans of need and telling me to hurry, while I lined up at her entrance and got my cock wet in the arousal just pooling there, waiting for me.

The plunge inside her was desperate and fast, but so fucking satisfying. I bottomed out inside her, and we both paused there, her gasping at the intrusion, me biting down on my lip to stop myself from shouting her name and waking the entire house up.

To distract myself from the fact her pussy was so damn perfect, and I was so hot for her I was ready to come after one stroke, I pushed my clothes off my bottom half, stepping out of my jeans and underwear and leaving them in a puddle on the floor.

She had the same idea about getting me just as naked as she was.

She yanked desperately at my shirt, unbuttoning it with greedy, fast fingers, and delivering kisses to my chest with every inch she exposed.

She reached the bottom, undoing the last button, and shoved my shirt off my shoulders.

But her kisses didn't stop. She kissed all over my neck and shoulders and pecs, every touch of her lips sending an explosion of pleasure and sensation through my entire body.

A gasp filled the tiny, quiet room.

I froze, my cock buried deep inside her, worry filling me that I'd somehow hurt her. My eyes flew open. "What? Are you okay?"

She stared at my chest.

Or more accurately, the Violet I'd tattooed over my heart.

Ah shit. I'd had it covered up when she'd last seen me naked but I'd ripped the bandage off it this morning. It had gotten loose and tattered and really didn't serve a purpose any more since the tattoo was completely healed anyway.

A part of me knew I'd been keeping it on because I hadn't been ready to show her.

But then last night, everything had changed.

Now all I wanted was for her to know exactly how I felt about her.

Because last night, I'd very nearly lost the chance to. If she'd died in that warehouse, she would have died never knowing how much she owned my fucking heart. How she was all I'd thought about since the very first letter.

She would have never known how damn much I loved her.

She stared at me. "You...you tattooed my name?"

I nodded.

She breathed out a slow breath, fingers trailing so lightly over my skin, if I hadn't been watching I would have thought I'd imagined it.

"Yes."

"When?"

"That night you met me up on the bluffs."

She screwed her head up. "The night you rejected me?"

I grabbed her chin, holding it tighter than I would have normally, but she needed to hear the words I was about to say.

I needed to know she heard them.

"I never rejected you, Violet. I only rejected the version of myself I knew wasn't good enough for you. I was stupid and selfish, I know that. But I loved you then, just like I love you now. And that tattoo reminds me every day."

She couldn't stop staring at it, her gaze flickering over every curve and twist of the stem, and the shading I'd attempted on the petals.

Awkward heat rose up the back of my neck, knowing she was seeing the imperfect lines I'd drawn because I didn't have the skill with a tattoo gun I wanted. "I know it's not perfect. It was really different than drawing with a pencil, and I need to get Dax to fix it—"

Her gaze snapped to meet mine. "You did it yourself?" There was a hint of awe in her voice that had me both awkward and my chest puffing up with pride.

"Yes."

Her eyes shone. "It's the most beautiful thing I've ever seen."

Her words were like a spear right through my chest, opening me up wide. If she hadn't already owned every inch of my heart, that comment would have done it.

I grasped the side of her face and tilted her head up, so I was staring down at her. "You are the most beautiful thing I've ever seen."

I lowered my head to kiss her slowly, and we

connected again, the words falling away when she kissed me back.

Our hips moved in unison, a rhythm igniting between us, one that was starting to feel familiar as we got to know each other's bodies and the way we liked to be touched.

I drew her in tighter, wrapping my arms around her so there was no space in between. Her tits pressed against my chest, every inch of us connected.

We'd been making out in the bathroom long enough that we'd both air-dried without any assistance from a towel, and I suddenly wanted her wrapped up in bed with me.

I lifted her, her mouth never separating from mine as I walked us to the bed and laid her down on it. I thrust into her while she stared up at me, both of us taking kisses whenever we felt like we needed them, her fingers trailing up and down my arms, braced either side of her, across my chest and down my back.

She never stopped touching me.

Never stopped moving her hips, showing me she wanted me inside her just as much as I did.

I pulled the sheet over our heads, blocking out the world, creating one where only she and I existed.

"I love you so much." I came, spilling myself inside her. My orgasm ripped through my body, sending pulses of pleasure with it that had me breathless.

But even if I'd only had one breath left, I would have used it to tell her I loved her. So I whispered it over and over again, talking her through her orgasm, feeling her clench around my cock, the sweet agony of feeling her come around me so damn perfect it was hard to imagine anything feeling better.

Beneath those sheets, she was mine. Not Whip's. Not X's.

Just mine.

Our breaths mingled, and we both came down from our orgasms, clutching each other close.

I rolled onto the mattress, taking her with me, settling beneath her with my dick still inside her, even though I was completely spent.

"I'm going to squash you," she mumbled sleepily, head resting on the light dusting of dark hair on my chest.

"You're going to lie right there and sleep. I'll be just fucking fine."

There wasn't a single other place I wanted to be more. Her weight on top of me was comforting in a way I had never experienced, and the idea of her ever moving off me felt like a fate worse than death.

So I held her there to me, making sure she knew her weight was never something I couldn't handle or didn't want.

And whispered that I loved her until she fell asleep.

It was only hours after staring down at her, sleeping on my chest, that I realized she had never said she loved me back.

18

VIOLET

The bedroom door crashed open so hard it bounced off the wall behind it.

Levi and I both jerked, twisting at the crash.

A soccer ball, followed by a small boy, flew into the room. Madden scooped up his ball, and then paused, finally noticing the two of us staring at him in horror.

"Mom!" he called back into the hallway. "Why is Uncle Reaper in Aunt Violet's bed?"

"Oh shit," Levi muttered. "I'm so fucking dead."

Madden shoved his hand on his hips. "Mom says we aren't supposed to say fucking."

I widened my eyes, but I was also biting back laughter.

Levi clutched me close to him, holding down the sheet which was the only thing keeping us from being completely indecent. He hissed at the little boy, "Madden! Don't say that."

The boy gave him a cheeky grin. "Say what? Fucking? Fucking, fucking!" He singsonged.

I hid my laughter. "Oh my God."

Fast footsteps came from the hallway, and then Rebel's head appeared around the doorframe, Fang behind her.

Rebel grabbed the shoulders of her wayward son. "I'm so sorry, I've been trying to keep them downstairs so you could sleep—"

Her gaze strayed to Levi beneath me.

Then she looked back up at Fang.

My gaze followed her, so I saw the moment Fang realized I was in bed with his best friend.

Rebel clapped her hand over Madden's eyes, but there was laughter in her voice. "Come on, sweetie. I don't think you need to see the massacre that's about to go down here." She picked him up and jogged down the hallway with him over her shoulder, him still singsonging variations of fuck all the way down the stairs.

I stifled a laugh, but it fell away when I realized Fang was really not happy.

He was all red in the face, and I could practically see the steam building in his chest so thick and fast it came out of his ears. It was just a matter of time before he'd explode.

"What the fuck, Levi!"

And there it was.

Levi kissed my cheek. "Well, we had a good run, right? Shame it had to end so soon. Bury me with my bike."

I couldn't hold in a laugh that time.

I clutched the sheet to my chest. "Fang. Stop."

The big man did nothing of the sort. He glowered at

Levi like a bull about to launch out of the gate and ram a sharpened horn right through the matador. I was almost surprised when he didn't paw the ground and snort.

Levi let out a sigh. "I love her, bro. I'm sorry, I know she's your sister, but I'm not just fucking her. I love her."

The warmest of glows spread around me, and I grinned at my brother.

He squinted like he suddenly had a migraine, his face all tensed up, lines deep between his eyebrows. He pinched the bridge of his nose to ease them. "No. No. No." He pointed at me. "You are five years old." He pointed at Levi. "And you are way too old for her."

I hid a laugh. "Haven't been five in a long time, big brother."

"I don't think it helps when you call him that," Levi whispered.

He shook his head at Levi. "There's fucking codes about this shit, Reaper! You know that! We don't mess around with each other's family!"

"To be fair," I interrupted. "We started 'messing around' before any of us even knew you and I were family, so I really don't think that rule applies."

Fang ground his molars, his fists still clenched at his sides. "I strongly disagree."

I sighed. He was being ridiculous. "If you want to challenge Levi to a duel or something, do it, but not on my behalf. He hasn't taken anything that I didn't willingly want to give him. There's no need to fight for my honor."

"It's not about that," Fang said quietly. "It's about him dragging you into a life you don't want. The club..." He screwed up his face. "The club is everything that's good, and everything that's bad all at once. You don't want a life with a biker, Violet. It'll mean a lifetime of always looking over your shoulder in case one of Reaper's enemies comes after you. Lockdowns when things get dicey. You'll never be one-hundred-percent safe."

I could see the worry in his eyes. Hear the sincerity in his plea.

But Levi had spent the night in my bed, making love to me and whispering words I'd never thought I would hear a man say. He'd washed my hair, stroked my skin, taken care of me like nobody else ever had.

He'd tattooed my freaking name right over his heart.

And he'd told me he loved me.

If Fang thought I would give that up just because he wanted to play big brother now, after all these years when I was a fully grown woman, then he had another think coming.

I leveled him with a stare. "Did you have all these concerns over bringing Rebel into your life?"

"Of course I did!"

"And you went and did it anyway?"

His jaw went tight. "That was different."

It wasn't, and we both knew it. I had him.

He blew out a long breath, and his gaze flickered back to Levi. "Fine. But I swear to Hades, if you hurt her I will kill you with my own two hands, with absolutely zero remorse."

Levi returned a solid gaze. "Brother, I promise you, if I hurt her, I'll stand there and let you."

The two of them stared at each other for a long moment, while I tried to find the feminist in me who should probably hate the two of them discussing me like I wasn't even in the room, but I couldn't bring myself to do it. I'd never had anyone but Toby care about me, and never in this sort of way. Toby and I didn't have a "touch her and die" sort of relationship. Toby's only weapon probably would have been a mascara wand. He could have sung musical soundtracks until my enemies' ears bled perhaps.

But there was something about a man declaring physical violence that just hit different. Fang's declarations made me feel young and protected.

Levi's felt like I really wanted my brother to go away so I could do some things with his best friend that no brother should ever see his sister doing.

Fang seemed to catch the vibe in the air, or maybe he was just satisfied with Levi's response. But either way, he closed the door, and I went straight back to showing Levi how much I loved the way he'd just fought for me, even if I couldn't bring myself to tell him the same three little words he'd said to me.

I'd been there with him once. And he'd broken my trust.

I wasn't quite ready to give it all back to him, no matter how many times his tongue and his lips and his fingers and his cock made me moan his name.

evi and I slept the morning away. I had no idea what he was supposed to be doing that day, but he'd made zero move to get out of my bed, his big body tucked around mine, his deep breaths rising and falling behind me.

It had been short-lived though, because I had a shift at Clean Sweep that afternoon, where Nyah and I had scrubbed Mrs. Lewersham's Providence mansion from top to bottom for four hours straight. Nyah had been back to her usual bubbly self, despite the events of the night before.

She'd taken all of that completely in her stride and gone on with her shift like nothing had happened. I'd tried talking to her about it a couple of times, but she'd just laughed it off like it had all been a grand adventure and said I didn't need to worry. That whatever me and Saint View threw at her, she could handle. That she'd seen and done worse.

She'd said it with such a straight face that I'd had no choice but to believe her.

Her family sounded terrifying. And I was glad she was here now, well away from them.

Which was saying something, considering Saint View didn't exactly feel too safe these days, if it ever had.

She dropped me off at Psychos on her way home, and I was well aware of X's ice cream van slowly tailing us, but we both pretended not to notice it.

If he was going to stalk people, he really needed to get a more inconspicuous ride.

I eyed the man sitting on the door at the entrance and stopped in front of him, cocking my head to one side, studying his expression. "Vincent," I finally determined, though really, it was an educated guess based on the fact the man just quietly stared at me, rather than jabbering a mile a minute or giving me a smug grin and cracking a joke about my little sexcapades the night before like Scythe would have.

Vincent gave a single nod. "Are you well?"

"Yes, thank you."

"I'm pleased to hear that."

I jerked my head toward the door. "Okay if I go in? I've got a shift tonight."

He held the door open, and I smiled at him while I passed. But I couldn't help but add, "You really are different to Scythe, aren't you?"

The corner of his mouth lifted. "We have a few things in common." His gaze drifted to Bliss, slinging drinks behind the bar, and something hard became soft in his eyes.

She noticed him watching her and she blew him a kiss, not waiting to see if he returned it.

He didn't, but it was very clear to me that Vincent loved Bliss in a way that calmed something inside him. Just one look from her had altered his whole being.

Oh, to have that sort of power over another person's happiness. I wasn't sure if it was a good thing or if the idea was terrifying.

But it clearly worked for them. Bliss radiated happiness in a way I couldn't imagine myself ever doing. I had no idea what it felt like to be that settled, that happy, that loved.

Though Levi's words echoed over and over in my head, I wasn't sure I could believe them.

He'd told me things in the past, and then it had all gone to shit. I didn't want to let myself believe him too quickly this time. I wanted to feel the glow of his I love yous, but I couldn't let myself be fully open to them just yet, the way Bliss clearly was.

That required a level of vulnerability I couldn't afford right now when my life was so messed up.

I gave Vincent a smile and moved past him, into the club. Unlike last night, the door to the cloakroom and the sex club behind it was closed, locked up tight. Psychos was back to the grungy dive bar it was most nights of the week, with sports playing on big-screen TVs mounted on the walls and the smell of fried food lingering in the air. People sat around at tables, drinking beer and eating chicken wings, a cheer going up as I passed a large group of college-aged guys, but when I glanced over at them, I realized they all had their gazes trained on the football game.

I slipped behind the counter and tucked my purse into the safety box Bliss had shown me on my first shift.

She wiped her hands on a towel and gave me a quick hug. "Are we okay?"

I blinked. "Of course. Why?"

"I wouldn't let you work last night."

I waved a hand around like it didn't matter, even though it kind of did. I didn't need people telling me what I did or didn't need. And yet I could respect that she needed staff who weren't going to be a danger to the public or her business.

Which was kind of a hilarious notion when I knew exactly what Scythe and Vincent were capable of, and they were here every night she was. But I could respect her need to protect her livelihood. And I had been a bit of a mess last night. I probably still was and would be for a long time. There would be no just "getting over" what had happened to Toby. I imagined I would still feel the loss of him until I was old and gray. There would be many more nights of crying myself to sleep, I was sure.

But keeping myself busy in between was what I wanted.

"You said I could come back tonight," I reminded Bliss.

She nodded. "I did, and I'll stay true to that, if you're sure."

"I am."

She threw the towel at me. "Then you're up. I'll get you to help with the bar and serving while we're busy. When it settles down you can switch to cleaning. Sound good?"

"As long as I have something to do all night, I'm happy."

Bliss jerked her head toward the room packed full of bodies, mostly male ones, all needing food and drinks. "I think we can keep you occupied." She pointed toward a table in the far back corner. "Could you start with that guy over there? He just came in, and I haven't had a chance to take his order yet."

"Of course."

I grabbed a notepad and a pen from beneath the counter and wove my way in between tables, ignoring the fact X had sat himself down in the middle of a table full of guys from Levi's club. They all clapped him on the back and welcomed him like he was a long-lost member, and I just shook my head, thinking about how nice it must be to be that extroverted.

I stopped at the table Bliss had pointed out and

poised my pen, ready to take the man's order. "Hey, I'm Violet. What can I get you?"

He lifted his head from the menu and peered up at me from beneath the brim of a white baseball cap.

My heart stopped.

"I know your name, Violet."

My fingers clenched so tightly around the pen the cheap plastic cracked. "Travis."

He chuckled with a deep laugh. "Why do you say my name like you're choking on it?"

Because I was.

I glanced over at X, surrounded by a table full of Levi's friends. And then at Vincent on the door. There were plenty of people here who had my back.

There was no need to make a scene, even though my gut wanted to scream that he needed to get out and leave me the hell alone.

But Bliss hadn't let me work last night because she'd been afraid of me breaking down and causing a commotion that could hurt her business. I didn't want to prove her right.

Didn't want to let anyone know my nerves were so frayed that just the sight of my foster brother had me wanting to sink to the floor, cover my ears, and rock back and forth until he was gone.

I sucked in a deep breath through my nose and let it out slowly through my mouth.

I wasn't going to let him get to me. He couldn't hurt me here, surrounded by all of these people.

He was just any other man. I forced myself to believe it before I spoke so my voice wouldn't wobble. "What can I get you?"

"What's good?"

"I don't know," I said honestly. "All of it." None of it. I didn't care. I just wanted him to order and leave.

He dragged his finger down the menu, all while staring at me. He stopped halfway down and tapped it. "This."

I bit my lip, hating that he was forcing me to lean in closer to him, just so I could read the text he was pointing at. "Buffalo chicken wings and beer combo. You got it." I spun on my heel, desperate to get out of his space.

Because even though he was just sitting there, it felt a whole lot like he was poisoning the air around him, and it was killing me to stand there and breathe it in.

"Wait. You didn't ask me which sides I wanted."

I pressed my lips together and turned back to him, trying to breathe deeply so I didn't explode. I tried to remind myself that the hidden dangers in my life, the psychopath playing murder games, was a whole lot scarier than this man sitting right in front of me with his patchy beard and beady eyes.

But the little girl inside me remembered exactly how cruel he could be. And that I needed to be on guard every second I was around him or bad things would happen.

I forced words out. "Which sides would you like?"

He leaned back, crossing his arms over his chest. "How about a side of 'heard you've got a rich new brother.'"

I stiffened at the mention of Fang but fought to keep that anger and fear out of my voice. "You can order your sides, or the kitchen can choose for you, sir."

He snorted on a laugh. "Sir? Is that what you're going

to call me now that you've replaced me with a real brother?"

"You were never my brother," I couldn't help myself from hissing at him.

His smile turned smug. "Good thing, too, 'cause otherwise me watching you in the shower would have been real creepy."

I shuddered. "Fries it is."

"I need money, Violet."

I didn't care what he needed. I was done talking to him. I moved back through the maze of tables, headed for the kitchen to put his order in.

X's gaze caught my eye, and even though he was smiling and laughing with the Slayers, I could see the concern in his expression. He must have been able to see something in my face, because he looked back at Travis and then back to me, one eyebrow raised questioningly.

I didn't even know what that eyebrow meant.

But whatever X was thinking, it would probably mean a scene and that would probably result in me getting fired. Which would be so incredibly awkward if I took this thing with Levi further and I had to see Bliss at every Slayers event.

I gave my head a slight shake and was relieved when X nodded back, accepting my decision for him to do nothing.

Travis was a pest, but he would leave, and I would finish my shift.

And that's exactly what happened. When Travis's food was ready, I grudgingly brought him his plate full of chicken wings and a glass of beer and set them down on his table without a word. When he tried again to bring up

Fang and the fact my brother lived in a fancy mansion in Providence, I ignored him.

Twice more he waved me over, and I went, because I could feel Bliss's gaze on me, watching me to make sure I was doing a good job, and I wanted to prove to her I could, but each time he refused to actually order anything. He just kept prodding about Fang and how much money he had.

Eventually, I set the bill down on his table and walked away without a word.

But I watched him from the corner of my eye as I wiped down tables and pulled beers for the guys at the Slayers' table.

Eventually Travis gave up, threw some money down, and stalked out without saying another word to me.

I breathed a sigh of relief, and while mentally praying he never came back, went to clean his table. I gathered up the money he'd left on the table, noting it was the exact amount of his meal and drinks and not a cent more.

Of course he was a stingy bastard and didn't tip. How unsurprising of him.

I picked up the bill he hadn't taken with him. The messy handwriting I remembered from when I was in my early teens was scrawled across the neatly printed paper.

No tip for you, rich bitch. I'll be back. I haven't forgotten what you owe me.

My fingers shook, and I crumpled the slip of paper into a ball, pushing it deep into the pocket of my apron.

I put the money into the register, and Bliss gave me a sidelong glance.

"Everything okay with that customer? You look a bit shaken up."

I forced a smile. "Just someone I used to know and wish I didn't."

Understanding dawned on her face. "Oh, an ex, huh? They're the worst. If you ever want to feel better about yours, ask me someday to tell you about mine. Because that story is a doozy."

I tried to laugh with her, but I knew it wasn't reaching my eyes and she would notice soon if I didn't get out from under her gaze. Bliss was so sweet and kind and attentive to those around her. All beautiful traits... until you didn't want anyone seeing what you were feeling.

"I'm just going to take a bathroom break," I told her.

"Sure, it's starting to die down now anyway."

I nodded, but I was already moving away from the bar to the hallway where the bathrooms were. I pushed inside, finding it thankfully empty, though that wasn't terribly surprising considering that Psychos' clientele on a regular night skewed very heavily male.

I locked myself in a stall and sat on the closed toilet lid, sucking in deep breaths of cold bathroom air.

At least it smelled reasonably good in here now, since I'd started cleaning the place regularly.

It was a much nicer place to have a mini mental breakdown than it had been a few weeks ago.

The main door to the bathrooms swung open, and I held my breath, not wanting anyone else to hear me fighting off a panic attack.

Honestly, there were about five women in this entire bar. And they had to choose now to go?

"Violet?" X hissed. "You pooping?"

I couldn't help but burst into laughter. "No, X. I'm not pooping."

He breathed a sigh of relief. "Oh good. I'm not very good with bodily functions. Piss. Shit. Vomit. Gag."

I rolled my eyes toward the ceiling. "Okay, good to know. Thank you. You can go now."

"Or I can stay with you."

A smile flickered at the corner of my mouth. "Why would you do that?"

"I just thought we should discuss the tiles. Truly hideous, don't you think? They should get one of those renovation shows in here. They could put in a farm sink, maybe some wainscotting and vaulted ceilings..."

I could barely conceal my amusement. "Do you actually know what any of those things are?"

"No, I'm just saying words I hear them say on those shows a lot because I don't want you to tell me to leave again."

I sighed and leaned forward to unlock the stall door.

It creaked open to reveal X on the other side, arms crossed, leaning against the bathroom wall watching me. "Who was that guy?"

"An old foster brother."

He studied my expression, and for once, was actually observant of what it meant. "I'm assuming you don't want me to send him one of our joint Christmas cards this year?"

I couldn't help my tiny smile becoming a big one. "We're sending joint Christmas cards?"

"Well, duh. Of course. We'll be married by then, and you'll be Mrs. X and I'll be Mr. Violet, and we'll have adopted a rescue kitty named Harold who is *really* ugly. But so ugly he's kinda cute. You know? Harold is also really mean, but Reginald really needs a friend, so it has to happen. We'll wear matching sweaters, even Harold and Reginald will have one, and we'll be kissing beneath the mistletoe." He winked at me. "And I'll be grabbing your boob."

I snorted on my laughter. "You've got it all planned out, huh? Very creative on the ugly kitty."

He frowned at me and then pulled out his phone, scrolling through it. "No, seriously. I've already got our names on him. Look."

He flipped his phone around. The little screen showed a nearby animal rescue website, and in the center, a photo of the most bedraggled, angry cat I had ever seen in my life. "Harold" was written beneath the photo, with an adoption date set for next week.

"He's brand-new on the site. But don't worry, I knew everyone would want him, so I got in there so fast. He's definitely ours. They just need to do some vet checks and things first. They said we can pick him up next week."

I stared down at the feral-looking cat that had a face I doubted even its mother loved.

There would be no one lining up to give this animal a home. Of that I was sure.

Nobody but X.

Because he saw beauty in things most people didn't. And I kinda loved that about him.

I passed him back the phone. "He seems like a great

cat. I'm not sure Reginald needs saving though. He has a pretty cushy life at the park."

He put the phone back in his pocket. "You're probably right. He also has no arms to wear a Christmas sweater, so he probably can't be in the photo anyway."

Laughter felt nice on my lips, but it faded away. "Travis would never be on my Christmas card list, whether Reginald is in our photo or not."

X nodded thoughtfully. "You want me to kill him?"

For a single, horrifying minute, I realized I wanted to say yes.

The realization left me cold. I knew if I said yes, X would do it. It wasn't just a joke to him, like it would have been with most other guys. If I told X I wanted Travis dead, then he would make it happen.

Then I would be responsible for ending a man's life, even if I wasn't the one who pulled the trigger or plunged the knife.

It would still be on me.

Just like Toby's death was.

I couldn't stand the weight of that, hanging around my neck like a second noose when the first one was already killing me slowly.

I shook my head. "No. No killing. He's mostly harmless. He's just a narcissistic asshole who wants money. He'll get bored and disappear when he realizes I don't have any."

X pressed his lips together in a way that made me think he didn't agree.

I really didn't want any more killing or death on my hands.

Unless it was the person who was watching us. The real person who was responsible for Toby's death.

They were going to die slowly and painfully, and I was going to be the one to do it. Toby's death wouldn't go unpunished. I refused to let that happen.

But Travis wasn't worth breaking a nail over, let alone anything more.

"I really don't want to think about my shitty ex-foster brother," I admitted to X.

"I could go down on you instead?"

I laughed. "I have to finish my shift. And anyway, I'm kinda still mad at you for what happened last night."

He raised an eyebrow, the one that had a scar running through the middle of it. "You weren't very mad when you were coming around my cock."

I glared at him. "No, I meant more about you introducing yourself to people as the licker of my pussy."

"Where's the lie?"

"You don't need to make that your whole personality, you know."

"I respectfully disagree. Offer still stands to go down on you right now before you finish your shift..."

The thought was incredibly tempting. My insides clenched at the very thought of having him down on his knees, my leg over his shoulder, his tongue on my clit.

The fact I wouldn't be thinking about Toby, or how I was going to pay my rent without him, or Travis walking back into my life at the shittiest time possible sounded appealing.

X was all smug bastard. "You totally want me." He linked his hands behind his head and leaned back against the wall again. "You're already mentally planning our wedding, aren't you? Just you, me, Reginald, and Harold, on some sort of tropical beach somewhere warm...we might have to plan it around Reggie flying south for the winter..."

I pushed up onto my feet. "I like you distracting me. Nothing more. We aren't getting married on an island with a wild duck and an ugly cat as our witnesses."

He pouted at me. But disappointment never seemed to register with X for long. He just bounced from one thing straight into the next. "Fine. But I do want to take you somewhere. There's no ducks or cats, so it won't be as good as our wedding, but I think you'll like it anyway."

I moved past him to the sink and squirted soap into my hands. "Where?"

"I want you to meet my family."

I jerked my head up so fast I was pretty sure I gave myself whiplash. "Your...family?"

"Yeah. Tomorrow night, if you're free..."

X was a psychopath who had murdered a man right in front of me. And not just in a regular sort of gunshot-to-the-chest way. No, he'd stabbed him repetitively until there was blood and guts and who knew what else all in a pool at his feet.

I'd let myself forget that more than once, but never had that memory been clearer than when he was standing in front of me, asking me to come home with him to meet the parents who had raised such a monster.

I opened my mouth to make an excuse. I was washing my hair. Or walking the neighbor's dog. Hell, I should have been packing a bag for Bermuda and getting the hell away from him.

He dug his teeth into his bottom lip, and then his

hands into his pockets. He couldn't hold my gaze and stared down at his feet.

I suddenly realized he was nervous.

And that was such an uncommon X characteristic that it stopped me dead, mid-refusal.

He lifted his gaze to meet mine. "Please? I really want you to meet them."

The look on his face was so ridiculously wholesome there was suddenly not one part of me that could refuse him.

And so I found myself saying, "I think I'd really like that."

19

X

I got changed three times before I settled on jeans, a white T-shirt, and a backward baseball cap. Variations of the same outfit were strewn across my bedroom, and I'd dropped to the carpet at least three times to do pushups, trying to make my biceps pop.

Levi and Whip watched me from my bed, neither acting terribly impressed by how jacked I was.

I winked at them in the mirror. "Don't be so depressed! We can't all have guns like these!"

Whip squinted at me. "I'm not depressed over your arms. I'm depressed by the fact you said you had an emergency, and we needed to get over here now, and really your emergency was you couldn't count your pushups yourself."

I stopped in plank position. "I had no idea what to wear, Whip! I can't make important decisions like that alone!"

"You made us choose between the white tee, the off-white tee, and the cream. That is not a decision that warranted an SOS text, X."

I grumbled beneath my breath, "I'll call Reginald next time. He's less grumpy than the two of you."

I glanced between them. They were about as far apart on the bed as they could get, neither looking at the other. There was a distinct chill in the air between them.

I dropped my knees down and sat up. "Did you two have a fight?"

Levi glanced over at Whip, but then quickly dropped his gaze back to his lap. "No."

"Ah." I nodded to show them I understood. "You had sex, and Whip didn't call you the next day?"

Whip glared at me. "Why are you so obsessed with me and Levi fucking?"

"We aren't fucking," Levi muttered.

Whip rolled his eyes. "Oh, sorry, I forgot the idea of that was so completely repulsive to you. I mean, I can jerk you off, and you can kiss me like you want me to roll you over and take you hard and fast from behind, but no. There's definitely no possibility of us fucking."

Levi glared at him. "Fuck off, Whip. You're being an asshole."

"I'm being an asshole? That's rich."

I glanced between them. "I kinda think you're both being assholes, because you asked me a question and then didn't let me answer it."

They both looked over at me, but it was Whip who wearily asked, "What question did we ask you?"

"Why I was so obsessed with you and Levi fucking."

Levi flopped back on the bed. "I don't think I want to know the answer to that."

I pushed to my feet. "Okay, cool, well, if you don't want to talk about my feelings on the subject, the least you could do is talk to each other."

"I'll talk to him when he stops being a prick," Levi muttered.

Whip shot back just as fast, "I'll talk to him when he stops pretending that anything between us is one-sided."

I moved for the door. "Well, I was going to invite you both to come out with me and Violet tonight, but now you're killing my vibe, and I think I'd rather lock you in here until you sort out your shit. There's lube in the top drawer!"

I closed the door behind me and slid the lock into place.

In a heartbeat, the door rattled, the handle twisting uselessly.

"Why the fuck do you have a lock on the *outside* of your bedroom door, X?" Levi shouted from the other side.

I grabbed my keys from the kitchen counter. "Some people have safety blankets. I have a reinforced door with a deadbolt." I tossed the keys into the air, and they jingled as they fell back down into my palm. "I have Doc lock me in there when I'm in one of my moods. Safer for the public, you know? Don't bother trying to get out. If I can't, you won't. Toodle-oo!"

"X!" Whip shouted. "If you leave us in here, I swear to God I will fucking rip you limb from limb when I get out!"

"And I'll help him!"

I grinned, pausing in the doorway that led to the hallway of my apartment building. "Aw! You're working together already! Good job, boys!"

I closed the front door on their complaining and practically skipped along the hallway. They'd feel so much better after they'd had some time out. I know I always did. There was water in the bathroom, and if they got hungry enough, there was flavored lube they could snack on.

Or do other things with.

Violet was waiting on Fang's front porch, a long skirt brushing her ankles and a cropped sweater covering her top half. When she lifted her arm in a wave, it showed off a tiny bit of her belly, and she quickly tugged the top back down, looking uncomfortable.

I just wanted to get my fingers all over it.

She ran across the lawn to my van, and I got out, opening up the passenger-side door for her.

"Your chariot, my lady. It doesn't even smell of horse."

"No, it smells like ice cream and sugar." She grabbed my hand and hauled herself up, pulling the seat belt across her chest and buckling it in. Then winked at me. "With maybe a dash of hyperactivity."

I loved how she just got me.

The blinds in an upstairs window twitched, and I waved at Fang, who I knew was probably watching me through the lens of a sniper rifle, just waiting for me to put a finger wrong.

But I wouldn't.

Tonight I was introducing my woman to my family, and it was going to be perfect.

I got back in behind the wheel and started the engine again.

Violet smoothed her hands over her skirt. "I'm really nervous. I've never met a man's parents before."

"Not just my parents. The whole family will be there. All my brothers and their partners. My grandma and her boyfriend."

She smiled but seemed a little green. "Really? I didn't catch that. All of them, huh? A whole party of your relation..."

"It's gonna be great. They're going to love you. Just like I do."

"You don't love me, X. You just love the idea of me."

And she called me insane.

She was the one who sounded crazy.

But I didn't have time to tell her yet again about how we were going to have four kids, a house in Providence with a white picket fence, and a birdfeeder so Harold had something to keep his psycho side entertained.

Like father like son, after all.

I couldn't wait to get that cat.

"So, tell me all your brothers' names." Violet took a notepad from her purse and poised a pencil over a blank page.

She was so freaking cute with her note-taking.

"Xavier is the eldest, after me. Suzanne is his wife, but don't call her Suzy. She gets crazy eyes when someone does. Lilith and Blake are their kids. Then there's Felix and Max, and Hendrix is the youngest of my brothers."

She wrote it all down diligently, then read over it. "You all have X's in your names."

"We do."

"That's why you go by X in the group?"

I shrugged. "When Trigger first found me and told me about the group, he said we couldn't use our real names. I had to choose fast or one of them would have chosen for me, and I would have ended up with a name like Tinker-bell. Or Lulu. Or...Bob. X was the only thing that came to mind."

"Your family doesn't call you X though, do they?"

I shook my head. "No."

"So I should call you by your real name, at least while we're in your parents' home?"

I hadn't really thought about it. This problem had never come up before because I had never wanted to bring a woman home to meet them.

But I wanted to spend a night with Violet. And knowing my parents were expecting us kept any desire to wrap my fingers around her throat at bay. I hated that I felt like we always needed a chaperone, but the memory of choking her in the shower haunted my every moment.

I wasn't ever going to put her in that situation again.

I needed a babysitter, whether I wanted one or not. And since Levi and Whip were too busy making "I want to suck your dick, even though I swear I'm straight" eyes at each other tonight, that chaperone was going to have to be my parents, my siblings, and my ninety-year-old grandma, Ruth, and her man of the week.

We stopped in front of my parents' home, and Violet peered out through the window.

"Wow. This is really nice!"

I got out to open her door again, taking her hand as she got herself out of the van. "Were you expecting the slums?"

She shrugged a shoulder, pink flushing her cheeks. "Honestly, maybe? I think I expected burnt-out cars on the lawn and guns and drugs littering every surface inside." She glanced at me. "Is it impolite to ask if your family all likes to kill people too?" Her cheeks were bright red. "I know you won't let them touch me, but it would be good to know, either way."

I snorted on a laugh. "You're so fucking cute."

I couldn't help myself. I snaked my hand into the back of her hair and drew her in close, my whole body lighting up when she didn't fight me and just went with it.

I dropped my mouth down on hers, kissing her slowly, savoring the taste and feel of her lips.

The door swung open in front of us, but I was powerless to stop kissing her, and she seemed to feel the same way. Or maybe she didn't notice my little niece standing in the doorway with her face all screwed up.

"Ewww! Mom! Uncle Knox is kissing someone on the front porch!"

I finally dragged my lips away from Violet and ruffled Lilith's hair. "Tattletale! You going to let us in? Or are you the bouncer I'm going to have to fight later once I've had too many drinks and made some bad decisions?"

Her face lit up, and she brought tiny fists up either side of her cute face. "We're definitely going to fight."

This kid was always ready for violence, unlike her older, much gentler brother.

Violet laughed at the small girl pummeling my thigh with her tiny punches.

But I gave my niece a sidelong glance. "I worry about you. I fear your parents might have started something by calling you Lilith."

The tiny demon herself didn't stop her attack to acknowledge me further, and I knew my brother was going to be pissed I'd encouraged her violent streak. So I picked the pipsqueak up in one arm, throwing her over my shoulder so her hair dangled down my back and her shouts of violence turned to giggles of laughter.

I wrapped my free hand around Violet's fingers and towed her along the hallway, into my parents' home.

Everyone was in the living room, all four of my brothers squished onto the three-seater couch, Suzanne cross-legged on the floor with Blake, my dad in an armchair with my mom perched on the arm.

And Grandma Ruth sitting on the lap of a man I vaguely recognized.

My mouth dropped open. "Silas Pearler?"

The guy peeked out around my grandma's bony shoulders. His face smoothed out into a smile when he recognized me. "Hey, Knox, right? We went to school together, didn't we? I think you were a few years younger than me, right?"

"I was a year older," I grit out through barely moving teeth.

Silas laughed. "Oh, right. Long time ago. Bad memory." He kissed my grandmother on the cheek. "We have that in common, don't we, sweetheart?"

I turned to Violet and pulled her in close, inhaling the scent of her hair like it was aromatherapy fragrances designed to calm me down. It only half worked. "I have rage," I whispered in her ear.

She stifled a laugh, but she squeezed my fingers, while I hid in her hair.

When I finally pulled away, my entire family was staring at us. My brothers and Suzanne with looks of complete and utter shock.

My mom with tears in her eyes and pure pride and happiness on her face.

She stood and crossed the room, and when she stood in front of Violet, a good ten inches shorter than her, she didn't hesitate.

She went straight in for a hug, wrapping her arms around my girl.

"Welcome to the family, Violet."

20

VIOLET

X's mom was a tiny woman, but her hug was so tight it felt like it could crush my bones.

It took me by surprise at first, but something inside me, the part that didn't remember my biological mother and who had never had a foster mother show her any affection, hugged X's mom right back.

Which made the hug go on for way longer than an introductory embrace should, but I found I couldn't let her go.

Or maybe we both couldn't. Because we stood there like that for a really long time, my arms wrapped around her, holding each other while her family watched on with confusion.

But when the woman finally stepped back, there was understanding in her eyes. And something I connected with.

I liked her instantly.

"I'm Jeanie. This is my husband, Lewis."

X's dad stood, and I instantly realized where X and his

brothers got their height because it certainly wasn't from their mother. Lewis was very tall and had the long, lean physique of a basketball player.

Lewis offered me a handshake, rather than the hug his wife had, which felt fitting, and then Jeanie went around the room, excitedly introducing me to each member of her family.

She paused when she got to Silas and Grandma Ruth, but they were busy making out, so she just pressed her lips together and tried to school her features into something that wasn't the pure horror written all over X's and his brothers' faces.

I elbowed him gently. "She seems happy," I whispered to him. "Stop staring."

"How can you tell?" he muttered back. "Her lips are being devoured by a washed-up football player who I'm ninety-nine-percent sure had a widely publicized case of gonorrhea in high school."

Grandma Ruth dragged her lips away from her much younger man's. "He had that taken care of years ago, Knox. And I don't want to hear any grief about it. We're both consenting adults."

X coughed. "Are you sure? Did you check his ID?"

The older woman frowned at him.

He instantly hung his head. "Sorry, ma'am."

"That's more like it." She patted Silas's cheek, but her words were for her grandson. "Be nice. He might be your new grandaddy."

X's mouth dropped open in horror. "The rage is back," he whispered, pulling me close again.

But Grandma Ruth winked at me, and I suspected the old woman was just having a bit of fun. I couldn't blame her. She was old, not dead. If she wanted to sit on the lap of a man forty or maybe fifty years her junior, then who were we to stop her?

Plus, I kinda liked having X wrap himself around me like I was his comfort blanket.

He'd been that for me more than once, and I drew just as many good feelings from his scent and the strength of his arms as he was currently getting from me.

Grandma Ruth clapped bony hands together. "Now that everyone is here, how about we get this game night underway?"

I grinned. "We're playing games?"

Jeanie nodded. "It's tradition. First Saturday night of every month is game night." She tucked her arm into mine. "You don't cheat, do you, Violet? We like to run a clean, fair game here."

I suddenly really wanted to make a good impression on this woman. I didn't want her to think I was lacking in moral character.

Even though I had sworn to bury the psychopath playing games with us. And I had meant it in the physical way.

"I'm not a cheater," I promised.

The thought of Levi and Whip suddenly flickered through my mind. Was I cheating? Levi and I had spent the night in bed together, and it had felt like a whole lot more than fucking.

And Whip? Every time I thought about him, something deep inside me yearned for his touch. He felt safe and calm, and I kept turning to him when I was scared.

I knew he wasn't mine, and yet I didn't want to give him up.

I had no idea what I was doing with any of these men, but they all knew about each other, and so far, none of them had asked me to choose.

Which was good, because I was pretty sure I couldn't.

Jeanie winked at me. "Well, that's a shame, because the rest of us are."

I laughed at her, and X sat me down onto the floor next to his nephew and sister-in-law and started setting up Monopoly pieces.

I watched on, the family all chattering with each other and laughing when one of X's brothers accused him of stealing an extra hundred from the bank.

He totally had, I'd seen it too, but when his brother turned to me for confirmation, I shrugged.

"I didn't see anything. Looked completely legit to me."

Hendrix just laughed. "You fit right in here."

I hid a smile, because fitting in with a family, especially one as loud and colorful and fun as the one I'd been introduced to tonight, felt like the biggest compliment in the world.

The game began, and I watched Suzanne from the corner of my eye, her son cuddled up on her lap, her daughter bouncing around the uncles, each of them vying for her attention, X included. Suzanne had gotten to marry into this family.

I wondered if she knew how incredibly lucky she was.

I was dead jealous of her. Of all of them, really.

There was so much love in this room, even though there was also a lot of trash talk, and play fights, too. I'd never seen anything like it. My only memories of family nights were my foster parents gathering all the kids in the house in the living room to scream about which one of us had drunk their vodka and refilled it with water.

I flinched at the memory of a belt cracking across the backs of my thighs because nobody had owned up. So they'd punished all of us.

I knew it had been Travis who'd done it. I'd seen him drinking with one of his friends after school one day, but he'd let us all take his punishment, and he hadn't even been a little bit remorseful for it.

I'd been too scared to tell our foster parents who it really was because I knew Travis's punishment would be worse than a spanking if I tattled.

X's fingers squeezed the back of my neck, bringing me back into the present. "What's wrong? We're winning."

I shook my head. "I'm fine."

But I wasn't. I was triggered by seeing Travis again and I knew it. I hated that he was back, ruining something else for me.

X took another long look at me and threw his Monopoly money down on the board. "We retire. I'm going to give Violet the tour of the house until dinner is ready."

He pulled me up with him, while his brothers booed him and Grandma Ruth made chicken clucking noises at him, taunting him for being too scared to lose.

X just ruffled her hair like she was a toddler as we walked by, and she swatted at him playfully.

I expected him to take me upstairs and show me his childhood bedroom or something, but he moved through the kitchen that smelled amazing, a big pot of something incredible simmering away on the stove, to the glass back doors.

He opened them, and we stepped out onto a deck. A large table sat in the center, surrounded by at least ten chairs. Fairy lights decorated the rail and lit the way down a set of stairs.

I followed X down them, our feet finding the soft grass of the lawn at the bottom.

"Your family is amazing," I said into the quiet night air around us.

His thumb stroked the back of my hand. "They're okay."

I tugged him to stop. "They're more than okay. They're perfect."

He sighed, focusing on a spot just past my shoulder. "That's kind of the problem. They're all perfect. And I'm...not." He dragged his gaze back to mine. "I love them with all that I have. They're the only reason I even know what love is. And I'm not complaining about them at all, because I know your childhood was so much worse..." He breathed out slowly. "It's just hard when I've spent my whole life keeping secrets from them. Always censoring myself so I didn't say something that one of them would find terrifying. I love them, you know? And the thought of my mother knowing what's in my head makes me sick. I don't want her to know any of that."

Shadows engulfed his face, but the fairy lights left enough of a glow that I could see his expression contort with pain.

"I spent so many years being scared I would hurt one of them. I'm still scared of that. It's the one thing I'm actually truly afraid of. Hurting them. Hurting you..." He swallowed thickly. "We shouldn't even be out here alone."

I laughed. "That's ridiculous, X. We're fifty feet away from your family."

His gaze hardened. "You think I couldn't snap your neck in the time it would take for them to hear you scream?"

A shiver ran down my spine at the sudden intensity in his eyes.

And I knew without a doubt he wasn't being dramatic.

He was danger and violence and unpredictability.

And I didn't care because somewhere along the way, I'd started trusting him with my life. He might be the bad guy, but he was the bad guy I kept running to.

I just needed him to trust himself.

I stared up at him and linked my fingers around his, drawing them up to my throat.

He hissed as he caressed the soft skin there, something deep and guttural that sent ripples of pleasure straight to the spot between my legs.

"Violet," he groaned, thumbs stroking over every inch. "What are you doing?"

"Trusting you."

"You shouldn't."

He was probably right. I'd seen how he could kill a man. Seen how once he started, he couldn't stop. He didn't trust himself, and it was stupid for me to think I knew better.

But I wanted his hands on me.

Wanted to give him that power over me.

Wanted his hand around my throat when he kissed me.

Our gazes met in the dim light, and I was sure mine were begging him for more.

My entire body was on fire. From my toes to my scalp, and all because he was too close, right there, so damn beautiful and funny and sweet and sexy and I wanted him.

He groaned and dragged me against him by my throat, pushing his mouth down on mine. He kissed me deep and slow, even though I wanted it fast and hard.

But I had wanted to give him that control, and now he was taking it in the way he wanted, so I didn't get a say in the matter.

He led, and I followed.

His tongue demanded entrance to my mouth, stroking my lips. He tasted of salt and sweetness, and I sucked in deep breaths through my nose, each one imprinting his scent on my brain until I knew I could never forget it, even if I lived to be Grandma Ruth's age.

God, I hoped he was still kissing me like this when I was in my eighties. I hoped he was kissing me like this until the day I died. My head spun, my body all feeling and no thought. Light and breezy and so blissed-out I wanted to stand like this, kissing in his arms forever.

Somebody cleared their throat nearby, and we both jumped apart like we were high school kids who'd been caught making out behind the bleachers.

Heat rushed to my throat, and I wasn't sure if it was embarrassment at being caught by his mom or if it was because he'd been squeezing it while we'd kissed.

I rubbed my hand over the spot absentmindedly, and X's gaze narrowed in on the movement, his teeth clenching.

I quickly dropped my hand and smiled at his mother. "Your garden is beautiful."

She chuckled. "Not sure the two of you have seen much of anything but close-ups of each other's faces, but thank you. It's a lot nicer in the sun. I hope you'll come over one day for lunch, maybe? I can show you all my plant babies."

X chuckled. "We just had a regular old plain backyard when we were kids. Nothing but grass and a pool. Then we all grew up, and Mom replaced us kids with her plants."

He grinned at her, letting her know he was just teasing, but clearly she had already heard this mock complaint from him or his siblings before.

She smacked his arm. "I didn't replace you. I just... landscaped. I no longer had five little boys running around, needing a backyard football field." She turned to me. "Can you imagine if I'd tried to have nice gardens when they were kids? They would have been digging in them to find caterpillars and making forts beneath bushes or trampling the flowers when they kicked the ball into them..."

X squinted at her. "How is that any different than when we play football out here now?"

She gave him a dirty look. "That's not an everyday occurrence anymore, so I can live with the odd occasion one of you dropkicks a pigskin into my rose bushes."

A fond affection passed between them, one that told me everything I needed to know about their relationship. She loved her son with her whole heart. And he loved her right back.

This was not the dynamic I'd been expecting from X's family. Not even a little bit.

I gazed around the darkened yard and then frowned at X. "You said you had a pool when you were kids. Did you get rid of it?"

An awkward silence settled over us. Jeanie glanced at X, biting her bottom lip. He was staring off into the darkness again, his entire body locked up tight.

I instantly knew I'd said something wrong. I just didn't know what. "I'm sorry. I didn't mean..."

I couldn't continue because I didn't really know what I was apologizing for. Only that I'd made the two of them uncomfortable and that was the last thing I wanted to do.

Jeanie caught my arm and squeezed it. "No, it's okay. You didn't know. Knox brought it up. It was an innocent question."

She glanced at her son; her teeth pressed into her bottom lip. She was clearly concerned by his reaction, and I was too. When he didn't say anything, she glanced at me.

"We had it removed about a decade ago. It just...it held some not very nice memories, and none of us had used it in a very long time before we decided to pull it out."

X snaked an arm around my shoulders and pulled me into his chest again.

I wrapped my arms around his middle, hugging him back, wishing I hadn't brought up the topic at all. It had killed the mood completely.

His mom walked away without any fanfare, leaving the two of us alone again.

X rested his head on top of mine. "It's my fault they

had to get rid of the pool. I can't swim. Not well anyway. They tried to teach me every summer, but I would just sink like a stone until someone yanked me back up. They never gave up, but I remember my father always being so baffled as to why I was so bad. My brothers all picked it up and were swimming laps around me while I was the eldest and forever stuck in the shallow end."

"You don't have to tell me any of this," I said quietly against his chest.

He gazed down at me. "I don't get to tell anyone anything. Those people inside that house? I love them with everything I have in me, but I can't tell them who I really am. They wouldn't believe me even if I did. And if I showed them..." His body gave an involuntary shudder. "That's not even an option. I don't want to think about them knowing what I need to do just to function."

I couldn't even imagine how hard that had been for him over the years. Never being his authentic self with the people closest to him.

"What about Levi and Whip? And the rest of your group?"

X scoffed, "We can talk about cleaning up a scene or dumping a body, but I can't talk about anything personal because we have rules against that. They can't know about the people in my life and I can't know about theirs. Do you know how superficial that makes a relationship feel? We aren't friends. You can't be friends with someone you know nothing about, other than they prefer guns to knives."

My heart broke for him. I could hear in his voice how isolated he felt, how the desires and urges inside him that he couldn't help had defined his whole life and left him feeling like he didn't truly have anyone.

"You can tell me," I whispered. "You can tell me all of it."

I wanted to know him. Wanted to know this version of him, who was quiet and open and not hiding behind chaos and violence and humor.

I wanted to know Knox. Not just X.

He shrugged. "I think I was about seven. It was an unbearably hot day, and the air conditioner inside had stopped working. I remember that specifically because normally Mom wouldn't have let us all in the pool when it was just her at home to watch us. There were too many of us, you know? Xavier and Felix could swim, but the other two were still in floaties, and I could stand in the shallow end but couldn't go any deeper. It was just too much for one person to watch over, so normally we only swam when our dad was home as well. But this day was so miserably hot, and there was no relief, and Xavier and I pestered Mom to go swimming until she eventually gave in and said we could."

I already had an idea where this was going. I didn't need him to say it. "You nearly drowned that day."

He nodded. "Hendrix got stung by a bee, and the last thing I remember was him crying and Mom grabbing his hand, trying to remove the stinger, the bee floating in the pool. Xavier was screaming it was going to kill us all. One minute I was standing in the shallow end while my brothers all splashed around me, trying to escape the bee. The next minute, the waves had pushed it closer to me, and I lurched back. But I was too close to the deep end and couldn't find my feet. The water was over my head so quickly, I don't even know if I flailed around. Even if I had, it wouldn't have caught my mom's attention. My brothers were all doing the same thing."

"But you were the only one who was drowning instead of swimming."

He swallowed hard. "Yes."

My chest felt tight, like I was the one who was being held in an underwater prison. The thought that he could have died that day messed with my head. If he had, I would be dead now. I would have been raped and murdered by Paul Jeddersen in that house on Olympic Drive, instead of standing here in X's arms in the moonlight.

I twisted my fingers in the back of his shirt and pressed my head against his chest, listening to his heartbeat beneath my ear. "How long were you out for?"

"I don't know. I just remember searing pain in my chest and then everything going black. When I came to, I was on the side of the pool and there was chaos around me. My mother screaming, my brothers all crying. And there was blood." He touched his eyebrow. "This happened when my mom dragged me out of the pool unconscious. She still can't remember exactly how it happened, but the paramedics guessed I probably hit my face on the edge of the pool when she was trying to get me out because I had some other scrapes too. But this was the worst one. It needed a couple of stitches and scarred."

I pushed his hand aside to run my finger over the scar through his eyebrow. "It's interesting that this cut is what you remember. But I guess you don't remember being unconscious...or whatever they had to do to bring you back."

He rubbed his hand over his chest absentmindedly. "I don't remember the CPR. Only the ache in my chest for days afterward while I was in the hospital..."

I cocked my head to one side. "Sounds like there's a but at the end of that sentence..."

He nodded. "But I remember being in that pool. Remember how it felt to be suffocating." He stared down at me. "Remember feeling...interested." He shrugged. "I don't know how to explain it. But it was the first time I remember feeling fascinated by death instead of scared of it." He smiled, more X again than Knox. "And that's the story of how I came to be a psychopath. Think the newspaper will want to do a feature on me?"

"Knox..."

He sighed. "I don't know if that day triggered something in my brain or if I would have been like this anyway. All I know is I won't even take a bath, let alone go in a pool." He grinned. "Even a puddle is pushing it."

He was smiling and joking, but I didn't miss the pain in his eyes. He clearly didn't want to talk about it anymore, and that was okay. There was nothing left to say anyway. He'd suffered something traumatic that may or may not have changed the hardwiring in his brain permanently. We would never know one way or another, unless he admitted to someone what he was really capable of, and they hooked him up with wires and machines and studied what made him tick.

And the thought of that was horrific.

Because it meant he'd been caught.

And he was probably in jail.

I didn't know why it hadn't really occurred to me before now that these men could be arrested at any minute. I could be okay with what they did, fall for them, be living out my fairy tale, only for it all to be snatched away by the cops or a knife or a bullet.

Getting involved with any of them was setting myself up for a heartbreak I wasn't sure I could recover from when my heart was already so broken over Toby.

X had opened up to me tonight, and in the process, I suddenly felt like I was shutting down.

I didn't want to lose him.

I didn't want to lose any of them.

But I didn't know how to keep them either.

21

LEVI

I threw my booted foot into the back of X's bedroom door and let out a scream of pure fucking fury and frustration when the damn thing didn't budge.

X hadn't been lying when he'd said it was reinforced.

I stalked to the window and stared down at the street at least ten floors below. This room was too small. Too hot. My skin crawled, and my chest was tight.

There was no air, and it was fucking suffocating.

"Don't bother," Whip said, lounging against the headboard. "Already checked it. Window doesn't open. And if he has a reinforced door, I'm willing to bet that window isn't going to be easily broken either. You could try it, of course, but even if you get it open, what are you going to do? You aren't fucking Spider-Man." His mouth turned up at the corner. "I mean, you'd look good in Lycra, but I don't think you have the athletic ability."

I glared at him, fingers clenched. "This isn't funny!"

His gaze strayed to my fists. "Didn't say it was. But if

you're gonna lose your shit, maybe don't aim it at me. Just sit. X will be back at some point."

God, he was a condescending prick. He had no idea what it felt like to spend six years of your life locked up in a box. He had no idea what it felt like to be caged in, feeling like the walls were shrinking with every moment, sucking up all the air until you choked. "Don't fucking tell me how to handle my shit. You didn't spend six years staring at concrete walls with a toilet two feet from your bed."

Whip's jaw clenched. "No. I spent it fucking strangers. We all have our prisons."

It wasn't the same thing. "That was a choice. Mine wasn't."

The pitying expression on his stupidly attractive face just pissed me off all the more.

"When are you going to take responsibility for your own actions?" he asked.

I stopped pacing. "What the fuck is that supposed to mean?"

He pointed a finger at me. "It means you like to blame everyone but yourself, don't you? The club threw you under the bus, so it's their fault you did six years in a cell. But from where I'm standing, Levi, you chose to be in that club. You chose that life. What did you think was going to happen? You were hardly an innocent in that situation."

I ground my teeth, irritation rippling up my spine because I knew he was right. I'd spent a long time holding a grudge against Army and the club, but I'd known what I was signing up for when I'd put on the jacket.

Whip's onslaught of honesty didn't let up. "And now

you're blaming me for what happened at the club the other night, aren't you?"

I just stared at him.

He stared back, never dropping his gaze from mine. "Admit it, Levi. You're blaming me instead of just admitting you fucking wanted me as much as I wanted you."

I scoffed. "You think I want you?"

Whip got off the bed so fast I barely saw him move. And then he was in front of me, the two of us eye to eye, my chest heaving from the panic attack I was verging on.

It had nothing to do with how close he was.

He leaned into my space, his warm breath brushing over my lips. "I *know* you do. You kissed me. I had my hand on your cock, and you didn't stop me. You fucking moaned."

I glared at him. "That was a mistake."

"Then make another one."

I blinked. Froze. The electricity between us so freaking sharp I could practically hear it crackling.

I grabbed his face and slammed my mouth onto his.

He kissed me back in a heartbeat, both of us all tongues and lips and teeth. It was the angriest I'd ever been while kissing someone, and we fought for control, both of us battling with the pace and depth of the kiss, our fingers grappling at each other's clothes, tearing at them.

I just wanted to touch his skin.

Needed something warm and real and alive that reminded me I wasn't back in that cell, alone.

I couldn't go back there. I wouldn't survive it.

My chest tightened, a band of steel wrapping its way around it that I couldn't shake.

I gasped, but Whip's lips were there to catch it, kissing me until the sound muffled, his hands dragging up my chest and taking off my shirt, me doing the same to him.

I just needed to feel his skin against mine. Craved the heat of another body on top of me, regulating my breathing, his touch forcing the demons out of my head.

The walls were too tight. There was no fucking air.

I kissed him harder, taking what I needed from him in a demanding press of lips I knew would be bruised tomorrow. But I didn't care. I couldn't breathe without it.

His fingers found the button on my pants, and he shoved them down my thighs, taking my underwear with them.

He dropped to his knees in front of me, and I hated it.

For the split second when he wasn't touching me, I felt like I was going to die.

And then he put his mouth around my cock, and every bad feeling I'd ever had disappeared.

I groaned, thrusting deep into his mouth, not giving a fuck if he was ready for it or not.

He took it, swallowing me down greedily, one hand coming between my legs to grip my balls, the other snaking around to grab a handful of my ass.

He urged me on, pulling me into his mouth, taking every thrust while I lapped up the feel of him. His mouth was hot and wet, and his tongue had me tilting my head back to stare at the ceiling, though my vision was unfocused and hazy so I couldn't see much.

I pushed my hands into the back of his hair, holding on to his head, needing something to anchor me and loving the feel of him there, while his mouth slid up and down my shaft.

"Fuck," I moaned, hips jutting forward, giving him every inch, feeling the tip of me hit the back of his throat.

He hummed his approval, the sound vibrating around my cock, and he squeezed my balls at the same time.

I was going to fucking come.

Too damn quick, but I didn't care.

He felt too good to stop.

The band lifted from around my chest, and I sucked in one deep breath after the other, filling my oxygen-starved lungs again. With every suck of Whip's mouth, my muscles loosened, an orgasm building low and sending sensation through my entire body.

I should have pulled away.

Should have at least fucking warned him.

But I was asshole enough that I didn't.

I just loosened my grip on his head so he could move away if he wanted to.

The orgasm gripped me hard, spinning my brain in circles. I shouted, spurting into his mouth, savoring in the feel of his tongue against my tip, licking off every drop.

He swallowed it all, and kept going, tongue fucking me until I was so damn sensitive and my knees buckled.

With a groan because I had no idea if I wanted more or needed him to stop, I pushed him away. My breaths came so hard I was sure I was going to hyperventilate again, but this time for an entirely different reason.

Whip got to his feet and stood in front of me.

I stared back, absolutely no fucking idea what to say to a man after he'd just blown me.

Thank you?

That was nice?

I got down on my knees instead, because it was a

whole lot easier than looking into his eyes or seeing the smug expression on his stupid face.

I dragged off his jeans. "This doesn't fucking mean shit," I grumbled at him.

"Whatever you say, Levi."

Oh, fuck him.

But it didn't stop me from pulling off his underwear and running my hand over his erection. He was glistening, slick with precum, clearly turned on from sucking me off.

"Want some instructions?" There was laughter in his voice.

He could go to hell. I gave him the middle finger.

The one on my hand that wasn't wrapped around his dick.

I knew what I liked in a blow job. I didn't need him acting like I was one of his sex students.

I wrapped my lips around the head of him, and that effectively shut him up.

He groaned, but he was clearly less of a prick than I was, because he didn't grab me the way I'd grabbed him.

Some part of me wanted him to. Wanted him to lose control, because he never fucking did. X was all hyperactivity and no thought before he acted. I was too fucking emotional, too in my head, always losing it because my feelings were too close to the surface.

Whip was a closed book. Always calm.

It was fucking annoying.

The sensation of having a dick in my mouth was new, but as I slid my tongue down his shaft, I found it wasn't unpleasant. My lips stretched wide around his cock, and I licked the underside of him, pressing him deeper and deeper into my mouth with each round.

Somewhere around the third or fourth plunge of my mouth, or maybe it was when I noticed his abs flexing and breathing change, I realized me sucking him was just as much a turn-on as when he'd done it to me. My balls were already tingling, and the familiar rush of blood to my cock was quicker than I would have expected, considering I'd just come.

I wasn't twenty anymore. It took me a few minutes to go twice in a row.

But, apparently, not when I was down on my knees for another man.

Wouldn't Whip have a field day with that information? Not that I would ever tell him.

I'd actually rather put a bullet in my brain than admit that.

But fuck. He was going to know anyway. Because there was going to be no hiding the boner I was sporting.

Great. Just fucking great.

I doubled down, sucking him hard and fast, both hating and loving I was so hard just from what I was doing. It was the same high I got when I was buried in Violet's pussy.

I'd had no idea I would feel the same when it was cock.

But, apparently, I did. So I guess we could all learn new things.

Whip pushed my head away, and I found myself staring up at him.

"What?" I narrowed my eyes. "If you tell me I'm doing it wrong, I swear I'm gonna punch you in the junk."

He rolled his eyes. "You aren't doing it wrong, dick-head. But you're hard again."

Heat rushed up the back of my neck, and I had no real idea why. "So? It's a biological response."

"Okay, sure, keeping telling yourself that. Let's say it's a biological response that I want to make you come again then."

The heat in my neck flamed across the sides, up my throat and straight into my cheeks. It only blazed brighter when Whip leaned across the bed and found the promised bottle of lube from X's top drawer.

I eyed it with my nose wrinkled. "You know that's probably covered in—"

Whip shut me up with a glare. "Don't say it."

Fair call.

He lay out on the bed, the bottle of lube on the mattress between us.

Fuck, he looked good. All muscled legs and abs and biceps. He wasn't as bulky as I was, but he wasn't as slim as X was either. He had the solid body that came to a guy in his thirties, but he'd kept it.

And he had the sort of cock all guys wished for. Big and thick.

Suddenly, the thought of him fucking me with that thing jumped into my mind.

My dick kicked at the very thought, and it was like a damn magnet, drawing me down onto the bed next to him, even though the idea was also fucking terrifying.

There was no way I was taking that thing in the ass.

And yet I was lying down next to him.

It was him who reached for me, grabbing me by the back of the neck and drawing me onto my side so we were facing each other. I moved so stiffly I was practically robotic.

Whip noticed and only shifted in closer. "Stop fucking thinking."

"I'm not."

"Bullshit. Your every thought is written all over your face. I'm not gonna shove my cock in your ass, Levi. Calm down."

The reassurance should have helped me relax.

And yet the feeling that rushed in was disappointment.

Yeah, wasn't fucking going to admit that one to him either.

He studied me. "Do you want to talk about the prison? What happened to you there?"

Oh, fuck off. I was not doing that with him. He could go play therapist with Doc. "I'd rather bite off my own dick than talk about that with you."

He sniggered. "Whatever, Levi."

I hated that I found myself leaning in to kiss him again. Told myself it was just to shut him up because I hated that he could read me, while I still couldn't read him. At least when we were kissing or I had my hand around his dick, I understood him. I felt the way he thrust into my lubed-up hand, and heard his moans and saw the sharp intake of breath when I rolled him onto his back and covered his body with mine. He didn't need to say a word for me to know what he wanted. What he felt.

It was obvious.

Because I wanted it too.

I groaned, burying my face in his neck and sucking him there while he writhed beneath me.

He spread his legs, opening them up for me, our cocks rubbing against each other until mine was as lubed-up as his was.

"Fuck," he groaned, panting hard. "You feel so good."

I couldn't talk, I was that damn hard.

I fumbled with the tube of lubricant and awkwardly squirted more onto my palm. Bracing my weight on one arm so I could use the other to get in between us. I stroked my cock, getting it slick, the lube mixing with both our precum.

Whip rocked his hips beneath me, searching out contact.

My dick slid along his balls and lower to press against his taint.

He grabbed my head, forcing his lips onto mine.

"Fuck," we both moaned in unison.

I couldn't stop.

A memory from years ago, when I was first sent to prison, rocketed into my brain.

But this time, it wasn't the walls closing in on me or the claustrophobic panic that swamped my brain whenever I was forced into a tight space.

It was a memory I'd locked up tight because it had only happened once and then I'd sworn I'd never let it happen again.

Whip's blue eyes stared up at me.

I couldn't look at them anymore.

I shoved him over onto his stomach and bit down on his muscled shoulder, my dick finding the crease between his ass cheeks.

He groaned as the tip of me prodded his ass, lubing him up.

God, it felt fucking good. I rubbed my cock there, moaning at the way he moved, encouraging me, pushing back against the pressure I was putting at his entrance, getting himself ready for when I thrust inside.

And fuck, I wanted to.

But my head was suddenly full of ghosts again.

Ones I couldn't get rid of if I just did what my body was screaming for and thrust deep inside him.

I reared back onto my knees. "I can't do this."

Whip buried his face in the pillow, so his words came out muffled but still understandable. "I'm fine. Do it."

God, I so wanted to. But something kept me rooted to the spot, even though my dick craved being back between his cheeks, thrusting across his asshole.

Whip lifted his head and twisted to look back at me clearly having a mental fucking breakdown.

A tremble racked my body, and I couldn't stop it. I stared at the wall above his head and tried to fight off the surge of panic that rushed in.

But I was back there in that prison cell, the first night I'd been shoved in there.

With a bag over my head.

And hands holding me down.

I couldn't breathe.

"Levi." Whip moved, rolling onto his back again and sitting up, squeezing my arm, bringing me back into the room.

I blinked. "There's no air in here," I wheezed.

"There is. You're okay."

I nodded fast, hating that I was doing this in front of him. I didn't want him seeing me like this. Didn't want anyone seeing me be this fucking weak.

So I kissed him instead.

He pulled back instantly, trying to talk, but I wouldn't give in.

I kissed him until he shut up and kissed me back. My hands found both our cocks and jerked us both in unison. I built us back up to a place where neither of us could talk, all we could do was feel.

We came at almost exactly the same moment, my balls drawing up, a delicious ache spreading through me, my grip tight. His dick jerked in my hand, his cum spurting from his tip, landing on his stomach.

I joined him a second later, spreading cum over the top of his, marking his abs and his chest and his thighs.

I stared down at the mess we'd made, breathing hard, the release feeling good but my head an open wound.

"Levi," Whip said.

I gave him a deadpan stare. "Don't fucking ask me to talk about my feelings."

"I wasn't going to."

"What then?"

He shrugged. "Are we gonna tell X what we did on his bed?"

22

WHIP

I turned down three client jobs over the next few days because I just couldn't bring myself to do them. I made the excuse that I was sick and rescheduled, but it was with a sense of dread I'd only felt once before.

Right before I'd taken my first job.

Guilt had plagued me. The feeling this wasn't right. That I was betraying the one person I'd ever fucking loved.

And now I felt like I was doing it all over again.

It was stupid. Violet and I weren't a couple. Levi and I definitely weren't. And yet all of a sudden, the thought of getting naked with anyone else had me feeling like I was cheating?

I'd gotten over it the first time. I would get over it again.

I checked the text on my phone one more time, wishing I had never gotten it. Or that I could ignore it.

But I'd made a promise when I'd joined Grayson's group. It was the number one rule we had.

No matter where you were, or what you were doing, when your phone went off, you showed up to the meeting.

You showed up for your brothers.

Though when I'd made that promise, I hadn't had any of their dicks in my mouth, so it had been a lot easier to make.

I hadn't seen Levi since X had gotten home to free us from his bedroom, and he'd rushed out without saying a word to anyone. I'd followed straight after because I hadn't had it in me to deal with X alone.

I'd lain low the last few days, just keeping tabs on Violet.

But seeing Levi at some point was inevitable.

I got out of my car and shut the door. At the iron gates of the Slayers' compound, Fang appeared on the other side and nodded his blond head at me.

The similarities between him and Violet were obvious. Their eyes. Their hair color. Their height.

But where Violet had a gentle softness about her, Fang was all brooding intensity that gave even me a slight pause.

Mostly because he knew I'd slept with his sister.

And that was awkward.

"Fang." I nodded at him. "Just here to see Grayson." I held up my phone like that explained everything. "He texted me."

Fang pushed a passcode into the control panel on the brick pillars holding up the heavy gates, and I gave him a small smile as I walked between them.

"They're down in the workshop. Grayson wanted somewhere private for you all to talk…or whatever it is you do at your meetings. Go down the hill, past the clubhouse, and the turnoff to Grayson's place. There's a big shed beyond that. Can't miss it if you stick to the road."

"Got it. Thanks."

I went to walk away, mentally trying to place where this workshop was on the compound, though it was a useless endeavor because, even though I'd been here half a dozen times for various reasons, I'd never gone any deeper into their vast property than the cabin Gray and his family had built here behind the safety of the fences.

"Whip?"

I was already halfway down the hill but turned back to Fang. "Yeah?"

"I like you. I really don't want to have to kill you. So don't fuck up whatever you and X and Reaper are doing with my sister, yeah?"

Even that sentence was complicated. And a promise I wasn't one-hundred-percent sure I could make. Because I couldn't see a future where I was in Violet's life in any meaningful way. If there was a competition for her hand, I was in dead last position and I knew it.

I didn't fucking like it. But I knew it.

"All I want is for her to be safe," I called back to her brother.

His lips flattened into a line, and I could tell my lack of promise wasn't exactly going down well, but it was the best I could offer.

I trudged down the dirt road until I rounded a bend and a huge industrial building rose in front of me. It was smartly positioned in the property, shielded by thick scrub and tall trees. I would have never even known it was there until I was right on top of it if the trees around it hadn't been thinned out by a fire I knew they'd had about a year ago. The garage looked new, probably built after the blaze, I guessed, maybe at the same time they'd built Grayson's place, but there was already a couple of old bikes and cars sitting out front, waiting for someone to work on or strip for parts.

There was a big roller door to one side, but a smaller regular one to the left. I beelined for that, taking a deep breath before I twisted the knob to enter, the sounds of talk from inside already filtering through the thin corrugated iron walls.

Doc raised a hand from the center of the open space, beckoning me over to the circle of chairs he'd made in the middle of the oil-stained floor.

There was only one chair left. The rest were taken up by Trigger, Ace, Torch, Scythe, X, and Levi.

Of course, the one open chair was right beside the man I'd very nearly had sex with just a few nights previously.

I didn't say anything to him when I sat. Didn't really acknowledge any of them. Just crossed my arms over my chest and sank low in my chair, the brim of my baseball cap pulled down on my head, shadowing my eyes.

Levi stiffened beside me.

A silence fell over the group, and even though I wasn't looking at any of them, I could feel their gazes on me.

The most irritating thing about a group of psychopaths was they were annoyingly in tune with other people at times. They watched shrewdly, and it was like it was a natural trait for them to pick up on any little weakness or vulnerability they might be able to exploit or use to their own advantage.

It didn't even surprise me they'd noticed the weirdness between me and Levi so quickly.

Ace waved a finger between the two of us. "What's up with you two? You're being weird."

"Nothing," Levi and I both said at once.

Fucking hell. We'd responded too quick. Too reactive.

I was right. The entire group pounced on the tension like they were kittens toying with a string.

Trigger shook his head. "Nah, something went down between the two of you. I can practically smell the secrets."

I wasn't giving them shit. I had made a promise to turn up to these meetings and support them in not going on mass murder sprees.

I hadn't promised to spill my personal business and bleed my heart all over the dirty cement floor.

X twirled a wrench absentmindedly that someone really should have taken off him in case he got the urge to throw it. "I might have locked Levi and Whip in my bedroom. Just to see what would happen."

A half-grin lifted Trigger's mouth. "So I was right then? Something went down?" He sniggered in my direction. "Or rather, someone?"

I raised an eyebrow, locking down my cool instead of answering in the heat of the moment like I had initially. "Are you implying we banged in X's bedroom while surrounded by his serial killer memorabilia?"

Trigger snorted.

But Ace glanced over at X. "What do you have in there? Like, just posters or collector's stuff?"

Even X ignored him. What had happened between me and Levi clearly a more interesting topic of conversation. He couldn't keep the laughter off his stupid face. "Aw. Did my emotionally stunted alpha boys have a little moment? Did someone hold the other and whisper, 'It's okay to feel things, bro'?"

Levi and I both gave him the middle finger.

I accidentally caught Levi's eye in the process and then had to fight an internal battle not to show how badly sitting by his side was affecting me. I didn't miss the way I was more grumpy than usual though. And that only annoyed me more. "Who called the meeting tonight anyway? Can we get on with it, because some of us have places to be."

"Got a hot date?" Levi muttered.

If I hadn't known better, I would have said there was a hint of jealousy in his voice.

"What do you care?"

Levi bit down on his bottom lip, white teeth pressing into the pink flesh I'd spent a lot of time kissing just a couple of nights ago. "I don't."

I rolled my eyes and turned back to the group, ignoring the fact they were all staring at us with stupid grins on their faces.

"What?" I snapped. "Get on with it before I'm the one who needs to be counselled out of a murder rampage. One I'll start in this room."

X opened his mouth, no doubt to make another joke at my or Levi's expense, if the laughter in his expression was anything to go by.

Grayson shut it down by clearing his throat and

giving X that dad frown he had down to a T now that he had a couple of kids of his own to practice on.

X sighed and raised his hand. "I called the meeting."

Ace rocked back on his chair, the front two legs lifting off the floor. "How many dead bodies did you leave in your wake before calling in this time?"

X screwed up his face. "Ha-ha, hilarious. Sheesh, you go on one little rampage—"

"There were at least three rampages, X," I threw in dryly.

He threw his arms up. "Fine! Three rampages, one of which was definitely not my fault, because that guy was chewing with his mouth open, and you know I can't handle things like that. But now you decide you don't trust me? That hurts, you know? It cuts real deep."

I snapped my fingers in his direction. "Focus, would you? If you haven't been leaving a trail of bodies around Saint View, why did you call the meeting?"

X had the decency to look a bit sheepish. "Okay fine. There was maybe one body..."

My groan mixed with those of the others in the room. I scraped a hand through my hair. "Was it at least someone on the list?"

X waved a hand at me dismissively, like I'd insulted him. "What am I? A newbie? I checked his ID. He was on this list."

Levi squinted as he followed X's explanations. "So where's the body now?"

X's trademark sarcastic grin fit itself back on his face. "He's just chilling in my truck."

I snorted on a laugh. "By chilling, do you mean..."

X nodded. "He's in the freezer, right next to the popsicles."

Levi wrinkled his nose. "Remind me never to buy an ice cream from you."

X pointed the wrench at him. "Hey! I'll have you know I have the best prices in town! I'm way cheaper than anyone else!"

Grayson rubbed the back of his neck, his agitation common during these meetings. His clipboard with his notes rested on his crossed legs. "Okay, so we have a dead body on site. That's great. My kids are asleep in their beds just down the road." He sighed. "How about you all sit here and think about your behavior while I go get someone to deal with that." He eyed X. "Seriously, you need a time-out. Don't freaking move until I get back."

He stood and went to the door, pulling it open.

X twirled his wrench like he was a cheerleader with a baton. "Uh-oh, I made Dad mad."

"You make all of us mad," I told him.

He leaned over and ruffled my hair. "Aw. I love you too, Whip."

"I will break every finger on your hand if you don't get them out of my hair," I said through gritted teeth.

He leaned in closer, giving my hair one last stroke and withdrawing his hand just in time to keep it. "It's okay. Even if I have no fingers, I can still get Violet off with my dick."

Levi made an annoyed noise in the back of his throat. "I can break that for you too, if you want?"

He didn't get to answer, because the workshop door opened again.

I twisted to see Grayson coming back in the door.

"That was quick. Did you sprint up to the clubhouse and back?"

He shook his head. "Didn't even get as far as the road. Found a *friend* hanging around outside eavesdropping."

All of us shoved to our feet, weapons drawn, muscles tensed and ready for a fight.

Grayson glanced over his shoulder.

Violet stepped into the open doorway, her cheeks pink but determination in her eyes.

My stomach flipped in a sickening roll. She was supposed to be at work. She'd been scheduled at Psychos tonight, and that's where she'd been because I'd watched Fang drop her off there hours ago. They had security, and on any given night, half the bar was filled with Slayers keeping an eye on Bliss or Rebel, so it had felt safe to leave Violet there without a babysitter.

But she was clearly not there any longer, and there was a dead fucking body up at the Slayers' gates, currently frozen along with the Ben and Jerry's.

Levi lurched forward, his face like a thundercloud, but putting himself between Violet and the rest of us holding guns. "What are you doing here?" He was clearly having similar thoughts to me and Grayson about having dead bodies anywhere near the people we cared about.

X seemed oblivious to it all, as usual. He just blew her a kiss, which she ignored.

She instead focused on Levi. "I want in."

X cocked his head to one side as the rest of us holstered our guns. "Into the squad or into Levi and Whip's newly discovered gay awakening? Because I have questions about both."

So did I, but I decided to focus on the Violet question

first, since she was standing right there next to Grayson, so incredibly tempting but also super out of place in the middle of a dirty workshop where a group of killers were having a meeting. "You shouldn't be here, sweetheart."

She narrowed her eyes at me. "Don't 'sweetheart' me. And where should I be, Whip? Hiding at home with one of you babysitting me?"

Irritation rose up my spine. She'd had a brick thrown through the car window the last time she'd followed us, but clearly that hadn't been enough to scare some sense into her. She was being reckless with her own safety, and frankly, it was starting to piss me off. That bubbled to the surface. "Preferably, yes!"

Her mouth flattened into a line, and she moved around Grayson, beelining for me until we stood pretty much eye to eye, me staring down at her just a few inches.

She poked me in the chest with a finger. "You aren't my keeper. And I can join your stupid group if I want to."

To prove her point, she sat down heavily in the chair Grayson had vacated.

All eight of us stared at her.

"You are not joining the group," Levi practically snarled. "No freaking way."

She raised an eyebrow at him, and then her hand followed. "I pledge allegiance to this group of emotionally unstable boys, who think murder is a love language." Her sarcasm was so thick it dripped from every word. "There. I'm in."

Scythe leaned in toward X. "That didn't sound sincere." He paused a second, then added, "And it is a love language, just for the record."

Grayson cleared his throat. "That isn't exactly how this works, Violet."

She glared at him. "Oh, isn't it? My bad. Is there an initiation I have to pass? Is it murder?" Her glare moved across the three of us who'd shared her bed recently. "I can think of a few people I wouldn't mind taking out right now because they clearly don't have my back, even though they promised they would."

The fight went out of all three of us and the shame sank in. It was like a literal deflation, all three of us dropping our gazes to the floor like dogs who'd just been told off by their owner.

It was a pretty spot-on analogy. It definitely felt like Violet owned me.

One by one, the three of us sat, the others all taking their cues from us and following. Grayson didn't seem happy, but he pulled over a chair with wheels from behind a desk filled with messy, oil-smudged paperwork, and we widened the circle a little to fit him in.

All of us stared at Violet.

She nodded, like it was exactly the reaction she had wanted, and I couldn't help the flare of pride deep in my chest for the way she was owning this. Where was the timid woman from the back of my car that first night we'd met? The one who'd been scared of her own shadow and too afraid to take her panties off for me?

She seemed far away tonight.

The Violet who sat at the head of our circle looked much more like some sort of Mafia don, owning the attention and respect of the eight men in the room.

It was hot.

Instantly, my brain started conjuring up all sorts of

things we could do in this workshop if there weren't currently seven other people in here. The workbench was just the right height for bending her long torso over. There was an old Chevy with a hood I could lay her on to bury my face in her pussy.

Levi behind me, finishing what we'd started the night before.

I swallowed down a groan at the very thought of being sandwiched between them like that, him taking me from behind, me going down on her at the same time.

Fucking hell.

"I heard everything you said," Violet announced calmly.

X turned sheepish. "I swear, it's still safe to eat my ice cream. The body is wrapped in plastic. Nothing is touching." He couldn't help but add, "Apart from Levi's and Whip's dicks."

Violet frowned at him. "You make jokes, but, X, someone tried to kill you. Someone tried to kill me. It's only a matter of time before someone comes after Levi and Whip too, if they haven't already."

She looked at the two of us.

I bit my lip but then admitted, "I think I was followed the other day. They backed off pretty quick when I turned around and confronted them. I don't know, maybe it wasn't connected to the list. Saint View isn't ever the safest place to be walking alone at night."

Violet wasn't convinced. "But it could have been someone targeting you because the sick fuck playing games with us is paying them to."

I couldn't deny it was a possibility.

She turned her attention to Grayson. "I want to see a copy of the list."

He shook his head. "Violet—"

It was Levi who spoke up. "She wasn't asking, Gray."

The two of them exchanged a look, Gray still hesitant, but Levi clearly willing to stand up for Violet, even if just minutes earlier he'd been objecting harder than anyone.

His mood swings gave me whiplash. But Violet had put him in his place, and he was backing her.

Just like X and I now were as well.

Jesus, this woman had all three of us so pussy-whipped. I knew it, and I didn't even care. It didn't feel like a bad thing to want to protect her, to give her what she wanted as well as what she needed.

Right now, she was asking for our support.

And we were giving it.

Grayson handed over his copy of the list. We all reported back which targets we'd taken out, and the list now had several crossed-through names, mostly all courtesy of Trigger, Ace, Torch, and maybe Scythe.

I knew Levi, X, and I hadn't contributed much, since we were too busy running around after Violet and fucking around in sex club camera rooms. But at least the body in X's truck would help toward evening up our tally just a little.

Violet ran her nail down the list of names, though I wasn't sure why. She was a nice girl. A good girl, who didn't hang out with criminals.

Well, she hadn't, until she'd met us, but that was beside the point. She wasn't going to recognize anyone on that list.

Except halfway down it, she paused, and her head jerked up. "I know this name."

I leaned in to peer over her shoulder. "Travis Jones."

Any humor that might have been lingering in X's expression faded away. "Travis? As in the Travis who was bothering you at Psychos the other night?"

She nodded. "Travis as in my foster brother Travis. I don't even want to know what he did to get himself on here. But I can imagine."

I gritted my teeth. I didn't know off the top of my head what he'd done either, but Grayson didn't put people on the list lightly. There was nobody on there who'd done time for a simple break and enter, or someone who had been sentenced for fraud.

The list was reserved for the worst of the worst. People we knew were associated with the most vile things humans could do to each other. Rapists. Traffickers. Murderers.

For her brother's name to be on there, he had to have done something reprehensible.

And the thought of her growing up in a house with someone who could do things like that sent chills down my spine.

I suddenly went from wanting to bang Violet up against a wall, to wanting to lift her in my arms, roll her in bubble wrap, and never let anything bad happen to her ever again.

She'd already been through too much. She'd been dealt so many shit hands, it just didn't seem fair she'd found herself square in the middle of another, just by being in the wrong place at the wrong time.

And I hated it was all because of us.

If she'd never met us, none of this would be happening to her and she and Toby would be living their best lives right now.

Except if X hadn't been there that day, to save her from Paul Jeddersen, the very man whose name had been scratched off the list she held now in her hands, she would be the one chopped up into little pieces and dropped off the Saint View bluff.

Everything happened for a reason.

And there was no turning back now.

"You need to use me as bait," Violet said quietly.

We all stared at her.

"It makes sense," she continued, like she couldn't hear the screaming in my head. "Either I'm a target for them, or they're using me because they know it will hurt all of you. Either way, they're watching me. So let them come. I'm sick of them having the upper hand and us always looking over our shoulders, wondering when they're next coming at us. We need to flip the tables. Take back the power."

The screaming in my head got louder. I managed to keep it from pouring out of my mouth, but I could feel the same sort of thing vibrating off X and Levi.

Nobody liked this plan. But nobody was willing to say it either, because all three of us wanted to have her back.

A tiny part of me really wanted the others in the room to object though.

Grayson nodded. "It could work. Something staged and well controlled with all of you working together. We've been picking off people from the list one by one, but it's not getting us anywhere. Maybe this will."

I sent a mental punch straight to Doc's groin. "Would

you be so quick to make Kara the sacrificial lamb?" I couldn't help but ask him.

We all knew he wouldn't.

But he didn't even get to answer because Violet answered for him, "Kara has two girls who need their mom." She swallowed thickly. "I don't have anyone who needs me like that."

"I do," I muttered.

She glanced at me. "Not like that, you don't."

I might not have been a little girl who needed her mom, but I was a grown fucking man who very much did need her.

She just didn't know how much, because until that moment, I hadn't even really admitted it to myself. I breathed out a long, slow stream of air, trying to get my shit under control.

Trigger's team was all nodding, in full approval of this new plan Violet was proposing. And slowly, X and Levi nodded, too.

Which left me.

Her gaze locked with mine, and there was a fire in it. One I knew was fueled by what Paul Jeddersen had done to her. What that trapped warehouse had taken from her. And from the shitty childhood that had stamped her down, beating her into the ground time and time again.

She needed this.

And I was never going to say no to anything she needed. Whether that be food or affection or sex.

Or murder.

I sighed. "I guess we're setting a trap for a psychopath."

23

VIOLET

Grayson eventually called the meeting over, and all nine of us filed out. Grayson strode ahead along the road with Scythe, the middle row made up of Ace, Trigger, and Torch, who were planning how best to take out their next victim from the list.

I walked in the last group, flanked by Whip and Levi, while X jogged in circles around the three of us, spouting the benefits of heart-healthy cardio and complaining we'd been sitting too long and we should all be working on getting our ten thousand steps in each day.

I suspected X probably did more than double that amount daily, considering the man really couldn't sit still for any extended period of time. That meeting had felt like it had dragged on for a lifetime. Even I felt like I had some energy to burn.

Though I was definitely not about to join X while he buzzed around us like a fly that needed swatting.

Even still, tension crackled through my body. Pent-up energy and leftover adrenaline from doing a very un-

Violet-like thing and storming a meeting of men and demanding to be heard.

They'd listened.

They'd agreed.

And that was going to my head.

Music and laughter filtered back from the Slayers' clubhouse. The evening air and being out in nature felt good. When was the last time I'd been surrounded by trees and open skies? I suddenly envied Levi for the fact he got to live here. It was a hell of a lot nicer than my shitty apartment in Saint View.

Levi's arm brushed mine. "Do you need to go back to work?"

"No. The bar was quiet, and when Fang told me there was a meeting happening, I asked for the rest of the night off. Nash told me to go, that he had it under control. Saves them on my wages when I really wasn't doing much of anything, other than wiping down bar tops that were already clean."

Levi's little finger linked around mine. "Stay here tonight then? We're having a party up at the clubhouse."

I raised an eyebrow. "A Slayers party? I've heard they're a bit...wild."

He chuckled. "They can be, if you want them to be. Or we can just go to my room and watch TV in bed."

The alternative was going back to Fang's place and hanging out with Vaughn and Kian while they changed diapers and sang "The Wheels on the Bus" a thousand times because it was the only way Lavender would fall asleep each night.

Or going back to my place and sitting there with my memories, all alone.

Alone and unprotected.

I'd just made a big show of being an independent woman and storming the meeting and being a boss bitch, who wouldn't take no for an answer, but going back to that apartment still made me feel sick.

Staying here with Levi for the night felt like a much more appealing offer. "Okay."

His fingers threaded through mine, and he led me up the hill.

I didn't miss the way he didn't invite the others to stay for the party though.

Nor could anyone miss the awkward tension that crackled between him and Whip.

Well, maybe X missed it. He was too busy yammering about zone something running and metronomes and other exercise-related words I didn't understand.

Grayson and Scythe were the first to reach the club-house, War meeting them at the top of the hill, a slow grin for his partner that heated even my blood so I could only imagine what it was doing to Scythe. Grayson kept going, disappearing inside, but Scythe stopped close to War, the two of them exchanging a couple of low words with their mouths close to each other's ears.

I couldn't see Scythe's face, only the back of his head, but I saw War's expression change from neutral to a sly smirk, and I had a feeling I could probably guess what the two of them were whispering about.

I doubted it was PG rated.

They threw off the same sort of chemistry as the two men walking either side of me did.

Not that my two would admit it.

I was more curious than anyone as to what had

happened between them in X's bedroom. But unlike X and his murder squad friends, I wasn't going to push them. They would tell me if and when they wanted to.

Even if my brain was in overdrive conjuring up a whole host of situations involving the two big men, hands and tongues everywhere, and whole lot of clothes hitting the floor.

That shouldn't have got me as hot as it did. It felt vaguely pervy and inappropriate and like it wasn't any of my business.

Except when I was sandwiched between them like this, and it was so thick in the air I could practically lick it, ignoring it felt impossible.

Still, I bit my tongue.

We reached the top of the hill just in time to hear War invite Trigger, Ace, and Torch to the party. They declined, in favor of going off on their killing spree.

It still surprised me how many of these people didn't even blink an eyelid at announcements like that. War just nodded like it was an every day occurrence and said he'd see them all later.

He turned his attention in our direction and jerked his head toward the clubhouse. "What about you guys? You staying for the party?"

X shook his head. "I've got a body to go deal with."

War nodded. "Grayson told me. I'll send a couple of prospects up to the gate to help you if you want?"

X saluted him. "Thank ye, kind sir. I can return the favor in ice cream. Only slightly blood-tinged."

War wrinkled his nose. "I think we'll just call it a no-strings-attached favor, yeah?"

"Suit yourself." X turned to me. "Love you. Miss you."

Then he lowered his voice to a stage whisper, as if it were only for me, though everyone around us could hear. "Find out which of them is the top and which is the bottom. I need to know these things so I can make them personalized Christmas presents."

"Is there a way your prospects could bury him while they're burying the body?" Whip asked War. "I'm happy to pay extra."

X walked backward with a shit-eating grin and pointing a finger at Whip. "You're just jealous because I was planning to give Levi the T-shirt that says 'Flip me over, Daddy,' aren't you?" He rubbed his hands together. "My Cricut machine is going to get *such* a workout."

War and I both bit back a laugh, but Levi and Whip didn't seem quite as amused.

X took up his jog again, catching up to Trig and his group as they continued on up to the gates where they'd all left their vehicles.

War looked at Whip. "What about you? You staying? Or you got bodies to bury as well?"

Whip smiled and opened his mouth to reply.

But Levi cut him off quickly. "He's busy."

Whip raised an eyebrow at him and then turned back to War. "I was going to say I had some things to take care of, but you know what? I'm suddenly in the mood for a beer and some company. So I think I will stay. Thanks for the invite."

He shook War's hand and moved past him, heading for the clubhouse door.

I could hear Levi's molars grinding, even above the music floating through the compound. He stormed after Whip, leaving me alone with War.

He winced. "Oops. Did I fuck up there?"

I grinned at him. "Not from where I'm standing. They have some...unresolved tensions they could stand to work out."

He turned and walked me into the clubhouse. "Ah. I know all about unresolved tensions." He grinned over at me and winked. "Get 'em drunk. Get 'em naked. Get in the middle. Guaranteed to fix all."

Heat flushed through me, partly out of embarrassment, but partly because the very idea of being in between the two of them was very appealing. "Don't think my brother would be too happy about that idea."

He winked at me. "He's already gone home for the night. He doesn't hang out here much when they have a new baby. Which is basically all the time. They need all-hands-on-deck with their tribe."

We entered the clubhouse, and War went straight to the bar, reaching over the top of it and pulling a beer from a bucket of ice. He shook it off before handing it to me.

"Drink. Have fun. Like Psychos, whatever happens at a Slayers' party, stays at the Slayers' party. Nobody is going to tell your brother what you get up to here." He clinked his beer against mine.

A tingle of anticipation ran down my spine. The room was already full of people. Most were familiar, and a few I recognized from Psychos stopped me to say hello. Drinks flowed freely, and chatter surrounded me.

War made his way through the room, smiling at everyone and slapping their hands, but the whole time, his gaze kept drawing across the room, and when I followed it, I found Bliss watching him with a small smile on her face.

I waved to her, but she was fully focused on War heading her way. She moved her ample hips sensuously in time with the beat, and I wondered if she even had any idea how effortlessly sexy she was. Her hair was out, all wild waves of beautiful auburn, and Scythe stood at her back, his head lowered to kiss her neck while she sipped her drink.

She had her free hand resting on his thigh behind her, her thumb stroking over the denim of his jeans while she waited for War to get to them.

When he did, she tipped her head back and kissed him deeply, zero shame or awkwardness that she was kissing one man while another kissed her neck.

I glanced around the room, and nobody was staring at them. They all just went on with their conversations like it was completely normal for the three of them to be making out in the middle of the room.

A warm hand wrapped around my wrist, spinning me around, which was a relief because otherwise I probably would have stood there all night, mesmerized by a woman who looked like me being so worshipped by multiple men.

Memories of the night I'd had three men in my bed, taking turns at having me rushed through my head, mixing with the pleasant buzz from the alcohol.

"What are you thinking right now?" Levi asked.

I bit my lip. "Nothing."

He raised an eyebrow. "Your face says otherwise."

I laughed at him. "Fine, maybe it does. But I don't need to tell you my every thought."

He sat on a cracked leather couch and pulled me down beside him. "Fine. How about I ask you again after you've had a few more drinks?"

The corner of my lips lifted. The beer tasted good, and I didn't drink a lot so one was already having a pleasant, relaxing effect on me that I was eager to continue. "Ask me again later and I might have a different answer."

"A different answer to what?" Whip asked, sitting on the other side of me on the three-seater couch that had more than enough room for him, considering I was sitting so close to Levi that I was practically on his lap. Whip had two beers dangling from one hand, and he took the empty bottle out of mine and swapped it for a fresh one.

I blinked in surprise. I hadn't even realized how quickly I'd been drinking it, but I wasn't sorry. I'd had a seriously shit couple of weeks, and there was something about being behind solid iron gates, surrounded by dangerous men who wouldn't hurt me, that made me just want to let loose.

Maybe it was the rush of commanding that meeting and getting my own way. Maybe it was just pure and utter exhaustion from a constant work schedule, combined with grief and uncertainty.

And there was more of that to come.

I'd freaking offered myself up as bait for a madman.

That was just...great.

But tonight, I was just going to sit here, drink a few beers, and pretend my life was normal.

That felt like the best plan I'd had in years.

I took another sip before I answered Whip's question. "Levi asked me what I was thinking." I tapped the side of my head with my forefinger. "But my brain is off-limits to the two of you right now."

Whip settled back, twisting slightly so his body was angled more toward me. "Bet I can guess what you're thinking."

I grinned. "Doubt it."

"You're thinking about what a badass you were at that meeting earlier."

I laughed. "You didn't think I was a badass when I first showed up."

"Fair. You took me by surprise, and I don't ever want you getting hurt. But, sweetheart, you put me in my place." He shrugged. "Not gonna lie, I thought it was hot."

A smug smile of satisfaction but also one of appreciation for him settled on my lips. "Thank you. But that wasn't what I was thinking about."

"My guess then." Levi shifted forward a few inches to put his empty beer bottle down. "You were thinking about how beautiful you look."

I snorted on a laugh. "Yes, that's definitely it. I think that every single day. Especially the days I wake up with one boob escaping my tank top, my hair a mess, and yesterday's mascara still smudged beneath my eyes, panda style. Super sexy."

Levi coughed and took another sip of his beer. "Fuck."

Whip groaned. "That's definitely what I'm thinking about now. Jesus."

I shook my head. "Trust me, boys. That is not anything anyone wants to see."

Whip pointed the lip of his bottle at me. "Oh, I very much disagree."

"I'm with him," Levi added.

I was sure X would have made a joke about that.

But I let it go. "At least you agree on something," I said cheerfully. "You both agree you want to see me first thing in the morning. Maybe you both should?"

That was definitely the second beer talking.

Whip raised an eyebrow and took a sip of his drink. His perfect lips wrapped around the opening of the bottle, his throat bobbing as he swallowed. "You inviting us to spend the night with you, sweetheart?"

Something inside me clenched.

Levi let out a long, slow breath, his gaze stuck on me, waiting for my answer. "That really what you were thinking, Vi? You were thinking about the two of us taking you to bed tonight?"

Was I that obvious?

Except I knew I was. My gaze strayed back to War and Scythe and Bliss, who'd moved into the corner, behind the pool table. They were mostly in shadows, but they weren't deep enough to completely conceal what they were doing. Bliss's tits were out of her shirt, War's hands and mouth all over them. Scythe's fingers gripped her hips, and he rubbed up against her from behind.

The scene wasn't even unusual. It was still early, and there were plenty of people just standing or sitting around, talking like Levi, Whip, and I were.

But Grayson sat side by side with another man in a Slayers' jacket. Grayson had his woman on his lap, but it was the biker who had his hands under her skirt. She was trying to keep a straight face, but it was very clear to me that she was very much enjoying whatever he was doing beneath it.

She too was a bigger woman, with thick thighs and belly rolls she didn't try to cover up as Grayson stroked his hands across her midsection. There was a tenderness in his touch and she snaked a hand to rest at the back of his neck. She twisted, drawing him in for a kiss, while the biker watched, his hand still busily working her toward an orgasm they didn't seem to care that everyone was watching.

A rush of excitement filled me, seeing these women with stretchmarks, and heavy breasts that weren't perky, and arms that jiggled. They had men who adored them. Men who worshipped the very ground they walked on. There were body shapes of all kinds in this room. Some of the other women were older, some younger. Some skinny with fake tits that didn't move, and others with barely any. They were tall and short. Thick and not.

But the one thing that was obvious to me was that they were wanted here. Accepted. The men outnumbered the women three to one, easily. And hell, maybe some of them just wanted to get their dicks wet, and whoever they took that night would be nothing but a quick fuck, never to be repeated.

But the overwhelming feeling in the room was one of respect I wouldn't have expected from a biker club.

I suspected it was a tone War had begun by being with Bliss, the way he was. His strong leadership had created this space, where women felt safe to be open and vulnerable with their sexuality.

And the vibe was contagious.

I realized I hadn't even answered Levi's question about whether I wanted him and Whip to take me to bed tonight.

Both of them were still staring at me, waiting on an answer.

Nerves suddenly rocketed around my belly.

My gaze strayed over Levi's shoulder at Bliss and War and Scythe.

All three of them moved in unison. Both men thrusting into her at once, their hips rolling, her head dropped back on Scythe's shoulder, her fingers clutching War for support.

How did that even work? Was one in her ass and one in her pussy? Were they both in her pussy?

I knew how big both Whip and Levi were.

I doubted I could do either.

Levi leaned in and kissed my neck. "Talk to us."

Whip inched closer, his hand pressing against my thigh. The heat of it radiated through my skirt, and his thumb rubbed along the fabric, bunching it up a little with each stroke. It lifted higher and higher, until the hem was just above my knee and he was stroking my skin instead.

In terms of what else was going on in the room right now, this was tame. And yet I burned all over, both with desire for more and shock that I was letting two men touch me like this.

Whip's hand slid a little higher, inching between my thighs, teasing them open with slow, gentle movements. His gaze bored into mine, so I knew he could see the desire there, hear the shocked, shallow breaths.

"Tell me to stop," he urged.

My pussy throbbed, aching to have him move his hands just a few inches higher. "I can't," I admitted.

Levi's hand squeezed the thigh closest to him. "Then say you want it."

His finger brushed over my panties, and my breath hitched.

I was in the middle of a room full of people, and though I caught the glances of a few, nobody sat across from us to openly stare. This wasn't exactly like Psychos, where that sort of behavior was encouraged. Sex was definitely in the air here, and Bliss's moans from the corner charged the room with a sexual energy. But Queenie and Aloha were slow dancing to an old song, their arms wrapped around each other. Grayson and his partners were too involved with each other to notice what anyone else was doing. Others were coupled off, and there was a group of guys, clearly the ones who weren't lucky enough to have a woman between them tonight, sitting around a table, a very intense game of poker going on.

They'd clearly seen this sort of thing a million times before, because none of them blinked an eye.

Bliss, Scythe, and War having a full-blown threesome in the corner didn't feel odd or even like a spectacle.

It just felt...hot. And bold. And...

Free.

That was a heady feeling, one I wanted for myself so badly. I was so sick of twisting myself into knots, wrestling with guilt over everything I did, wondering if I was embarrassing myself or if people were staring at me. I had always hated how tall I was, how thick. It drew attention I didn't want. Made me stick out of a crowd when I just wanted to blend in.

But here, with a few beers swirling in my system and

danger looming on the horizon, I couldn't care about any of that.

There was a high probability of me dying before I even had the chance to really live. It was just fact. I no longer felt like I was going to live forever. Toby's death had put a big fucking dent in that notion.

If I was going to be bait to draw out this freak playing games with us, then I was going to fucking enjoy the time I had left.

I spread my thighs a little wider and lifted one hand to the side of Levi's face, making sure I was looking him in the eye. "I want it."

He groaned into my neck and slid his fingers that inch higher, tucking them beneath the elastic of my panties and stroking over my bare pussy.

Instantly, pleasure erupted there, and I wanted to close my eyes and sink into it. But I covered Whip's hand, dragging it up to meet Levi's. "I want you both."

I knew that this would play over in my mind once I was sober. I would probably be embarrassed and awkward, dying on the inside that I had been so bold and obvious. My foster mother's condescending voice in my head scoffed and laughed at me for thinking I, a fat woman, could have two beautiful men want me.

My stomach suddenly lurched as her voice filled my head with taunts about how every person in this room thought I was fat and ugly and making a fool out of myself.

Whip's voice cut through all the noise. "Thank fuck." His fingers slid higher. "Because all I can think about is how much I want to make you feel good. Just open your legs and let us."

Levi pulled my thigh over his leg and drew my panties to one side.

Whip pushed two thick fingers straight inside me, filling the ache I so desperately needed filled.

"Oh!"

I tried to keep my cry quiet, so I wasn't drawing the attention of the entire room, but Levi was in my ear, whispering the reassurances he didn't know I needed while he held my panties between two fingers and rubbed my clit with a third. "Do you have any idea how beautiful you are, Violet?"

I shook my head, not because I was being coy and just wanted compliments.

But because I wanted to believe him, and I just didn't. How could I? I'd never had anyone treat me like he did.

Like *they* did.

I still mostly didn't believe him or Whip or X were even real. Some part of me was just waiting to wake up from the dirtiest, most detailed dream I'd ever had in my life and go straight back to watching *Grey's Anatomy* on the couch with Toby.

But Levi felt so damn real. So warm. His fingers on my clit were perfection.

And yet the doubts in my head never stopped. "I'm fat. Not beautiful."

Whip paused, his fingers still buried inside me. "I fucking hate that you think you can't be both."

I blinked at him.

He leaned in and kissed me so damn hard I was sure my lips would be bruised tomorrow. His tongue demanded entrance, taking what he wanted, spinning my head in the process, his fingers finding the spot inside me that electrified my body.

I gasped, but his mouth swallowed the noise. He pushed me further, he and Levi now working together, their fingers moving in time, stroking, rubbing, sliding through my folds, taking me higher, driving me toward the edge.

Whip's lips slipped from my mouth, dragging along my jaw to the soft skin beneath my ear. "You're so fucking beautiful, Violet. You can be both."

His words broke something inside me.

He wasn't telling me I wasn't fat. I hated when people did that. I wasn't blind. I knew that I was.

Whip was acknowledging what all of us already knew.

And telling me I was beautiful anyway.

It was the sexiest thing I'd ever heard in my life, and it was his words in my ear more than their fingers between my legs that pushed me over the edge.

When I went, I fell hard, my head tipping back, brain spinning, entire body convulsing around their fingers.

Shit, were they finger fucking me together?

The realization sent me into another shock wave of pleasure, until the room around me blurred and the people in it disappeared.

"Fuck…"

I was vaguely aware of Levi groaning.

"I need you naked, Vi. Need to see every fucking inch of you the next time we make you come."

I couldn't even respond. I was completely boneless, blissed-out, riding the high of the orgasm wave all the way to the shore because it was one of the best I'd ever had.

When Levi lifted me off the couch, I didn't even freak out over the fact he was carrying me.

I didn't protest about how much I weighed.

I just reveled in the knowledge that he could. That he wanted to.

And that I could be both fat and wanted.

24

WHIP

*L*evi going all caveman and picking Violet up and carrying her to his room shouldn't have been as hot as it was.

But fuck, it was.

I tried really freaking hard not to notice the flex of his biceps or the way the muscles across his back and shoulders rippled as he carried her down the hallway.

My fingers were still wet from Violet's pussy, and I could barely think about the way he'd slid his fingers inside her, joining them with mine, until we'd sent her into an orgasm. Both two fingers deep in her sweetness.

My dick was so hard.

Bliss caught my eye from the other side of the pool table, her men still all over her but a soft smile on her face for me. She jerked her head toward the hallway Levi and Violet had disappeared down. "Go!" she mouthed.

I grabbed another beer from the ice bucket on the bar and headed down the hallway after them, ignoring the offered high fives from some of the younger club guys who played poker at the table. I moved past the closed bedroom doors, mentally kicking myself for getting distracted watching Levi walk away and not following instantly, because now I had no idea which one was his room.

If I had to knock on all of them to find them, I would, but that would be awkward.

I doubted the bikers who had taken women to their rooms already would appreciate me asking for fucking directions to my threesome.

But I stopped dead in an open doorway.

Realizing Levi had left it open for me.

He already had her laid out on the bed beneath him, her thick thighs wrapped around his middle. They were both fully clothed but grinding against each other slowly, their kisses deep and so erotic I just leaned against the door and cracked the top on my beer, taking slow swallows while I watched them.

"You in, or you out?" Levi growled after a moment, seemingly pissed off that he had to lift his mouth from Violet's to even ask me.

I stepped in, kicking the door closed behind me as my answer.

But I couldn't stop watching them together. He hadn't pulled back the sheets, he'd just laid her straight down on the comforter. The bed wasn't big, and it was old enough that it creaked beneath their weight, the sound as rhythmic as the rocking of their bodies.

I dragged out the desk chair and straddled it backward so my elbows had somewhere to rest. I sipped my beer again, enjoying the buzz of alcohol not nearly as much as the two of them making out.

Levi reared back on his knees, yanking his shirt off.

I bit back a groan at the ridiculously chiseled body he had beneath.

I was sure I'd look like that too, if I'd spent six years with nothing better to do than work out. But fucking hell, there was no denying how cut he was. How big. How the muscles across his abs were impossible to deny, and the V lines running either side of his hips were like flashing neon signs, leading the way to the good stuff beneath his pants.

My heart stopped at the sight of the tattoo over his heart.

A tattoo he'd clearly gotten for her.

The rush of something came over me. Maybe shock, because until that moment, I wasn't sure I'd actually truly comprehended the depth of how much he cared for her.

Maybe disappointment, because yet again, this felt like the Levi and Violet show.

That they were what was meant to be, and I was just getting in the way.

As much as I wanted them, it was clear they wanted each other.

"Whip," Violet moaned, reaching a hand for me. She dragged her mouth away from Levi's, and her gaze connected with me.

Something passed between us.

Something I couldn't walk away from.

So when she whispered, "Please," even though I knew it was going to burn when she chose him over me, I went.

As long as she wanted me, I would always keep going.

The realization hit me hard. There was only one other woman I had ever felt like this for.

And when she'd died, it had nearly fucking killed me.

Yet, I couldn't ignore the damn magnetic force that drew me toward that bed, the connection I felt with Violet so strong it eclipsed any rational thought. I set my nearly finished beer down on the bedside table and pulled off my shirt. I yanked at the laces on my boots, loosening them until I could toe them off along with my socks.

Levi pushed Violet's shirt up, exposing her belly and bra. With greedy hands, he lifted the shirt over her head and drew the bra straps down her shoulders. He didn't even bother sitting her up so he could undo the clasps, just flipped the cups down and lowered his mouth to her nipple, sucking one into his mouth, squeezing the other between his forefinger and thumb.

He worked her tits, but it was me she reached for, wanting more.

Her fingers undid the button on my jeans and lowered the zipper.

I shoved them down my legs and sucked in a breath when her fingers found the edge of my underwear and removed them as well, freeing my cock.

I didn't miss Levi's gaze straying from Violet's tits to watch me kneel on the mattress near her head.

We both watched her stroke me, her velvet-soft hands wandering over the hardened length of my erection. I was already so ready for her, but it was a torturous sort of pleasure, having her touch me slow, having her test the way her hands could make me move.

Until she drew me in, dick first, so she licked the tip of me.

I braced myself on the wall, leaning over her so she could take my dick in her mouth.

Levi gave us room, moving down between her legs, taking off the skirt and panties I'd wanted to rip off her earlier.

I wanted to watch him go down on her. Wanted to see his tongue flick on her clit and then drive into her channel, but all I could concentrate on was the wet warmth of her mouth around my cock.

She stared up at me, the tip of me bobbing in and out, but the angle had my dick pressing against her cheek instead of the back of her throat so she could only take shallow thrusts.

And I wanted so much more than just the tip of me inside her.

I straddled her chest, pinning her arms beneath my shins. She lifted her head so I could put a pillow beneath it, and settled back, all her beautiful light-colored hair spreading around her like a goddamn halo.

How she had ever thought she wasn't beautiful was beyond me. Her eyelashes were so dark and long, framing the prettiest eyes I'd ever seen. Her cheeks were full, her face rounded. The pink blush that was so often present on her cheeks was now flush across every inch of her skin.

I braced myself on the headboard, and this time when I thrust into her mouth, she could take so much more of me.

"Good girl," I murmured, staring down at her, watching inches of my dick disappear into her mouth, only to come out wet and shiny from being pressed to her tongue. "You're taking it so well."

She moaned around me, the vibrations so sweet my balls clenched.

I allowed myself to go a little faster, a little harder, thrusting into her mouth until the leash I kept myself on was ready to snap.

Her moans of encouragement didn't help.

Though maybe the noises she was making were more courtesy of what Levi was doing between her legs.

Fuck. I didn't want to come in her mouth. I wanted to feel that perfect pussy clench and pulse around me.

I pulled out before I could come, breathing hard, giving myself a break to get my shit under control. I got behind her, lifting her so she was sitting.

Levi raised his head from between her thighs, his lips glistening with her arousal. He kissed her hard, grabbing the back of her neck and slamming his mouth down on hers, making her taste herself on his tongue.

She didn't seem to mind. She crawled forward onto her knees, and he mirrored, the two of them now kneeling on the bed, his arms wrapped around her while they kissed, hers dragging down his pants to free his erection.

I leaned on the headboard and picked up my beer from the bedside table, taking a long swallow while I watched them, because if I so much as even thought about my own dick right now, I knew I would come.

I didn't want to. Not yet. I wasn't done playing with her.

Or done watching him.

He grabbed two handfuls of her ass, fingers kneading and molding her cheeks, dragging her closer to him, until he settled on his ass.

She instantly spread her legs, straddling him, and sank down on his cock.

They both shouted at the fast engulfing of his dick.

Jealousy surged inside me, but I knew if that had been me, I would have come instantly and then this would have been over.

I didn't want it to be over. I didn't want them to realize she was just as in love with him as he was with her. I didn't want Levi to storm off again and pretend there wasn't some sort of fucking chemistry between us that had me wanting his body as much as I wanted hers.

I'd walked away from hundreds of naked, warm, willing bodies over the years and never thought anything of it.

But walking away from the two of them didn't feel possible.

So I sat there, watching them move together, watching them kiss, watching them fuck, and drank my beer.

God, they looked good together. Levi's tattooed arms a stark, dark contrast to Violet's unmarked skin. He dragged his hands up and down her back, pushing them up into her hair, and pulling it, tilting her head back to give him better access to her throat. He licked and kissed his way across it while she rode him, her rounded ass rising and falling as she impaled herself on him over and over.

It wasn't long before he was demanding her lips again though, and together they fell back on the mattress, kissing wildly, her chest pressed against his.

It gave me the best fucking view of her ass, and every

time she rose off him, I caught a glimpse of his thick, glistening cock, her pussy stretched around it.

She trailed her lips off his mouth and buried her face in his neck.

His gaze skated down her back and straight onto me.

Neither of us turned away. Violet moaned and writhed between us, but the heat between Levi and me was just as scalding.

"Fuck," I groaned, kneeling.

I wanted in.

In her.

In him.

Fuck.

The drink in my hand felt like the only thing grounding me. It was almost empty, only a few mouthfuls left. I had no idea what possessed me to do it, but I rolled the lip of the bottle along Violet's spine.

She moaned at the touch of something new, and my dick got way too fucking excited.

And my brain got way too fucking dirty.

I tipped the bottle up, letting a tiny bit of cold, amber liquid trickle onto her skin.

She gasped, then moaned when my warm tongue was there to lick it away.

So I kept going, dribbling liquid down her spine and tonguing it off, getting lower and lower, until the last few mouthfuls of beer trickled in between her ass cheeks.

The moan she let out when I followed the tiny river I'd made was the most satisfying noise I'd ever heard.

"Whip! Oh my God, you can't..." Heat radiated from her skin.

"I can't what, sweetheart? Tongue fuck your ass?" I

chuckled. "Yeah. I can. And I'm going to until you beg me not to stop."

If she'd been going to complain, she had stopped real fucking quick.

Levi's eye caught mine, and there was a fire in them I'd never seen before, but I couldn't keep my eyes on him when I was too busy making sure Violet knew how good anal could be if you did it with someone who knew what they were doing.

I flicked my tongue against her tight rear hole.

Her moans satisfied something deep inside my chest.

But my dick ached, dying to get in on the action.

She wasn't ready for that yet. She ground back against my face, losing herself to the pleasure, and I slid a finger inside her opening.

She paused for a moment, but this wasn't the first time she'd taken this much. She moved again, almost as quickly as she'd stopped. "More," she groaned.

I had no idea if she meant more of me or more of Levi. But it was damn hard not to line my cock up with her entrance and give her both of us.

But I refused to go too fast and hurt her. I was big. A lot bigger than a finger or an ass plug. She needed to take one of those before I could even think about giving her my cock.

Without a word, though like he was having the same thoughts, Levi jerked his head toward the bedside table I'd had my beer resting on. I opened it, hoping for a plug.

The thought of Levi jerking his cock in here alone, working a plug in his free hand, nearly had me coming on the spot.

But of course, Mister I'm Not into Guys didn't have a shiny silver plug sitting in his drawer.

But there was a tube of lube.

I plucked it up, squirting a dollop of it between Violet's cheeks and rubbing it in with my fingers.

"Oh God," she moaned. "Whip. Fuck me. Please."

I shook my head. "Not yet, sweetheart. Soon. But I gotta make sure you can take me there."

She panted and moaned, fighting the grip Levi had on her hips.

She wanted to be fucked fast. I could see it in the strain of her muscles. She was close to coming, and she wanted to get over the line.

But Levi and I were both on the same page. He still had his cock buried deep in her pussy, but he was clearly getting off on drawing this out as much as I was. He'd slowed her right down, so she was full of him, but she wasn't getting the friction she needed to come.

Not yet anyway.

I was about to push a second lubed up finger into her ass, but the empty beer bottle that had fallen onto the mattress stopped me.

The narrow opening and gradually widening neck was not entirely unlike the plug I'd been hoping to find in Levi's drawer.

Precum wept from my tip, my cock desperate to be the one inside that opening I'd widened with my fingers.

But the bottle was a good in-between.

And suddenly all I could think about was fucking her with it.

I picked it up and dragged it down her spine again.

But this time I didn't stop. I drew it between her ass cheeks, coating it in the lubricant I'd squirted there.

She froze.

I nudged it against her hole. "Trust me," I whispered.

"I do," she murmured back.

A sick sense of satisfaction rolled through me at the complete and utter honesty in her voice. She was such a fucking good girl, and she clearly liked being directed in bed.

And I liked bossing her around.

Liked that she didn't fight me, the way Levi did.

Though even he wasn't fighting me for once. We were instinctively working together, making sure this was all about Violet.

I ran my hand along her spine, guiding her back down onto Levi.

"Kiss her," I demanded.

He shot me a dirty look over her shoulder, clearly pissed I was bossing him around too, and the corner of my mouth flickered in amusement.

Because for all the big, hardened, ex-prisoner was complaining, he did what I said, putting one hand to the back of Violet's neck and drawing her down toward his mouth again. He whispered words of encouragement to her, until she fell down on his lips, the two of them reconnecting there, while his cock was still buried deep in her pussy.

But neither of them moved, other than their mouths.

Violet's sweet, curvy, dimpled ass was right there, open to me, just begging to be filled.

I nudged the tip of the bottle inside, unable to take my eyes off her body as she took it so easily.

She was into this. *So* fucking into it.

But I went gently and slowly anyway, giving her tiny little movements, stroking her insides with the smooth glass of the bottle, edging more and more of it inside her and watching her ass stretch around the gradually widening neck.

"Ohh," she moaned on Levi's lips. She turned her head, so I saw her eyes roll back. "Oh, God!"

"That's it, baby," Levi murmured, slowly starting to grind beneath her again. "Just relax. Let us do all the work."

Her legs trembled around him, and he started up a slow thrust in and out of her pussy. I matched it with the bottle, obsessed with training her ass to take more and more of it, and faster and faster, until my thrusts were just as fast and deep as his.

I found my dick with my free hand, pumping it in time, all three of us in unison. My fingers were still slick with lube, and I thrust into them, needing the fucking release that was building so deep inside me it felt like it was strangling my balls.

"Whip!" she shouted. "I need to come!"

I was a greedy asshole, but I wanted that orgasm on my cock. And she was taking so much of that bottle I knew she could take me just as well.

"I want to fuck your ass, sweetheart. Tell me I can."

"Yes! Oh God, yes!"

The bottle fell to the floor, bouncing off the carpet and rolling away under the bed.

And I replaced it with my dick, sliding inside her as gently as I could but groaning hard when I bottomed out, because of the way she thrust back against me.

Her scream of pleasure ripped through the room. Her orgasm squeezed my cock tight, and there was zero hanging on for either me or Levi. Both of us had been on edge since the moment we'd walked in here, and I could tell from the agonized look on his face that he was battling for control just as bad as I was.

But Violet coming meant the two of us could let go as well.

I came hard, thrusting into her ass, trying to be gentle but probably giving her too much for her first time. But I couldn't stop, her moans of pleasure fueling me, urging me on, telling me she wanted this just as much as I did.

And so I let go of everything.

Let go and just let myself feel whatever it was I felt.

I was still feeling it when, completely spent, I got off the bed, grabbed my clothes, and got the hell out of that room, the door slamming behind me.

25

LEVI

*V*iolet sat up, still impaled on my softening cock, her eyes huge. She stared at the door Whip had just slammed behind him, and then gazed down at me. "Did I do something wrong?"

She covered her tits with one arm, suddenly self-conscious, the other hand grappling for the sheets.

A hot rage filled me. I bucked my hips, flipping her down onto the mattress and kissing her mouth hard. "You are fucking perfect. He's what's wrong."

I pulled out of her with a groan and grabbed my pants.

"Where are you going?" She tucked herself into the sheet.

"To ask him what the hell his problem is!"

"Levi! You don't need to—"

But I was already storming out of the room, barefoot, trying to do my pants up as I went.

Everyone still left in the common room looked up as I crashed through it, all eyes on me. I did a quick glance around the room, searching for Whip. But I already knew he wouldn't just be there, hanging out and drinking beers.

He'd left the room like he wanted to be anywhere else.

I ran for the door, and once I was outside, I hooked right, knowing he'd be headed for the gates, his car on the other side of them.

"Whip!"

He stiffened, his form barely visible in the dark night. The road to the gates wasn't lit, but the light from the clubhouse and a full moon helped.

"Go back to Violet," Whip said quietly. "I'm going home."

I ran along the path, not exactly sure why, just knowing it pissed me off that he was walking out like Violet was one of his clients he could just fuck and then leave.

Like *I* was one of his clients he could fuck and then leave.

Even though I was acutely aware it was exactly what I'd done to him after I'd blown him in X's bedroom.

I didn't care. The two of us hurting each other was one thing. Hurting Violet was a different story altogether.

"Whip!" I ignored the rocks stabbing at the soles of my feet. "Fucking hell, would you just stop for a second?"

He didn't, but maybe he slowed, because I caught him, grabbing his arm, spinning him back to face me.

We both breathed hard, me from the run, him from I didn't know what.

We were so fucking close our breaths mingled.

"What the fuck was that?" I forced my brain to make

coherent words, even though being this close to him did things to me that made it really hard to concentrate.

His voice was low and sharp, with a strong hint of bitterness. "It was sex, Levi. Get over it."

"Get over it?" I reared back, blinking at him. "I'm not going to fucking get over it. You just walk out without a word? She's in there asking me what she did wrong. What the fuck am I supposed to tell her?"

The clubhouse door banged open again, but neither of us turned back to see who it was.

Whip shook his head. "She didn't do anything wrong. Go tell her that. Fuck. She did everything right. Too fucking right." He ran his fingers through his already mussed-up hair. "I need to go."

Maybe it was the alcohol.

Maybe it was the way I hadn't been able to keep my eyes off him while he'd been inside her. Watching him fuck, watching him lose control...I'd been jealous of Violet in that moment. Jealous of his hands on her body. Jealous of the time he'd taken with her, building her up, always concentrating on her.

All I'd been able to think about was what it would feel like to have his hands and attention all on me.

To trust him with my body the way Violet had trusted him with hers.

Now I was fucking glad I hadn't, since apparently, he could fuck like that and then just walk on out like it hadn't meant anything.

"You're such an asshole," I swore at him. "What the hell is your problem?"

His fist connected with my face so fast and hard I didn't even have time to react. I stumbled back, surprise hitting me just as abruptly as his fist had. The force of it threw me into a soft body behind me. On instinct, I grabbed her, steadying us both so I didn't take her down with me.

But I didn't understand any of this.

Since when did Whip lose control like that?

I hadn't even seen Violet come out of the clubhouse. But she was there, wrapped in nothing but the sheet from my bed.

"What the hell, Whip?" Her gaze ran all over me. "Are you all right?"

I gave a curt nod, though one side of my face where his fist had connected throbbed. But I'd had worse. I was fine, apart from a burning need to punch Whip in the dick for being such a cunt all of a sudden.

But I didn't get a chance. Because Violet was all over him, her anger palpable.

She turned blazing eyes in his direction. "You're punching him now? What are you doing?"

He swore, his regret was written all over his face. He threw his hands up. "I don't know. Okay? I don't know!"

She was a bigger person than I was because something instantly softened in her. It took me a few seconds longer, but the anguish in his voice, and the way he tugged at his hair, eventually got to me too.

He scrubbed his hands over his eyes. "I don't know."

Violet stepped in, pulling his hands away and peering up at him. "What did I do wrong?"

That got him. He stopped and cupped both sides of her face. "Nothing. Absolutely nothing. This is all me, not you. You..." He sighed. "Fuck, Violet. You are so fucking perfect."

"I'm not, or you wouldn't be running away from me right now."

He groaned, dragging her in tighter. "It's not you—"

"Yes, it is," she cut in. "I've heard the 'it's not you, it's me' speech a thousand times. I know it's me."

He kissed her fiercely, claiming her lips so passionately I felt like I was intruding and had to look away.

"It's not you," he said again. "It's how much I want you. And how much it's going to kill me when you pick him."

I lifted my head, my gaze meeting his.

Violet opened her mouth and tried to answer, but Whip shook his head.

"I had a wife once. Two kids. A family. A normal life." He sucked in a deep breath, trying to continue, even though it was clearly agony for him. "People I cared about. And when I lost them, I died too."

Violet didn't say anything. Just stared up at him, her fingers wrapped tight around his, like that might keep him from running away again.

"What happened to them?" I asked bluntly.

He stared at me, his eyes broken. "A drunk driver hit our car one night when we were on our way home from my son's Little League game. It was barely five in the evening, and this guy was six sheets to the wind." He swallowed hard. "Car flipped. The three of them were killed. I walked away without a scratch."

My stomach sank, twisting with a sick feeling of regret and sorrow and pain.

Violet's gasp was only muffled by the way she clapped her hand over her mouth. "Whip..."

I shoved my fingers into my pockets. "Shit. I didn't know..."

Whip lifted a shoulder. "Nobody does. First rule of murder squad. No personal details, right?" He laughed bitterly. "Except I screwed that up. Kissing you. Fucking around with you. I kept blurring the line, and now I've crossed so far over it I can't even see it."

He gazed down at Violet. "I just can't do this again. It hurts too fucking much. You love Levi. You have since the day I met you. Whatever we just did...it's only going to end in both of us getting hurt. And that's the last thing I want for you." He gave her a tight smile and tucked her hair behind her ear.

He let her go and stepped back toward the gates again.

Suddenly, I was really fucking scared that if I let him walk through them, then I might never see him again.

"What if she didn't have to choose?" I blurted out.

They both stared at me.

But it was Whip who saw through it first. "What if Violet didn't have to choose?" He swallowed hard. "Or what if you didn't?"

His words hit deep. Too fucking deep, in a place I wasn't ready to fully admit to. I didn't know what I wanted from Whip.

All I knew was I didn't want him to walk away.

That it might end me if he disappeared in the night, and I didn't know where he was or if he was okay.

Fuck.

I didn't know how to say any of that. My tongue felt ten sizes too big for my mouth, and I couldn't get out the words.

Violet took pity on me. "It's late. We've been drinking. Nobody is going anywhere tonight." She swallowed hard. "Nobody has to choose anything right now. I need you both. Tomorrow, or next week, or sometime soon, I'm going to be offered up on a platter for a psychopath. But for tonight, I'd really like to forget about that and sleep knowing I don't have to keep one eye open."

She stared up at Whip, clearly already knowing I wasn't going anywhere. "Please stay. I don't want you to leave."

His resolve crumpled. "Okay, sweetheart. Whatever you want." He put his arm around her neck, drawing her into him, breathing deep the scent of her hair.

They walked back toward me and the clubhouse.

I readied myself to trail behind them, following them back inside.

But Violet, with her sheet tucked in on itself so she didn't have to hold it up, caught my wrist as they passed, her fingers sliding down, palm pressing against mine until we were holding hands.

That's how we returned to the clubhouse. Whip's arm around her. Her fingers wrapped around mine.

A public declaration that nobody was choosing anything.

At least not tonight.

I woke to the creaking of the bed, my back smushed up against the wall but Violet's soft, curvy, very naked body curled up in front of me. I snaked a hand around her belly, barely awake, but my fingers heading straight down to cup her pussy.

She moaned in her sleep, and without even opening my eyes, I massaged her clit.

"Are you leaving?" she asked.

"Are you insane?" I mumbled into her shoulder, inhaling the scent of her skin. "I'm not going anywhere."

"She meant me."

I cracked open an eye to see Whip off the bed and putting on his clothes. "Oh. You."

He rolled his eyes but leaned down, sinking his palms into the mattress so he and Violet were face-to-face.

Though how he could keep his eyes off her exposed tits and the sheet slipping down her thighs so I could get my fingers in between them was beyond me.

"I've got some things I need to sort out this morning," he told her.

She swallowed hard. "Do you have a client?"

I paused my assault on her clit, waiting to hear his answer.

"No. I've cleared my schedule for the next week."

I let out a sigh of relief I didn't deserve. It was bad enough I got jealous watching Violet touch him. I was going to give myself an aneurism if I let myself think about his clients all over him.

The vision of other women, other men, trailing their hands all over his body, wrapping their fingers and mouths around his cock had me suddenly wanting to punch holes in the wall.

But I took a deep breath, pressing my mouth down on Violet's shoulder so I didn't say something stupid.

Like begging him to get back into bed and start fucking my ass the way he had with Violet last night.

The thought was so fleeting and hot it seared.

The part of me that was still firmly clinging to being a complete virgin when it came to guys quickly dumped a bucket of cold water over me.

As if to prove the fact, my morning wood found its way between Violet's thick thighs, searching for her entrance.

Like I needed it to prove I was still straight.

Fucking hell, I was so not straight. Straight men didn't lie here, getting as turned on by his body as I was by hers.

He needed to put a fucking shirt on.

"Levi."

He also needed to stop saying my name, because even his voice got me going.

"What?" I snapped at him, instantly regretting it because it wasn't his fault I was having a midlife crisis. Or a bi awakening. Or whatever the hell this was.

Was I into all guys now?

No.

Just him.

Fabulous.

Whip seemed like he was going to say something different, but the harshness in my tone had him shaking his head. "Fuck her good."

I nodded, knowing that hadn't been what he was going to say at all, but I'd ruined it by being a dickhead.

He kissed Violet goodbye. "I'm going to go find X and check on him. Make sure he got rid of that body."

She put a hand up on his cheek, holding him to her, making the second kiss last longer. "Thank you."

He nodded and walked out of my room, closing the door behind him.

I rolled Violet onto her back and covered her body with mine. She spread her legs instantly for me, and I settled there, my hips against hers, dick sliding through her wet folds and gently inside her.

Her fingers traced over my chest while I warmed my dick inside her, not thrusting, just needing to connect with her.

There were so many things we needed to talk about. But just being inside her, staring down at her was enough for now.

Until Whip brought X back, there was no point thinking about what we had agreed to let Violet do. That was a plan for the four of us to come up with together.

Her fingers traced over the tattoo of her name. Her voice turned breathy with something that sounded like amazement. "That's my name on your chest, Levi. In permanent ink."

I caught her hand, holding it over the artwork I'd etched into my skin for her. "That's your name on my heart. And it was already there, long before I inked it."

Her eyes watered.

"I'm in love with you, Violet," I admitted softly. "So fucking in love I can barely breathe when you aren't around. I always have been. I fell in love with you with every letter you wrote. Every word." I touched my lips to hers. "I know Whip said last night he can't lose you. But fuck, Vi, neither can I."

A tear rolled silently down her cheek.

I brushed it away. "Don't cry."

She smiled. "I'm not. I'm happy." She pressed up, kissing me back. "I love you too, Levi. I always have."

A vise I hadn't realized was around my chest suddenly freed me from its grip, and I felt like I could take a deep breath for the first time in months.

Maybe years.

I buried my face in her neck, kissing her there, moving slowly inside her, not an inch of space between us as me warming my dick turned into making love to her.

It was soft and gentle, her staring up at me, quiet moans on her lips that I kissed away or replaced with my own. Her body melded to mine, until we fit perfectly together, both of us building the other up into an orgasm, me holding mine off until she was ready to come with me.

There was no screaming each other's names. No wild bucking of hips or slapping of thighs.

It was just gentle whispers from my lips, promising her over and over again I loved her and I always would.

And her promising the same in return.

There was no going back. No changing my mind. She was mine. Maybe she was Whip's and X's as well, but it didn't matter, because loving her was all I wanted. And that meant giving her whatever she needed.

If she needed them too, then that's what I'd give her.

"Levi," she whispered. "What are you doing at this club? Your art…"

I shrugged. "The club is what I know."

"But not what makes you happy."

Wasn't that the truth. I loved my brothers. But I was too fucking old for them to be my whole world. Especially when the woman beneath me had wholeheartedly stolen that position.

What I wanted was that little house with a picket fence and sure, a motorcycle in the driveway.

But my woman and our kids inside.

And my art on the walls.

And on her skin.

"I want to tattoo," I admitted. I followed the lines of her body with my palms. "Fuck, what I wouldn't give to mark up all this pretty virgin skin with a tattoo gun."

She smiled. "Do it."

I laughed at her. "Do it? You're just going to let me draw all over you in permanent ink? What if I draw X's face right in the middle of your back?"

She laughed, and the sound was sweet. "He'd probably love that, and I would congratulate you on your realistic portrait skills."

I grinned and moved my hand between us, cupping her sweet, bare pussy. "What if I tattooed you here?"

"What would you put there?"

I answered in a heartbeat without even thinking about it. "My name."

She moaned. "Do it."

But that was so permanent, and in a place on her body that was so intimate. "You'll have to ask me a lot more times than once for me to do that to you."

"How many times do I have to ask?"

I shrugged. "At least three."

She opened her mouth. "Tattoo—"

I stopped her lips with my finger. "At least a week apart."

She pouted. "I could just get Dax to do it."

My gaze darkened. "If you want me to fucking kill him, then sure, you could ask him."

She laughed, leaning up to kiss me again. "I'm joking! Nobody is tattooing my pussy except for you."

I groaned, wishing she hadn't said that. Because now it was all I was going to think about. Fucking hell, I had a tattoo gun right there in the damn drawer. I could do it right now, claim her with my name in permanent ink.

But then I wouldn't be able to go down on her.

And that seemed like a pretty good consolation prize. So instead of arguing, I put my mouth where I really fucking hoped I would one day get to put my name.

26

VIOLET

When it hit midmorning and I hadn't heard from either X or Whip, I started to get worried.

I paced the length of Levi's bedroom and tried calling, but both their phones went straight to voicemail. Whip's was very professional, clearly stating his legal name and he'd get back to me promptly.

X's personal phone didn't give his name but did say: *Hey, I can't come to the phone right now because I'm duct taped to a ceiling fan. I'll call you back when I stop spinning.*

I glanced at Levi hopefully. "Can I call their squad phones? Grayson gave me the numbers last night." Admittedly, it had been grudgingly, but he had eventually handed them over. "I'm worried. And I really think we need to talk about the plan."

He shook his head and kissed me instead. "You want to call their squad phones because their girlfriend hasn't heard from them in a few hours and wants to discuss making herself bait for a psychopath? I don't think that counts as an emergency."

I sighed because he was right. He'd explained to me how their group phones were sacred and that using them meant business.

But I kind of liked the sound of him calling me their girlfriend.

Which of course was actually ridiculous when I'd just spent half the night whispering I love yous to Levi.

I couldn't be doing that with him, and then in the space of hours, preening on the inside over being Whip's and X's girlfriend too.

But Bliss did. Kara did. Rebel did. All three of them had multiple partners, and not one of them seemed to be questioning their life choices like I was. They were just enjoying the benefits.

But I couldn't imagine walking down the street with three men. What would date night look like? Me, sandwiched between the three of them in a café booth, or making out with all of them in the back row of the movies?

And why did the idea of both seem so appealing?

At least it did until I started thinking about what the people outside these clubhouse walls would think.

I knew exactly what my foster mother would have said.

Slut.

Whore.

Any other derogatory word she could have come up with.

Hell, she'd called me those things when I was a virgin too. Every time I'd even turned in the direction of my foster dad, she'd called me a little ho. It was where I'd learned to keep my eyes on the floor.

Levi watched me pace from the bed, and on what was probably my hundredth lap, he caught my hand. He leaned over and found a motorcycle helmet beneath his bedframe and pushed it toward me. "Put that on. Let's go for a ride."

I hesitated. "We should wait for them to get back. The plan—"

"You're going to wear a hole in the already pretty threadbare carpet if you keep pacing like that. Us sitting here isn't going to get them back any faster. And we can't talk about any sort of plan without them."

I still hesitated.

He raised an eyebrow. "It's either that or I spend the rest of the day going down on you."

I laughed. "You say that like it's a punishment."

"It will be when I don't let you come." He smirked, but it settled into something gentler. "Put the helmet on. I fucked you so many times last night and this morning, you have gotta be sore."

I had to admit, I was. But I didn't regret a single thing I'd done. The two of them...the things they'd done to my body, and then Levi again this morning, telling me he loved me...I was going to remember every second of that for the rest of my life.

The gentle throb of my pussy, reminding me how well it had been used, was nothing to complain about.

But maybe it could use a break.

Though straddling a vibrating motorcycle and wrapping my arms around Levi's thick midsection to feel up his abs while we rode didn't exactly seem like giving the old vajajay a breather, but whatever.

I took the helmet and tugged it on. "Let's go."

When I'd gotten on the back of Levi's bike, I'd expected a cruise down the bluff road that ran along the beach and connected Saint View to Providence. Or maybe in the other direction, to the city.

But Levi took the road that led into the center of Saint View.

It wasn't exactly much of a drive, and it certainly wasn't picturesque. The main strip that ran through Saint View was as dingy as it ever was.

But Levi stopped the bike outside Saint View Tattoo, and a tiny bit of smug satisfaction curled through me. I waited until he'd turned the engine off and then said in his ear, "You changed your mind about Dax tattooing me then?"

He twisted and pulled me forward by the chin strap on my open-face helmet. He kissed my mouth. "Not a fucking chance is that man looking at your pussy after I spent all morning pounding it."

I laughed. "Charming. Why are we here, then?"

Levi sucked in a breath. "I'm going to ask him for a job."

I widened my eyes. "Really?"

He nodded, even though he looked a little green. "Apparently." He stared up at the tattoo shop like it might suddenly grow teeth and snatch a bite out of him. "Shit. This seemed like a good idea at the time."

I shoved him toward the door. "It's a great idea. The worst he can say is no, right? But what if he says yes?" Excitement lit up inside me for him. I had no idea what I wanted to do with my life. I doubted I wanted to clean for the rest of my days.

But Levi knew.

At least his heart did. He'd sent me hundreds of drawings over the last year, each one better than the last. Art was his calling, and watching him realize that, and now actually follow through filled me with a pride and joy I'd really only felt for Toby in the past.

But I liked the way it felt. And it made me want to find that thing that lit me up the way art did with Levi.

I pulled him toward the door, my heart racing, suddenly as nervous as if I was asking for my dream job.

I wanted this for him so bad.

A bell above the door tinkled when we went in, and it was probably a good thing, because if it hadn't I wasn't sure Dax, with Nyah grinding on his lap, would have even noticed. The two of them both looked up guiltily.

I raised an eyebrow. "Well, well, well. What's going on here?"

Levi grinned. "Taking a little personal time in the middle of the day, huh?"

Nyah's pretty face flushed pink, and her eyes sparkled. She went to get up off Dax's lap, but he banded an arm around her middle, holding her there.

I practically saw the love hearts form in her eyes as she watched him reach his free hand out to Levi so they could shake.

When she finally dragged her gaze back up to me, she

was so full of happiness it was impossible not to feel it as well.

Dax glanced between me and Levi. "What brings you two in here today? Want some new ink? Maybe a piercing?"

"No," Levi answered quickly before I could say a word.

I hid a laugh.

Levi shifted his weight from foot to foot uncomfortably, the tension radiating off him. I wanted to reach out and squeeze his fingers for reassurance, but I didn't want Dax to think Levi needed me for emotional support either. So I made out like I was really interested in the art on the walls instead.

Levi cleared his throat. "I wanted to ask for a job."

Dax paused. "Here?"

Levi nodded. "I don't care what I'm doing. I'll sweep floors or answer the phone or go on lunch runs. Whatever you need. You don't need to pay me much. I just need the bare minimum to survive."

Dax shook his head. "Levi..."

I squeezed my eyes shut, my stomach dropping. Shit. I didn't want him to say no.

Levi shoved his hands deep in his pockets. "Yeah, sorry. Right. I knew it was a long shot. Don't worry about it."

He reached for my hand, and this time I was there, wrapping my fingers around his and squeezing them reassuringly.

I was sure I was just as disappointed as he was.

It hit me hard that this was what it felt like to love someone. That it wasn't all tummy butterflies and hot sex.

But feeling their sadness and disappointment as if it were my own. Sharing that burden and lightening the load just a bit by being there for him.

God, I loved him.

In that moment, I was surer than I ever had been.

Dax untangled himself from Nyah, lifting her off his lap and setting her down next to him so he could stand. "Christ, Levi. The first thing we're going to have to work on is your listening skills. Or maybe your confidence. You didn't even let me get a word out before you'd written yourself off and were walking back out the door."

He wasn't wrong.

Levi stopped and faced Dax.

He smiled. "What I was going to say is you're too fucking talented to be sweeping my freaking floors. I don't need a cleaner." He eyed Levi. "But if the rest of your drawings are as good as the one you brought me a few weeks back then, brother, you need an apprenticeship."

Levi lifted his head. "Seriously?"

Dax shrugged a shoulder. "Pay is shit. Hours are shit. Yeah, you probably will end up cleaning and doing lunch runs, but when I see someone with talent like yours, I'd much prefer to train them up and have them as a part of my team than have them go work for someone else and then kick myself in a few years when they're making bank for another store." He glanced around the empty room. "I know it doesn't seem it right now, at ten in the morning, but it does get pretty busy around here. So we could use the help."

"I'll take whatever you're offering," Levi said quickly.

Dax nodded. "I'm offering you a career. Work hard.

Practice your skills. And we'll let you get a gun on some real skin in no time."

"He already tattooed himself," I couldn't help but add proudly. "It's really good."

Dax raised an eyebrow. "Let's see it then."

Levi hesitated then let go of my hand to pull off his shirt.

"Oh wow," Nyah squeaked, staring up at my name on Levi's chest. "That's so pretty." She shot a look at me and mouthed, "Oh my God."

I couldn't help but grin.

I felt the same way every time I remembered he had my name permanently etched in his skin.

Dax leaned in and inspected the fresh ink in a much more clinical manner.

"It's not perfect," Levi said self-consciously.

Dax stepped back and shoved his hands in his pockets. "No, it's not. But fuck, man. It's pretty damn good. A hell of a lot better than my first tattoo. You'll start this weekend, yeah?"

Levi grinned as he tugged his shirt back on over his head. "Whenever you want me to."

The two of them shook hands, sealing the deal.

Just like that, Levi had landed himself his dream job. And I couldn't have been happier for him.

Nyah clapped excitedly. "We should go out and celebrate! We can double date!"

That seemed bold of her, considering she and Dax had what? Hooked up at Psychos and now again this morning? It was quite a leap to go from there to a double date.

But Dax was also nodding. "That'd be fun. Maybe not

right now in the middle of the morning, but one night? Dinner and drinks?"

Levi glanced at me. "What do you think?"

All three of them turned to me hopefully. "I've never been on a double date," I admitted.

Nyah tucked her arm into mine. "It'll be fun. We can get drunk and dance and the guys will watch us from the bar, and when other men come to try to dance with us they'll storm over and be all, 'get your hands off my woman!'"

Levi and Dax both frowned at that, but Nyah ignored them.

"Say yes," she begged me.

"Of course, yes. Sounds fun."

The guys fell into a conversation about inks and what hours Levi would work, and Nyah announced she and I were going to walk down to Clean Sweep to pick up the jacket she'd left there at our meeting earlier in the week.

Levi glanced up at me worriedly, but I waved him off.

"It's one block, in broad daylight. I'll be fine."

He didn't seem sure, but I needed some girl time, and he and Dax had business things to sort out.

The moment Nyah and I got outside, I pounced on her. "What the hell is going on with you and Dax? You two are acting like an old married couple."

Her smile was so wide it looked like it had to hurt. "I know! I've never met anyone like him. I did exactly what I said I was going to and just dropped by his store the day after that night we had at Psychos, and we basically haven't been apart since, other than for me to go to work." She wrapped her arms around herself. "I've never met anyone like him. He's so nice! Like, actually a really decent human being, you know? Who doesn't kill people for sport like all of my exes, and every other man I ever knew back home. In just the space of a few days he's bought me flowers and taken me out to dinner." She clutched my arm tighter. "And the things he has done to me when we're alone and naked. Holy shit, Vi. I think I'm going to marry this man."

I laughed at her, but at the same time I was so happy for her. She was thick in the early excitement of a new relationship, and it looked good on her. And on him. When I glanced back over my shoulder, both men were watching us walk away.

I couldn't help my smile as Nyah and I rounded the corner.

"What about you?" she asked, side-eying me. "You and Motorcycle Man are cozy all of a sudden. Don't think I didn't see you get off the back of that man's bike, Violet Garrisen." She grinned. "I know what that means to guys like him. Shall we make it a double wedding?"

I shook my head at her exuberance. "No weddings."

She pouted. "Aw. Why not?"

I bit my lip but I couldn't keep the words in. "Because the law kind of frowns on marrying more than one person at a time, and last night, I had a threesome with him and Whip, and both of them are saying I don't have to choose, and so now..." I blew out a long breath. "Now, I don't even know."

Her eyes widened, but then she laughed and raised her hand for a high five. "Not to mention you and X getting down and dirty in that cam room at Psychos the other night. Is he on board with you having three boyfriends as well?"

I raised a shoulder. "I don't really know but I kind of think so?"

We both burst into hysterical laughter.

We'd reached Clean Sweep, and I pushed on the door, holding it open for her. "This is so insane."

Francine glanced up from behind her desk. "What's insane?"

I pressed my lips together, embarrassment rising up my neck. "Nothing."

But Nyah was too overexcited to keep the news to herself. "Violet has three boyfriends."

I elbowed her. "Nyah!"

She laughed. "Girl, stop being so modest. If I had three boyfriends, I'd be telling everyone I know. Wouldn't you, Francine?"

I waited for it. The judgment I knew was coming. It was one thing for me to tell Nyah about the man-hopping I'd been doing the last few weeks, but Francine was older. Maybe the same age as my foster mom.

And every insecurity that woman had ever put into my head was right there on the surface, while I waited for another woman just like her to pass judgment on me.

I didn't want to hear it and yet I felt like I had been trained to stand there and take whatever disapproval Francine threw my way. To be the good girl who respected her elders.

But Francine's disapproval didn't come. She just leaned back on her chair. "Whatever makes you happy, Violet."

Nyah nodded. "Agreed!"

But I couldn't let it go that easily. "Really?" I cocked

my head to one side. "You don't think it's weird I'm dating three men at once?"

I just couldn't imagine someone of her age thinking this lifestyle was acceptable.

But Francine just went back to her pile of paperwork. "I might be older than you ladies, but I'm not dead. And who you date, Violet, isn't any of my business."

Nyah leaned on the edge of her desk. "I bet you have a hot man waiting for you at home, huh, Francine?"

I nudged her. "That's not your business either."

But Francine was smiling down at her paperwork.

Both Nyah and I stopped to stare at her.

And even I couldn't help but get involved in the gossip. "Wait. You do, don't you?"

Francine chuckled to herself. "There might be a new man in my life, yes."

Nyah slammed her palm down on the table. "I knew it! Go, girl! Is he a silver fox? Ooh, is he a younger man? Tell us all, Francine!" Nyah glanced over at me. "Maybe she could come on our double date? Make it a triple?"

Francine waved us off. "You don't want a middle-aged woman like me cramping your style. Go on. I've got to get back to work anyway."

Nyah and I left her to it and emerged back out into the early morning sunshine, with the addition of Nyah's jacket over her arm. "I bet Francine is super freaky between the sheets," Nyah said as soon as we were out of earshot.

I made a face. "I don't need that visual, thank you."

Nyah laughed, but I couldn't stop thinking about the way Francine hadn't shamed me when we'd told her I was dating three men.

Something warm settled inside me. Something that reminded me not every middle-aged woman had the sharp, vile tongue of my foster mom.

And that some could just be happy for a girl who was finally finding herself with the help of three men.

I walked back to the tattoo shop with a lighter step and the hope maybe Levi and Whip were right.

That I could have my cake and eat it too.

That society wouldn't make me choose between three men it felt impossible not to fall for.

27

VIOLET

ours later, every barstool and seat at Psychos was taken, despite the fact it wasn't party night. It was a mostly Slayers crowd, as it often was, their motorcycle jackets slung on the backs of chairs, their bikes all lined up in a neat row in the parking lot.

But Travis was in the mix as well, this time sitting at the far end of the bar, shooting me pointed looks whenever I turned in his direction.

Bliss eyed him. "Say the word and I'll throw him out."

But I didn't want to cause a scene, and he wasn't even doing anything, other than sitting there, reminding me he existed and he wanted money.

Didn't mean he was going to get any. Hell, did he really think I would be working two jobs if I had any money to give? I wasn't going to hit up my brother and ask him for cash for me, let alone for the foster brother I had no desire in having a relationship with. I knew how it would work. If I gave him a dollar, he'd just come back and ask for two. It was better to just ignore him entirely.

He'd lose interest eventually when he realized I wasn't the payday he was hoping for.

Anyway, he wasn't going to be doing anything when Levi was sitting at the bar, catching my hip every time I moved past him and drawing me in for a kiss.

It was terribly unprofessional behavior, but I was powerless to stop it. I craved the trail of his fingers and kept finding reasons to be near him so I could feel it again.

Despite Travis being in the room, I was happy.

Levi made me happy.

His drink was empty, and I poured him another, pushing the beer across the bar top. He wrapped his hand around mine and leaned over, kissing me as a thank you.

Bliss sighed beside me. "You two are so cute."

I smiled against Levi's lips. I wasn't sure how a biker who'd done six years in a prison would feel about being labelled cute, but if he objected, he didn't say anything.

The bar door opened, letting in a gust of cool night air, and butterflies mixed with relief lit up my stomach at the sight of Whip in the doorway. On the other side of the front windows was X's ice cream van.

Levi followed my line of sight and raised a hand in Whip's direction.

Recognition lit up Whip's features, and he quickly made his way through the crowd to Levi's side. He gave me a quick smile and a, "Hey, sweetheart." But I didn't even get a chance to respond before his gaze was back on Levi. "Can I borrow you for a minute?"

I eyed X outside, leaning against his van. He waved to

me, but he was stiff, and didn't make a move to come inside. His attention was focused on Whip and Levi.

X and Whip had been gone all day. Which I couldn't argue with, even though it had made me feel sick for hours wondering where they were, and if they were okay. They had lives of their own and didn't report to me, but last I'd heard from them, they were off burying a body.

"Is something wrong?"

Whip shook his head and cleared his throat. "No. Just want Levi's advice on something."

I didn't want to pry into something that Whip clearly didn't want to give me details on. We weren't married. I wasn't privy to every conversation they had.

They were allowed to have conversations without me.

I leaned in, grateful for the noise of the bar that drowned out individual conversations unless you were standing right next to the person. "Can X come inside then? I really want to talk to you all about the 'making me bait' plan. I've been thinking about it all day, since we all agreed it was a good idea."

Whip leaned over the bar top and kissed me. His hand found the back of my neck, holding me in place, his tongue pressing at the seam of my lips.

Instantly, all words fled my brain, and I was kissing him back, my relief that he was standing right here in front of me after being gone all day too great to do anything else.

I was dizzy and slightly breathless when he let me go.

"Hold that thought, sweetheart," he murmured. "I can't stay right now, but I'll come back at the end of your shift. Okay?"

I nodded, pressing my finger against my lips. "Sure."

Whip gave Levi another look and jerked his head toward the door.

X was positively twitchy out by the van. I was suddenly concerned, more than suspicious.

Levi clearly noticed as well. "Will you be okay for a bit, Vi? Aloha and Fang are here if you need anything."

I waved my hand in a shooing motion. "I'll be fine. Go."

He took one last swallow of his drink and set it down.

I slowly picked it up and rinsed it in the sink, watching Levi and Whip head back outside to X. The three of them stood in front of the van, X and Whip doing a lot of talking, and Levi's expression changing from neutral to strained almost instantly.

"That doesn't look good," Bliss commented idly from beside me, where she was cutting up limes.

"No, it doesn't," I agreed.

Both of us stared as Whip yanked open the passenger door on the van and Levi hauled himself inside, Whip and X following.

Bliss raised an eyebrow as they peeled away from the curb with a spin of tires.

"I guess they're in a hurry to get somewhere," I muttered.

Bliss put the knife down. "Or they're in a hurry to get away from the conversation you were trying to have with them." She raised her shoulder in a half shrug. "Sorry. I wasn't trying to eavesdrop. Scythe told me about what you're planning though."

"No, it's fine. I shouldn't have been trying to have a conversation like that in the middle of a bar while I was on shift." I stared at the empty space where X's van had been moments before. "It's just they seem to be trying really hard to avoid talking to me about it. Whip and X were conveniently gone all day, even though what they were doing shouldn't have taken that long. And that's the second time they've distracted me with affection when I was trying to talk to them." I frowned, disappointed in myself for letting them bamboozle me with hot kisses and promises of delayed gratification.

Bliss gave a little laugh. "Ah yeah. The 'distract her with an orgasm' technique. I know it well. War has definitely used that one on me a time or two."

I smiled at her, so grateful to have another woman who could actually relate to the weirdness my life had become. I had barely scratched the surface on everything Bliss had been through, but she was where I wanted to end up. Happy. Successful. With men and children who loved her.

It didn't seem like too much to hope for, and yet it felt so very far away.

Bliss leaned her ample hip on the edge of the sink. "You know they're never going to let you offer yourself up as bait though, don't you?"

I paused, my hand midway to the dishwasher. "No. We talked about it last night. We all agreed it was the only way." I pulled her a few steps away, toward Nash's office behind the bar. "There're people after them. Me. The same people who are responsible for Toby's death."

Bliss's teeth sank into her bottom lip in worry. "Violet, that sounds really dangerous."

"I know. But I can't just keep being the victim either. Never knowing where this guy is going to show up or how. It's driving me insane. I need to know who it is and why they're targeting me." My heart squeezed. "I owe Toby that much."

My throat got all blocked up at just saying his name.

I missed him so freaking much.

Bliss and Nyah and Rebel were great, but Toby was the one I wanted to be spilling all my secrets to. It was Toby I wanted to sit on the couch with and dissect every detail of whatever I had going on with three men.

And I was never going to get to do that again because some psychopath wanted to play games nobody could win.

I couldn't just spend my whole life waiting for the next time he'd come out of the woodwork.

I needed to face it.

And the guys had agreed. But now they seemed hell-bent on doing just about anything other than actually talking about how we were going to make it happen. What on earth could they have possibly been doing all day that was so important? There's no way it took twenty-four hours to bury one body. I'd been around them long enough to know they worked a hell of a lot faster than that. And they'd clearly been keeping something from me just now.

"I'm going to have to do it myself, aren't I?" I asked Bliss.

I couldn't blame them for wanting to keep me safe. That was noble of them.

If I had to make a bet, it would have been the three of them were off working out how to find this guy and cut me out altogether.

The idea didn't fill me with the peace I needed.

They weren't there.

They hadn't been the ones to listen to that count-down. To know your life was about to end and there was nothing you could do about it.

They hadn't been the ones to hold Toby while he'd died.

I didn't just want the person responsible dead.

I wanted to take their life with my own two hands. To stare them in the eye and make them feel the fear Toby had felt in his last moments.

Bliss let out a long sigh. "You don't have to do it alone, or with them. We can go to War. Or Fang."

I shook my head. "They're just going to go straight to Levi, and then we'll be back at square one with them kissing me and...doing other things until I forget I was trying to have a conversation with them."

Bliss nodded. "Vi, I'm not encouraging you to do this. I just know I've been in your shoes. And that guys like Levi and Whip and X..." She sighed. "I know men like them. It's like they're born with double the dose of protective genes. They aren't deliberately trying to keep you in bubble wrap, they just can't help it. The idea of you being in danger short-circuits their brains and makes them dumb."

I stifled a laugh. "Sounds about right." But then I sobered. "But I need to do this. They don't know what it feels like to be the victim. To have all your power stripped away." I stared at her with big eyes. "I need it back. I can't stand feeling this scared and sad and pathetic."

Bliss pulled me in for a hug, and I let her because I needed it. I was terrified of doing this alone, but I'd been terrified in that warehouse with Toby dying on my lap too.

I'd survived, but I'd never gotten to look the person responsible for his death in the eye.

And I needed to.

"I need to draw them out," I told Bliss. "Somewhere public, but private enough that other people won't be there in case…"

In case things went badly.

I didn't want any more innocent people getting hurt.

"The bluffs." Bliss peered through the window in the direction of the road that would take me up there. "There's a storm coming in. Nobody will be up there when the weather is shitty. Visibility drops to practically zero as soon as the clouds roll in."

My stomach churned at the thought of doing this tonight. I wanted to run to the bathroom and be sick, but I also knew if I didn't do it tonight, I might never do it. "I'll text the guys right as I'm leaving. Telling them to meet me up there. To hide themselves in the trees." I swallowed hard. "I won't be alone. I'm just forcing their hand."

Bliss cringed. "What if they don't get the message in time?"

"They will. I'll use their group phones. They religiously carry those with them at all times in case they need each other." I shrugged. "This time, it'll just be me who needs them. They'll be there. If I tell them any earlier than that, they'll try to stop me."

"Agreed," Bliss said. "I don't like it, but I can see why it needs to be this way." She grabbed my hand and squeezed. "I'll come with you."

"You absolutely will not. You have kids to think

about." I swallowed hard. "And this is something I think I need to do for myself."

I wanted the guys there to back me up. But it needed to be me who put herself out on the line.

Toby had done it for me, paying the ultimate price for my safety.

It needed to be me.

Bliss dropped my fingers reluctantly. "Okay. So that just leaves the question of, how do you get this guy to follow you up there? You could put a public post up on social media maybe? Say you're going up there to say goodbye to Toby?"

My gaze bounced around the room, eyeing the familiar and unfamiliar faces, and finally settling on that of my foster brother. I had no proof he was involved, and yet my brain screamed warnings every time he was near.

It was awfully convenient that he was back in town right as all of this started happening.

And he was on the list.

I dragged my gaze back to Bliss. "Whoever this guy is, he's followed me before. He'll follow me again."

28

———————

X

Ten minutes earlier.

I paced the sidewalk in front of Psychos, catching little glimpses of Violet talking to Whip and Levi inside. They were taking too long. They were probably talking about all the hot, dirty sex they'd had while I was out digging a shallow grave in hard soil with a couple of Slayers prospects who kept gagging at the sight of the dead body.

Amateurs.

Whip found me at some point after I'd told the prospects to go home and take a chill pill. He'd helped me fix that problem.

Only then, we'd walked into a few new ones.

Hence why were here now, needing Levi's help. Rather than sweeping inside, plucking Violet up into my arms, and whisking her away somewhere romantic since I was due some X and Violet time.

Levi and Whip had gotten theirs last night.

Which I would not be thinking about because the idea of them all over her, when I wasn't around to watch, made me feel vaguely like murdering someone.

Though to be fair, I'd already done a whole lot of that today, so the urge was a tad bit dramatic.

A couple rounded the corner and strolled toward Psychos. It was only as they passed beneath the streetlight that I realized they were two men, and they were both wearing police uniforms.

Well, that was just great. I motioned for Whip and Levi to hurry up.

Then got distracted waving at Violet.

She was so pretty.

"That your ice cream van?"

Well, fuck. Apparently I'd gotten distracted long enough for the cops to walk right on up to me. I not so casually leaned over and pulled the shade down over the window that read, "Closed." "Sorry, boys. I'm off duty tonight."

One of them peered up at the list of flavors and sundaes I had painted on the side of the van. "Shame. I could have gone for a banana split." He looked at me hopefully, like I might open up the van just for him.

But if I opened that van door, he was going to get a lot more than just a bit of dessert.

There was a dripping sound, and I really hoped it was the misty rain beading and sliding off the sides of the van.

And not blood dripping from inside it.

Maybe I could pass it off as raspberry sauce?

When I didn't respond, the cops lost interest and wandered off, continuing their patrol through the backstreets of Saint View.

Whip, with Levi close behind him, stepped back out onto the street.

Whip hissed at me. "Are you for real?"

"Geez, Whip, I don't know. Should we ask Geppetto if I'm a real boy now or should we just assume?"

Whip's stare turned into a glare. "Please tell me I did not just see you close the serving window on a van that we have full of bodies! While you were talking to two cops! Jesus fuck, X, you didn't think to do that before they showed up?"

I shrugged. "You never know when you might make a sale."

"You do realize you're the entire reason I'm gray, don't you?"

"You should thank me for that! Your whole appeal is the silver fox thing!"

Levi clapped a hand over my mouth and pinned Whip with a glare. "Do you think the two of you could stop arguing for one minute and tell me why the fuck you just said you have a van full of bodies? You said one body, X! And you were supposed to bury it last night! What the hell have the two of you been doing all day?"

I dragged his hand down off my mouth. "I did, thank you very much. Don't accuse me of being a sloppy murderer." I cringed at the blood that was very definitely dripping from inside the van, out through the seals on the door and into the gutter. "Apart from that. That's not my fault. It's probably from one of the ones Whip shot."

Levi's eyes widened at Whip. "What the fuck?"

Whip jerked his head toward the van door. "Can we please not have this conversation on the street outside a very busy bar where Violet is watching us, and just around the corner from a couple of patrolling cops? Maybe all the talk of dead people would be better off done in private?"

I quoted one of my favorite movies in an eerie tone. "I see dead people..." Then added, in my usual cheerful one, "Mostly because I put them there. But, hey, semantics. I've basically been Uber for corpses all day."

Whip tapped the van's window. "If you lie down beneath the tires, and I let the parking brake off, do you think the van would just roll right on over you and crush your windpipe? Or would that be a wasted effort and you'd act more like a speed bump?"

I made a face at him. "Very creative."

"You two are giving me a migraine," Levi complained.

Whip opened the front passenger door. "Just get in, would you? We can't stay here. Christ, if this is the way I get caught, I'm never going to live it down. How fucking embarrassing."

Levi got in first, and I jogged around the front of the van to get in behind the steering wheel. Whip got in and closed the door on the passenger side.

"Nope," Levi said from space between the two front seats that formed a walkway so you could move to the back of the van where the freezers were. "Nope. Nope. Nope."

I started the engine. "What? It's not like you've never seen a pile of bodies before."

"I'm not sitting back here with them! You're in the back, X."

"It's my van. I drive!"

Levi shook his head. "Move."

I looked at Whip. He jerked his thumb toward the

back. "You're still in disgrace for the way you left the freaking window open."

I rolled my eyes. "Geez, you try to give a few dead bodies a bit of air to breathe—"

"Dead bodies don't breathe, X!" Whip shouted.

I waved my hands at him and swapped positions with Levi. "All right, all right. Don't get your knickers in a knot. Men your age are at much higher risk of a heart attack, and I already have enough bodies to deal with tonight. Don't need to add yours to it."

"Just bury me now," Whip said to Levi. "Seriously, like, bury me alive. Dirt in my mouth and nose and suffocate me. It would be less painful than this conversation."

"And they say I'm the dramatic one." I swapped spots with Levi. Only because I really didn't feel like digging more graves without his help.

"Where to?" Levi checked the mirrors and pulled out onto the street.

Whip sighed. "There's too many of them for us to start from scratch. The group has a dump point in the woods for situations like this. We can leave them there for now and go back and move them when we can."

Levi's lips pressed together into a thin line. "Does somebody want to explain how we ended up with a pile of dead bodies in the back of an ice cream van?" He glanced over his shoulder at me.

"Hey! Why do you automatically think it was me who went off the rails?"

He turned back to the road, but I still saw the raised eyebrow in the rearview mirror. "Oh, I'm so sorry. Did I mislabel you as a serial killer?"

I grinned, ignoring his sarcasm. "No. I wear that label with pride. But this wasn't my fault."

"Never is, huh, X?"

Actual irritation prickled inside me, and just the edge of my good mood slipped. I didn't say anything.

Whip filled him in for me. "I was dropping him home after we went to get some food. They jumped him in the alley outside his apartment building. If I hadn't looked back—"

"If you hadn't looked back, I would have killed five people tonight instead of three," I growled. "I left two of them for you because I was feeling generous."

It wasn't quite the truth, and Whip and Levi both knew it.

I was good with a knife. And I had zero remorse for taking a life. Especially when that life belonged to people hunting me down.

But any five-to-one fight wasn't an even match.

And men from the list, ex-crims and violent felons, were generally no strangers to brawls and weapons either.

I'd been lucky Whip had been there to back me up.

But I didn't have to admit that when they were both being fuck nuggets.

"We're fairly certain at least two are from the list," Whip said to Levi. "The rest were probably roped in to help. They all look like gangbangers."

Levi clenched the steering wheel harder. "That's two attacks on X in less than twenty-four hours."

Whip's jaw clenched. "I've been watching the security footage on my place too. A couple of guys came to my house with guns last night while I was at the clubhouse. They walked right up to the fucking porch and knocked on the door like I was going to ask them in for tea."

"And they were going to respond with bullets instead of offering to bring a sponge cake." I shook my head. "No manners on thugs these days, is there? You know, back in my day—"

"You're barely thirty, X. Shut up." Whip pinched the bridge of his nose.

"Sorry we aren't all in our eighties, Grandpa," I muttered back.

Levi turned the van off the main road, onto a dirt track Whip and I were both familiar with, though it had been months since I'd been down here.

"So they're escalating." Levi eased off the accelerator a little to account for the uneven road. "That's just great. We need to warn the others."

Whip nodded and pulled out his phone, then tossed it onto the dashboard. "Signal is shit out here. We'll get it back when we get a bit higher up."

The van jolted over a bump, and one of the bodies shifted, slapping me on the leg with a rapidly cooling dead hand.

I fought back the urge to gag.

It was going to take forever to get the stench of death out of the back of my van.

Whip eventually pointed to a spot and told Levi to stop.

"Thank God." I jerked open the sliding back door. "Dead bodies are disgusting."

Whip got out of the passenger seat and reached for the first one off the top of the pile we'd made. "I'll never understand how you can like killing so much and yet be so grossed out by it at the same time."

"I like the killing part, not the sloshing, leaking, decomposing part. I'm unhinged, not unhygienic." I grabbed the second guy by the arms and hauled him down onto the ground. My guy was smaller than Whip's, so I overtook him quickly, grinning at him as I passed. "Zoom, zoom!"

Rain drops rolled down my face, mixing unpleasantly with the sweat of dragging another fully grown human male around who was too dead to provide any assistance. I squinted in the darkness, trying to remember where the hell the site was. I'd been here a couple of times since I'd joined the group, though it was really more of Ace and Torch's favorite spot.

It was tempting to just leave the bodies here with no cover at all and call it good. Especially since the rain had set in and this was starting to feel like *Groundhog Day*, me doing the same thing over and over.

Kill a man. Bury the body. Repeat.

But just dumping them here was sloppy and kind of disrespectful. If you were going to borrow another guy's burial spot, then the least you could do was be considerate and clean up after yourself.

"Do you see it?" Whip breathed hard, his hands on his hips. "Visibility is shit."

I pulled out my phone, switching on the flashlight function and bouncing it around the ground ahead of me. I froze, stopping the beam of light, and then glanced back at Whip. "Do I see you needing to do more cardio, or do I see a pile of dead bodies who very much do not look like targets from the list?"

Whip caught up to me and snatched the light, walking ahead a few paces to light up the scene better.

There were at least ten of them. Their legs and arms a broken, tangled mess. Naked. Marks all over their bodies.

Long hair. Pretty faces. Eyes that stared, unblinking, frozen forever in the fear they'd felt before they'd taken their last breaths.

Women.

Levi stopped at my side. "Those aren't approved kills from the list, are they?"

"No." I stared down at the mutilation of breasts and genitals that made it clear to me these women had been murdered for sick, sexual gratification. "Fuck, I'm going to be sick."

And I really hated vomit.

But I hated the sight of those women more.

I turned away, doubling over, gagging but grateful I hadn't actually gotten to eat the food Whip and I had picked up earlier. At least our dinner being interrupted by men trying to kill me meant I now had nothing in my stomach to actually bring up.

One of those women could have been Violet.

The thought left me so cold I could barely breathe. It was like my blood had instantly turned to ice and no amount of rubbing my arms would make me warm again.

"Who dumps bodies here?" Levi asked.

Whip swallowed thickly. "Trig. Torch. And Ace."

"You think these are their kills?"

Whip's lips thinned into a line. "I fucking hope not. But I couldn't say for sure they're not. You saw how hard it was to get in here. The road peters out. You have to know where you're going to find this place. But we know people are watching us. Maybe they're watching them too."

"Or," I mused. "We've been looking at people on the list this whole time. When maybe we should have been looking at people inside the group."

Both of them turned to stare at me.

Whip shook his head. "No. The other guys didn't do this. This...This is fucked up. This isn't just running a knife through someone's gut to watch them bleed so you can take the edge off your own demons. This sort of shit is the thing we fight back against. This was done by someone on the list. Someone trying to frame us."

I shrugged. "Or the reason this guy has always been one step ahead of us is because he *is* one of us."

"Shut up, X," Levi muttered. "That's not helpful."

Maybe not, but I had a point, and they knew it, even if there was nothing we could do right now. We already had three of the bodies out of my truck, and I wasn't going to try to get them back in so we could go find a different burial spot. I needed to get out of here. I closed my eyes briefly, not wanting to see the bodies of the women anymore.

In my mind, all their faces were Violet's.

I stalked back to the van, yanking out the next guy by his arm and letting my mouth run because that was the only thing that blacked out the images burned into my brain. "Maybe there's a simple explanation for this. Ace might have picked up one of those reward cards. You know, where you buy nine coffees and get the tenth free. Maybe he got confused."

Whip gaped at me, watching me drag my next body

over to the pile. "And what? Thought it was some sort of dead body loyalty club?"

I heaved my guy farther through the dirt, wrinkling my nose at the trail of blood he left behind. "He's not real smart. I don't know if he can read that well. It's a possibility!"

I stalked back to the van, irritated I was doing all the work while they shot down my ideas. "Maybe Torch got bored? You know how he gets when he's not allowed to set things on fire. Or maybe, and hear me out, Trig started a sex cult side hustle. And they have Murder-orgy Mondays."

Levi exploded out of the blue. "What the hell is wrong with you, X? There's a pile of dead, brutally murdered women here and you're making jokes? You're as messed up in the head as whoever the fuck did this!"

Whip's anger was just as palpable, and all of it directed at me. "You're unbelievable, you know that? This isn't a fucking joke! Either someone is trying to frame us for these murders, or somebody we thought we knew and trusted isn't who they say they are. Either way, do you actually comprehend how fucked we are right now? How this is going to blow up in our faces and we are yet again farther away from working out who's doing this, rather than closer?" He threw his hands up. "Honestly, X, you're a liability. You need to be fucking locked up."

His words felt like a slap in the face.

Because by being locked up, I knew he didn't mean in prison.

He meant in a psych ward.

And he was just saying out loud the very thing I had worried about every day.

He'd gotten inside my head and yanked out my deepest, darkest fear.

Then rubbed it in my face.

My heart beat too fast. My chest was too tight to pull in enough air.

I stared down at my hands, coated in someone else's blood, with Whip's words ringing in my ears.

I turned stiffly and walked back to the van, slamming the sliding door closed. I got in behind the steering wheel and closed that door too.

Levi had left the keys in the ignition.

I turned them, and the engine came to life.

Without looking back, I put my foot down on the accelerator, leaving the two of them behind. Their shouts were lost in the roar of the engine when I pushed down harder, needing to put distance between me and Whip's words.

But the space didn't help the pain and fear threatening to engulf me.

You're a liability. You need to be locked up. You're messed up in the head.

I groaned, the pain inside me a sharp, physical ache I couldn't ignore. It carved through me, as deadly as a knife, chiseling away my insides until it felt like there was nothing left.

No amount of stupid jokes and bad humor was going to make this feeling go away.

I just had to sit there and bleed, while Whip's and Levi's words sliced me open.

Everything they'd said was right.

And I knew it.

I didn't know how long I'd been driving or how long

my phone had been beeping for when the sound finally registered. But it was a welcome relief from the onslaught of thoughts in my head, and so I steered to the side of the road and opened the message on my phone.

Violet: *Meet me at the bluffs. It's happening now. I'm the bait, and we're going to catch a killer. Don't be mad. You all know you were never going to let me help.*

I stared down at the message.

"No. No. No." I punched Violet's number on my phone, holding it up to my ear with shaky fingers, silently willing her to answer.

But I knew she wouldn't. She wouldn't want to be talked out of it.

I slammed the heel of my hand against the steering wheel and let out a scream of frustration that echoed around the van.

Violet was up on the bluffs, offering herself up to a madman. And I'd left Levi and Whip stranded in the middle of nowhere with no way of getting to her.

VIOLET

I'd put the message up on my social media, with Bliss looking over my shoulder. And then worked the rest of my shift with trembling fingers, not one-hundred-percent convinced I was going to go through with it.

I hadn't missed the fact Travis had disappeared not long after I'd closed down my app.

Though he had also finished his meal and paid his tab to Bliss, so I couldn't say with one-hundred-percent certainty that it wasn't a coincidence either. A lot of people had left around the same time, their meals finished and the football game on the screen at a disappointing forty-point advantage.

Nobody was sticking around to watch that, and maybe that's why Travis had left.

Or maybe it was him I'd be facing off against on the bluffs later that night.

The idea had left me cold. It was one thing to see him

here in a crowded bar, where I knew he couldn't do anything to hurt me.

But seeing him alone. In the dark. Knowing what he was capable of.

It was that thought that had me reaching for my phone, texting the guys, and telling them what I was doing.

X called almost instantly, and I silenced the phone, not wanting to be talked out of it.

I'd come this far. Set the wheels in motion. I needed this to end. I was so sick of being scared. So sick of always looking over my shoulder.

So sick of missing my best friend.

He'd died so I could live. And I wasn't going to let him down. I wasn't going to walk around these streets, just waiting for something evil to jump out of the shadows.

I was going to lure them out. Meet them face-to-face, on my own terms.

And then put a bullet through their heart.

Bliss had given me her gun.

I had very little idea how to use it, and if I wasn't in point-blank range, I knew I would miss. But she'd pressed it into my hand anyway and said I couldn't go up there unarmed.

She'd hugged me tight and eyed Fang and War still sitting at a table with the other Slayers, and led me to the back door. "They're going to notice you aren't here pretty soon, and I won't lie to them when they ask."

I nodded. "I wouldn't ask you to. Please don't tell them until then though? I just need a head start."

She still seemed uncertain, but I grasped her fingers. "They'll stop me if they know. Once I'm up there, they can back me up all they want. Hell, send the entire club up. I'm not on a death mission here."

Bliss looked at me carefully. "Are you sure about that?"

I nodded. "I don't want to die. But I don't want to watch any more people I love die either. And that's what's going to happen if we don't face this head-on."

Bliss nodded, her tone turning hopeful, like she was trying to reassure herself as much as me. "They might not show up anyway."

"You're right. They might not. I might just end up staring out at the view."

Except we both knew that was unlikely.

I could practically feel eyes on me, even though Bliss and I were the only ones around, the parking lot in front of us empty of people.

The darkness watched.

It drew me in.

Begged me to follow it.

So I did.

I took Bliss's SUV up the road that ran along the Saint View beachfront and up into the hills. My fingers tapped the steering wheel, and my leg bounced the whole way. But I didn't falter. I kept my foot on the accelerator, following the winding road until we were at the top.

The rain picked up the higher I went, and the trees whipped back and forth with the force of the rain.

Everything inside me said I should go back.

But everything inside me also screamed I should go forward.

Bliss's gun sat on the seat next to me. I steered into the

bluff parking lot, and a clap of thunder drowned out the nervous chatter of my teeth.

I put the car in park, grateful that as Bliss had predicted, the lookout was completely empty of other cars. The storm picked up as I sat there with the doors locked.

Like that might keep out a bullet.

I was no safer in this car than I was outside of it. I glanced around, peering into the shadows, just praying Levi and Whip and X were here somewhere, watching.

I'd given them thirty minutes. That had to be enough.

I didn't dare check my phone.

Because some part of me knew that even if they weren't here, I was going to have to do this myself.

"Get out of the car, Violet." I muttered to myself, picking up the gun and shoving it into my jacket. "Get out of the fucking car and be the woman Toby always said you could be."

He'd loved a mantra. He'd had me repeat more than one of them. That I was bold. Brave. Fearless. Fantastic.

I hadn't believed any of them then. Repeating the words hadn't meant anything when I didn't feel it inside.

And yet somehow, when I whispered them now, they felt entirely different.

They felt like weapons. Like armor.

Like truth.

I pushed open the door and got out, slamming it behind me and striding forward to the edge of the cliff. I shuffled my way along the rock that loomed over the swirling ocean, careful not to get too close to the drop. Lightning cracked over the water, and power surged in the atmosphere around me.

Or maybe that was something inside me. I didn't know. But I suddenly felt like I had Mother Nature on my side. Like I was the storm. I was the wind. I was the ocean churning beneath me.

I checked Bliss's gun in my pocket. Ran my fingers over it, reassuring myself it was still there. Then yelled, "Come on, you miserable assholes! Show yourselves!"

The bluff remained empty.

I scanned the darkness. Were the guys there, watching? They had to be. I didn't dare turn my phone back on to text them. It was too late for that. I'd turned it off, not wanting them to talk me out of it, and now I had to follow through.

Headlights bounced down the road, lighting up the trees whipping around in the wind. I clutched the gun in my pocket, reminding myself this wasn't the time to pull it out. That car could be anyone.

It could be one of my guys.

I filled my lungs, the thought of accidentally shooting one of them so horrific I wanted to toss the gun straight off the ledge behind me.

But I wanted it to be one of them. Wanted to know they were here, fighting side by side with me against a faceless, cowardly evil.

The headlights lit me up, and I shielded my eyes with my arm, trying to see through them.

I prayed for it to be X's van.

Except it wasn't. When the headlights dimmed, a plain white van with the darkest tint I'd ever seen sat in front of me.

The same one that had been used when they'd thrown the brick through my windshield. I was sure of it.

I'd been seeing that van in my nightmares, right alongside headless men and Toby sacrificing himself for me.

They all played over in my mind again now, and I shoved them away.

Now was not the time to lose focus.

"I'm here," I shouted to the person inside the van. I spread my arms out. "This is what you wanted, isn't it? I'm here!"

I held my breath, waiting for a response.

Or for the guys to creep out of the shadows and surround the vehicle.

Nothing happened.

Fear rose up my throat, threatening to cut off my voice, but anger came right along with it. And it was the driving force. The one that overpowered everything else.

The man in that van was responsible for Toby's death.

"Get out and face me!" I screamed. "Get out and show yourself, you coward! Because that's what you really are, aren't you? A scared little boy, getting off on terrorizing others. A sick, sad, son of a bitch who probably lives in his mommy's basement." My chest heaved, the wind stirring up the sea behind me into a frenzy that fed the one pounding through my blood.

A primal shout ripped from my chest. "Get out and face me, you fucking asshole!"

Nothing happened. The person inside the van didn't move.

The storm inside me exploded, like lightning had struck and obliterated everything in its path.

I yanked out the gun and squeezed the trigger.

The gunshot splintered the night, the crack so loud my ears rang, and my hands vibrated from the recoil.

But my aim was true. The van too big a target and too close for me to miss.

The shot bounced off the windshield, leaving barely a mark behind.

I didn't even have time to flinch or wonder where the bullet ended up. I just stared in horror at the fact it hadn't even left a dent in the glass.

Bulletproof glass.

Dread filled me. Who the hell were these people? But more than that, it was the realization that I was alone.

If X or Whip or Levi were hiding somewhere in the shadows, there was no way me firing a gun wouldn't have drawn them out.

I was entirely fucking alone, in the dark, with a psychopath.

My fingers shook, the gun slipping from my grasp, and I didn't even stoop to pick it up. I couldn't move.

The driver's-side window lowered, and I held my breath, waiting to hear his voice. Waiting for him to show himself.

I needed to know who it was. The not knowing was worse than the fear.

But he didn't get out.

A recorded message played through the van's speakers.

"Step where you shouldn't, and boom goes your breath.
Run if you dare, and you'll dance into death.
Each stone's a secret, each step a mistake.
One wrong move, and the cliff will break."

My blood ran cold. "No," I whispered, staring down at

the ground below me with the horrible realization that if the poem was true, then they'd rigged some sort of explosives that could detonate if I stepped in the wrong spot.

And last time, the poems had all been true.

I frantically searched the dirt for any signs it had been recently disturbed. That there might be explosives buried somewhere there, but it was impossible to tell amongst the long shadows and the rocky, uneven terrain.

I jerked my head up and screamed at the person in the van, over the top of the recorded message playing on repeat, just like the one in the warehouse had.

I knew what came next.

A countdown.

Bile rose in my throat. I spun around, staring down at the swirling ocean below me. I could jump without taking another step. And I could swim, but I had no idea if I could swim in a sea like that. In the cold, in the dark, in my clothes. How long would it take for me to get to the shore? What if I never found it?

My lungs got tight at the very thought of being smacked in the face by waves, over and over until I was pushed beneath them, the sea claiming their victim.

But I couldn't move my feet either. Couldn't run.

How could they have rigged the bluff with explosives that quickly? I'd only posted about coming up here at most two hours ago. Was that enough time?

It couldn't be, surely. They had to be bluffing.

Except we'd thought that once before.

I'd underestimated them, and it had ended with a man being decapitated right in front of me, a blade dropping from a ceiling that had sliced clean through his neck.

Underestimating him again would be stupid.
And just like I knew it would, the message changed.

> *"Jump for the sea or run for your life,*
> *Either way ends in panic and strife.*
> *We're bored of waiting,time to play,*
> *Sixty seconds. Run or pay."*

I couldn't jump.
I couldn't run.
All I could do was stand there, locked in by fear, and the miserable realization there was no way out.

30

X

I pushed my creaky old van as fast as it would go. My accelerator foot to the floor, I steered around the bends of the bluff road, peering through the rain smashing against the windshield.

Headlights coming up the other way made the visibility worse, and I swerved around a car in front of me that was going too slow.

All I could think about was getting to Violet.

And I'd royally fucked up in leaving Levi and Whip behind.

That thought played over and over in my head, urging me on, despite the rain and people who drove too slow in it.

I took the dirt road that led down to the bluffs, but there was more than one entrance, and I had no idea if this was the one she'd meant or if she'd been at the one farther up the mountain.

This was the one closest to Psychos. It *had* to be this one.

"Please, Violet. Don't be dead when I get there," I muttered. "That will be really fucking upsetting."

It would be a lot more than upsetting. It would be throw myself off the fucking cliff devastating.

But I couldn't let myself go there.

Maybe she was just joking. Maybe this was an elaborate prank to get me up on the cliffs and she'd just have a nice romantic dinner set up there, with candles and moonlight.

And a big ugly white murderer van right in the fucking middle of it.

"Fuck!" I screamed, stomping my foot down on the brakes. I scrambled for the door, yanking the handle, falling out and trying to find my feet again on the uneven road in the dark.

Numbers filled the air in a robotic voice.

"X!" Violet screamed from her position on the edge of the cliff.

Her voice ripped through me, the fear in her tone leaving behind a gaping wound.

Because I would never unhear that terror. It would play over and over again in my nightmares for the rest of my life, I was sure of that.

The white van's tires spun, kicking up a spray of rocks and mud in my face. I shielded my eyes with my arm but kept running, only managing to slam my fist against the van door before it peeled away along the road.

Frustration flooded me, and I let out a scream, an internal war battling inside me, between the desire to get back in my van and chase them down so when I caught them, I could gut that fucker slowly and painfully, making him beg for his life for hours before I eventually ended it.

And going to the woman I loved.

It took less than an instant for the desire for her to win out over the desire to kill.

I ran toward her. "Violet!"

Her hands stretched out, palms facing me. "No, X! Stop! Don't come any closer."

I stopped in my tracks, having learned my lesson from her. When she said stop, I needed to stop.

She let out a sob. "There's explosives. They've rigged the cliff with something, and if I move, I'll set them off." She drew in a ragged breath. "I have to jump."

I shook my head fast at the very thought of her diving over the edge. "No! No, you're okay. We'll call the cops. Get the bomb squad up here. Whatever it is they do. Just stay there." I was already pulling out my phone, my heart sinking as I watched her eyeing the edge.

The storm only howled louder, like it was urged on by her fear.

By mine.

That fucking water was practically calling her name, whispering it seductively, luring her down.

If I could hear it, so could she.

I faltered with the phone, all my concentration on her. "Just stay there, Vi. It's going to be okay."

"I can't," she said miserably. "There's no time. You can't hear the countdown." Her sob almost drowned out her words. "But I can. It's in my head. *He's* in my head."

She stared at me across the gap. It was barely twenty feet, but neither of us could move, both of us frozen.

"I have to jump," she said again.

I couldn't let her do that. I still remembered what it felt like to have the water suck you down. To have it in your nose and ears and mouth. To feel it seep inside your body until it was in your lungs, the searing, crushing pain suffocating you while you fought to live.

"Run to me Violet," I begged her. "*Please*. Run to me."

"I can't." She just stared at me. "Ten," she practically whispered, her mouth moving but the sound barely reaching me. "Nine."

I shook my head. "No! Violet, run!"

She stepped toward the ledge, her decision clear.

She was going to fucking jump.

She could hear the countdown in her head. That much I could see. And I'd heard enough of it before the white van had sped away to know that she was right.

We had seconds.

But I only needed one to make a decision.

I ran for her. Sprinted across the gap, wrapping my arms around her and dragging her back.

We both landed in the dirt and mud, my body cushioning her fall, right as she whispered, "One."

I covered her, protected her, praying to whatever fucking god there was that this wasn't the night He took her from me.

Or that if it was, He took us together.

Because I was so fucking in love with her.

Not in the stupid, playful way I'd told her before.

But in the soul-destroying, all-encompassing way a man loved a woman when he fell so hard there was no coming back.

If she was dying tonight, then so was I.

We both waited for the explosion. Her tense beneath me, both of us barely breathing, waiting for it to end.

Nothing happened.

I counted to ten silently in my head, my breaths suddenly so fast they kept time.

Still nothing.

"Did we die?" she whispered beneath me.

I cracked open an eye and was flooded with glaring brightness. "I think so. I see the light."

"X, that's your van's headlights."

"Oh."

31

VIOLET

X gingerly peeled himself off me and helped me to sit up. He wiped the mud and tears from my face, though his hands were caked with it as well, so I was sure he was really only making it worse.

But I appreciated the gesture.

And the fact he was here, and we were both still alive.

The countdown in my head was well past the sixty seconds the psycho in the van had started. And a new anger raged inside me, hating that I'd fallen for another of his games.

"Why is he doing this?" I asked X, both of us just sitting there in the mud. I knew if I tried to stand, my legs would give out. Adrenaline still pumped through my body, leaving me shaky.

He put his arm around me and rubbed my shoulder. "I wish I knew."

We both looked up as another car bounced along the road. X moved in front of me but sat back down wearily when he recognized it wasn't a white van, but Levi's bike, with Whip on the back. Levi dumped the bike on the ground, and they both rushed over.

X grinned at them. "You know, Whip, I think in biker terms, you and Levi just got married. Isn't that what putting someone on the back of your bike means?"

I expected Whip and Levi to laugh, or at worst, tell X he was an idiot.

But Levi stormed right over to me and crouched to cup my face. "You're all right? You're okay?"

I nodded quickly. "I'm fine. I—"

He didn't even let me finish. He slammed his fist into the side of X's face.

"Levi!" I shouted, scuttling away on instinct.

But Levi was losing it and didn't hear me at all. He hauled X up by his shirt and slammed his fist into his face again.

X's head whipped to the side under the impact, his nose erupting with blood.

It was like Levi didn't even see me.

"Whip!" I shouted. "Do something!"

But Whip was just as mad as Levi.

Which seemed like a complete overreaction to some teasing about being an old married biker couple.

Whip glared at X. "You fucking left us out there in the middle of nowhere? Do you ever think before you act? Violet needed us, and we couldn't get to her because of you! What the fuck is wrong with you?"

Levi's fists were wrapped in X's soaking shirt, and he shook him hard. "God, I can't believe you. You're a child, you know that? You could have gotten her killed!"

Anger bubbled up inside me, and I ran to X's side,

blocking him with my body and facing off against the two other men. "Stop! He hasn't done anything!"

Whip paced, and Levi breathed so hard his chest heaved in the moonlight.

He glared at me. "Don't protect him. You have no idea what he did tonight! You could have been killed!"

The ocean screamed behind me and X, echoing my fury as we faced off with the other two.

I glared at Levi. "And I wasn't! Because of him! So don't—"

A boom from somewhere beneath us cracked through the air.

It took me longer than it should have to feel the earth shift beneath my feet.

And then X's hands on my back, shoving me at Whip and Levi.

Before the cliff face gave away completely.

Taking a pile of rocks and soil and shrubs down the swirling sea below.

And X with it.

A scream ripped from my lungs, the boom of the explosion ringing in my ears.

Shouts mingled with it all, chaos swirling around me, and that angry, feral ocean practically laughing as she swallowed up the man I loved.

The man who'd saved me, more than once.

Whip and Levi hauled me away from the broken edge, their eyes wider than I'd ever seen, their mouths moving in shouts, but all I could comprehend was the sheer terror on X's face as he'd dropped away, eaten up by the darkness.

I threw myself toward the edge, fighting against Levi and Whip to dive over it.

Levi caught me around the waist. "Violet! No!"

Whip stared over the edge and tried to talk sense into me. "The fall isn't that far. He'll be okay. He'll swim around." He turned and nodded at me. "He'll swim around," he repeated, like he was trying to convince himself.

"He can't swim, Whip! He can't swim!" I choked on a sob, punching and scratching at the hold Levi had on me. "He can't swim."

That last one was more of a sobbing plea than anything else.

Levi and Whip both stared at each other in horror.

Without a word, both of them dove off the edge of a cliff and into an inky black ocean, determined to take everyone, and everything, I loved.

The end...for now.

The Saint View Murder Squad series concludes in book three, Reaper and Ruin.

For a free spicy bonus scene of the night Dax and Nyah met at Psychos, Click this link or visit the bonus content tab at www.ellethorpe.com

ALSO BY ELLE THORPE

Saint View High series (Reverse harem, Bully Romance. Complete)

*Devious Little Liars (Saint View High, #1)

*Dangerous Little Secrets (Saint View High, #2)

*Twisted Little Truths (Saint View High, #3)

Saint View Prison series (Reverse harem, romantic suspense. Complete.)

*Locked Up Liars (Saint View Prison, #1)

*Solitary Sinners (Saint View Prison, #2)

*Fatal Felons (Saint View Prison, #3)

Saint View Psychos series (Reverse harem, romantic suspense. Complete.)

*Start a War (Saint View Psychos, #1)

*Half the Battle (Saint View Psychos, #2)

*It Ends With Violence (Saint View Psychos, #3)

Saint View Rebels (Reverse harem, romantic suspense. Complete)

*Rebel Revenge (Saint View Rebels, #1)

*Rebel Obsession (Saint View Rebels, #2)

*Rebel Heart (Saint View Rebels, #3)

Saint View Slayers Vs. Sinners (Reverse harem, romantic suspense.Complete)

*Wife Number One (Saint View Slayers Vs. Sinners, #1)

*Torn in Two (Saint View Slayers Vs. Sinners, #2)

*Three to Fall (Saint View Slayers Vs. Sinners, #3)

Saint View Murder Squad (Reverse harem, romantic suspense.)

* X's and O's (Saint View Murder Squad, #1)

*Whips and Chains (Saint View Murder Squad, #2)

*Reaper and Ruin (Saint View Murder Squad, #3)

Saint View Strip (Male/Female, romantic suspense standalones. Complete.)

*Evil Enemy (Saint View Strip, #1)

*Unholy Sins (Saint View Strip, #2)

*Killer Kiss (Saint View Strip, #3)

* Caged Bird (Saint View Strip, #4)

Dirty Cowboy series (complete)

*Talk Dirty, Cowboy (Dirty Cowboy, #1)

*Ride Dirty, Cowboy (Dirty Cowboy, #2)

*Sexy Dirty Cowboy (Dirty Cowboy, #3)

*Dirty Cowboy boxset (books 1-3)

*25 Reasons to Hate Christmas and Cowboys (a Dirty Cowboy bonus novella, set before Talk Dirty, Cowboy but can be read as a standalone, holiday romance)

Buck Cowboys series (Spin off from the Dirty Cowboy series. Complete.)

*Buck Cowboys (Buck Cowboys, #1)

*Buck You!(Buck Cowboys, #2)

*Can't Bucking Wait (Buck Cowboys, #3)

*Mother Bucker (Buck Cowboys, #4)

The Only You series (Contemporary romance. Complete)

*Only the Positive (Only You, #1) - Reese and Low.

*Only the Perfect (Only You, #2) - Jamison.

*Only the Truth - (Only You, bonus novella) - Bree.

*Only the Negatives (Only You, #3) - Gemma.

*Only the Beginning (Only You, #4) - Bianca and Riley.

*Only You boxset

Add your email address here to be the first to know when new books are available!

www.ellethorpe.com/newsletter

Join Elle Thorpe's readers group on Facebook!

www.facebook.com/groups/ellethorpesdramallamas

ACKNOWLEDGMENTS

There's an ever growing group of people who make these books possible and they all deserve the hugest thank you.

Thank you to the Drama Llamas. You guys make my days fun. If you aren't already a member, it's a free reader group on Facebook where I share all sorts of stuff. Come join us, everyone is welcome. www.facebook.com/groups/ellethorpesdramallamas

Thank you to Montana Ash/Darcy Halifax for writing with me every day and being the best office buddy/work wife ever.

Thank you to Sara Massery, Jolie Vines, and Zoe Ashwood for the constant support, friendship, and book advice.

Thank you to the cover team:
Wander Aguiar and his team for the photography.

Thank you to my editing team:
Emmy at Studio ENP, Karen at Barren Acres Editing and Lori Parks.
Dana, Louise, Sam, and Shellie for beta reading. Plus my ARC and street team for the early reviews.

Thank you to the audio team:

Denise and Marnye at Audio Sorceress for producing this series. Thank you to Kelsey, Gregory, Sean and Theo for being the voices of The Saint View Murder Squad Series.

And of course, thank you to the team who organize me on the home front:

To Donna for taking on all the jobs I don't have time for. Best admin manager ever.

To my mum, for working for us one day a week, and always being willing to have our kids when we go to signings.

To Jira, for running the online store, doing all the accounting, and dealing with all the 'people-ing.' Not to mention, being the best stay at home dad ever.

To Flick and Heidi, for helping pack swag, and to Thomas, who refuses to work for us, but will proudly tell everyone he knows that his mum is an author.

From the bottom of my heart, thank you.

Elle x

ABOUT THE AUTHOR

Elle Thorpe lives in a small regional town of NSW, Australia. When she's not writing stories full of kissing, she's wife to Mr Thorpe who unexpectedly turned out to be a great plotting partner, and mummy to three tiny humans. She's also official ball thrower to one slobbery dog named Rollo.

When she's not at the office writing, she's probably out on the family alpaca farm, trying not to get spit on.

You can find her on Facebook or Instagram(@el-lethorpebooks or hit the links below!) or at her website www.ellethorpe.com. If you love Elle's work, please consider joining her Facebook fan group, Elle Thorpe's Drama Llamas or joining her newsletter here. www.ellethorpe.com/newsletter